Chasing

Marisol

LAUREN GIORDANO

BLUEPRINT FOR LOVE SERIES

LOVE UNDER CONSTRUCTION . . .

Construction executive Jefferson Traynor has zero problems attracting women. Until now. A blow to his ego, the sexy, beautiful Marisol seems immune to his superpower charm.

Marisol Ortega is on a mission— build the safest women's shelter she can negotiate on her shoestring budget. If that means playing along with the gorgeous, cocky stud building it— then game on. A single mom to foster son Hector, Mari can't afford the distraction of the crazy hot man pursuing her.

Chasing Marisol was supposed to be a fun, no-strings interlude while Jeff builds a safe shelter for the strong women he has grown to admire. Falling for Mari and Hector wasn't in the blueprint. But can Marisol ever move past old fears to risk building a shiny, new life with him?

DEDICATION

This book is dedicated to all the beautiful, strong women who have ever struggled with domestic or partner violence. Don't ever doubt you are worth so much more. A portion of the proceeds of this book will be donated to Safe Harbor Shelter. Assist them at safeharborshelter.com

CHAPTER 1

She had a run in her pantyhose— left leg, inside the ankle. Not usually one to notice such a small detail, Jefferson Traynor momentarily forgot the phone in his hand— fascinated by the shapely limbs transporting his next girlfriend quite ably across the hotel parking lot.

"Earth to Jeff— you still there?"

"I'm here. Wasting time at Dad's charity thing." His slow assessment had yet to reach her face, and in a way, Jeff was reluctant to continue. The rest of her couldn't possibly hold his attention so readily. "Jake, when I said I wanted more responsibility— I meant at work. Can't you stick this charitable stuff with Jenna?"

His brother launched into the *many* reasons why his presence at a charitable board meeting *was* important to Specialty Construction. With a sigh, Jeff resumed his perusal of the lithe body heading toward him, praying her destination would coincide with his.

Wow. He'd been wrong. If possible, the face was more stunning than the body. A Latin supermodel. . . right here in Arlington. Jeff's pulse ricocheted as she drew closer. His presence at the board meeting might be delayed while he scored her number.

"So, Dad dumps the homeless shelter gig on you and now you're sticking me with it." The spark of interest he'd experienced as she approached morphed to inferno level awareness. When their eyes finally met over the wobbly stack of files she struggled with, he drew a breath of dismay.

Her eyes were wide-set and shimmering blue. Had they been welcoming, they would have reminded him of the clear turquoise of a tropical sea. Instead, her challenging, *don't-even-think-about-messing-with-me* stare told him what she thought of his perusal. When she turned haughtily toward the hotel entrance, he was left to admire long, chocolate curls that bobbed with every step.

Damn— he should be offering to grab the door for her instead of wasting time arguing with his brother. "Jake— are you gonna pull this four-kids-excuse forever? Because it's getting a little old." Pocketing the keys to his bike, he hustled after the supermodel. Jeff managed to reach the door as she jockeyed her briefcase with the precariously sliding stack of folders.

"We'll argue later. I'm late for this stupid charity thing." In one motion, Jeff stuffed his phone into his pocket and reached for the door handle. Offering her one of his patented Traynor smiles, he winked. History being what it was, Legs would be unable to resist for long. "You look as though you could use some assistance. Allow me to get the door, Miss-"

Ignoring his blatant end run, she responded with a smile, but it was the kind meant to freeze out— not invite in. And it most definitely didn't reach her eyes. "Thank you."

Okay— maybe a little too obvious. Truth was— most women approached him, not the other way around. But her voice held promise— husky, melodic. A touch of an accent. Definitely worth another try. Not the least deterred, he fell into step beside her.

"Can I carry something? I'm heading into a meeting but I always have time to assist a beautiful woman." Eventually they all caved. The Traynor charm was damn near irresistible.

"Only the beautiful ones? What a shame." She eyed him with amusement. "Many women need assistance." She turned for the bank of elevators. "Thankfully, I'm not one of them."

"What is *wrong* with you?" Marisol Ortega muttered as she rode the elevator to the third floor. Her arms were moments from snapping under the weight of her briefcase and the load of presentation materials she carried. An absolutely stunning man offers assistance and what does she do? Accept gracefully? No— that would be too easy.

Absolutely stunning and completely full of himself, she amended, entering the carpeted hallway. Remembering his expression, she smiled. Gorgeous, hazel eyes had registered something akin to shock. Perhaps it had been worth it after all. Motorcycle Stud wasn't familiar with being rejected— for anything. Despite his disarming smile and the drool-worthy build his expensive suit couldn't hide— everything about him screamed 'player'. Mari had too much experience with that type to ever be tempted again.

Sexy and conceited were only attractive for a short while. Inevitably, the inherent shallowness left her bored. Her next relationship would be with a plain, earnest man. Maybe even a bit dull, Mari decided. No— not dull. She needed someone to laugh with. So— plain, earnest and funny. And gainfully employed, she added— after a brief flashback to Nick. Employed would be a major plus.

A little bitter, Mari? Because that definitely sounded like sour grapes. And what did it matter anyway? She had enough problems to manage without adding a high maintenance man to her list. Besides— she had Hector to think of now.

Annoyed with herself, she shook off the ambivalent mood. It would not serve her well to head into this board meeting with an attitude. She needed cooperation— and lots of money. Otherwise, the shelter would suffer for her bad temper. The wealthy patrons who showed up for these meetings expected to feel noble about the money they parted with. With the exception of a few hardworking board members who truly embraced the mission— most wanted to hear a sad story, learn how their specific donation would make the difference, then write their check and leave.

Setting the stack of PR materials on the table inside the room, she massaged her aching arms. Her practiced eye noted the fine china coffee service, the tray of expensive pastries that would barely be touched by the toothpick-thin wives of the wealthy executives she courted. Yet, if the trappings weren't there, her shelter would appear less worthy— less photogenic to the corporations she solicited. She continually walked a fine line between wasting valuable resources on the elaborate trappings required to gain more donors and appearing too lowbrow to merit their attention.

Hearing the rustle of footsteps behind her, Mari shelved her thoughts. Pasting on a smile, she turned to face her arriving guests. "Good morning-"

"So, we meet again."

Her smile faltered as she met the discerning gaze of the sexy fratboy from the lobby. What were the odds? "What a pleasant surprise," she lied. "I'm Marisol Ortega from the New Beginnings Shelter. And you?"

"Jeff Traynor, from Specialty Construction. Nice to meet you."

Her hand was engulfed in his. She noticed he took his time before releasing it. It was a nice hand, she admitted reluctantly. Sturdy. Capable. "You're related to Linc and Mona? They're wonderful people." Who couldn't possibly have spawned such a self-indulgent charmer. Perhaps her original impression had been wrong.

"My parents— and they are pretty great. They speak very highly of the shelter. On behalf of Specialty, I look forward to helping in any way we can."

Mari couldn't help her smile. "You realize our shelter is the very one you referred to in the parking lot as 'being stuck with the homeless shelter gig'?"

His expression chagrined, he raised his hands. "Guilty as charged. But try not to let my initial impression sway you."

"You've suddenly realized a previously undiscovered interest in the homeless?" Warm, green eyes sparked with what she could only term mischief. How could a man his age have the capacity to appear as though he'd been caught with his hand in a cookie jar? "Perhaps you had an epiphany in the elevator?"

"Go figure." A slow grin flashed. "Seriously, the shelter means a great deal to my parents. Therefore it means a great deal to me."

"Where is Mr. Traynor? He's well, I hope?"

"Dad's out of town this week. He asked me to sit in for him. Something about an addition you're planning?"

"Yes, we've been working together for months on the final plans." She chewed her lip at the realization there would be yet another delay. With Linc out of town, she would make little progress. "I'd hoped to spend a few minutes with him after this meeting to finalize a few outstanding issues-"

"I'll be happy to review the plans with you," he persisted.

Jeff's grin revealed dazzling, movie star white teeth and a winking dimple. A lethal combination. Thick lashes and a panty-dropping smile. No wonder he was full of himself. Mari hesitated— knowing the flare of interest in his eyes was not a sudden fascination with the city's homeless population. "Perhaps I should wait for Linc-"

"I insist," he interrupted. "He'll be ticked if he thinks I'm the reason your project is delayed. Dad said I should do whatever you asked."

Thankfully, a sudden cluster of new arrivals crowded the doorway. The tall, likeable man standing before her was a little too charming. Nodding to Jeff, she drifted to the door. "Very well. I look forward to working with you."

Nodding as introductions were made, Jeff tried to contain his smile. A private meeting with a gorgeous woman— a project that would keep them in close contact. He owed the old man big-time. He couldn't have planned the situation better himself. Marisol. An unusual name for a beautiful woman. She'd be charmed. Grateful for his assistance. By the time the project was ready to break ground— she'd be his for the taking.

"As most of you are aware— the homeless population in Arlington has only grown since the downturn in the economy forced people further outside the District-"

Jeff had every intention of paying attention. But each time she passed his table, her scent drifted over him, tantalizing him with the spice of cinnamon and . . . vanilla? Whatever it was had his senses prickling with awareness. She was making it very difficult to concentrate.

Discreetly checking his phone, he rearranged his schedule for the next several hours. They would review the plans . . . flirt a little. Invite her to lunch. Easy enough to extend their *work* discussion over a meal. Then shift their conversation to the personal side-

"Despite having seven homeless shelters in this area— over one hundred people are turned away each night for beds. That number will more than double or even triple when the weather gets colder."

Glancing up, he discovered Marisol staring at his phone as she spoke. Damn. What had she just said? That last statistic sounded ridiculously high. Sliding his phone into his pocket, he vowed to pay closer attention.

"At New Beginnings, we serve over three hundred meals each day— not including those that are prepared for the residents at the shelter."

"Is this shelter unisex?"

Marisol acknowledged the woman with a gracious smile. The simple act sent his pulse into overdrive. "The shelter is for women and their children only. But our daily meals are open to anyone. We serve breakfast, lunch and dinner to the area homeless. At night we have a separate living area that serves as short term housing for women in transition."

Transition? Jeff raised a brow. He smiled a moment later when someone asked the same question.

"We offer temporary housing to women who are experiencing domestic violence and must make a quick escape-"

"How often do those situations occur?" Jeff surprised himself with the question. Her beautiful eyes shifted their focus to him and he experienced a punch of heat.

"At New Beginnings we receive at least three calls a week from agencies asking to place women— sometimes alone— but usually mothers with children. Typically, they have escaped their situation with only the clothes on their backs." Marisol's voice grew husky, her expression serious. "Currently, those are hard for us to accommodate. We have limited space and we don't have separate apartment units for mothers to care for their children."

Wishing he'd taken the time to review the plans his dad had dropped off earlier in the week, Jeff frowned. "Is that what this addition is all about?"

She nodded. "We hope to expand the homeless shelter to better provide an appropriate setting for mothers to care for their children— somewhere they will feel safe from harm— safe from being discovered— as they work to get back on their feet."

Nodding his thanks, he jotted notes as others asked detailed questions about the expansion and the financing. He had several construction-related questions— most of which would be answered once he took a good look at her drawings.

Her voice washed over him as she calmly answered each question, at times, her sexy accent more pronounced. Had she been raised in the States? Marisol was painstaking in her answers— yet unvarnished. He was left with the impression of a woman would not couch the truth in pretty words. Nor would she paint an extremely dire picture— even though making the situation appear worse might be helpful in securing donations. From what he'd heard so far, she was straightforward. Her eyes sparkled with intelligence and compassion for the women she assisted.

Jeff glanced around the room. She had them eating out of her hand. Hell— after thirty minutes in her presence, she'd reeled him in, too. He'd entered the room resentful about having to waste his time. Now— he was eager to review the plans. Discover what changes needed to be made. Research what engineering could be accomplished to shave costs without hurting design. She'd won him over to the challenge— just as she'd won over several others in the room. He watched as several heads nodded, agreeing with the point she was making.

His thoughts drifted to their conversation by the elevator. When he'd been busy launching a standard pick-up line, her response had been decisive. *Many women need help. But I am not one of them.* Marisol was tough. He'd bet she was protective of her clients at the shelter. She'd probably seen just about everything humanity had to offer.

Jeff allowed himself a grudging smile. She represented an interesting challenge. His usual game plan would require tweaking. She wasn't a typical one-and-done pushover. Marisol would demand effort. Well-planned and highly coordinated. Though subtlety was a tool he'd rarely been called upon to utilize in the past, he was smart enough to realize he would need it now. But with a little Traynor elbow grease— and maybe some advice from his sisters-in-law— he could pick up a few pointers. By the time he was finished, Marisol Ortega wouldn't know what hit her.

Mari sank back in her chair, resisting the urge to kick off her pumps. Soon enough she could slip back into the jeans and sneakers that were her uniform at the shelter. The men and women she served didn't care how she dressed. They worried about the roof over their head and the hot meal in their belly. They cared whether they would be privy to the same luxury the next day. And the one after that.

Checking her watch, she waited for Jefferson Traynor to return. For a part of her job she didn't enjoy performing, she was rather adept at soliciting donations— of both time and money to assist the New Beginnings Shelter. About to undertake her biggest challenge, it was fortunate she performed so well. Adding a wing to the shelter had been her dream for nearly five years. She was down to the last half million they needed to complete the addition. More important, they finally had enough money to get the project *started*.

The remaining hurdle was securing the contractor who could make it happen for the lowest price, in the shortest amount of time. The shelter had been overcrowded for months. Every night, people were turned away. That situation would only intensify by the time winter rolled around again.

Marisol rose when she saw Jeff in the hallway, wrapping up his conversation with a colleague. It was the ultimate irony that the annoying man she'd met in the lobby was the unlikely savior who would be the catalyst to her dreams for the new wing. But if she could parlay his interest in her into lower prices . . . a shorter schedule . . . better equipment. Mari smiled. She didn't mind using sexual attraction to gain what the shelter needed.

He re-entered the room with the same crackling energy he'd shown earlier. Though he hadn't eaten, he reminded her of a sugared-up kid due for a crash. Shrugging free of his suit jacket, he tossed it on the chair. "Okay - let's take a look at these plans."

"How about back here?" She cleared one of the tables, unable to contain her frown as she noticed the mountain of untouched pastries on the tray.

His gaze followed hers. "You hungry? I'll get the waiter to bring us more coffee."

She shook her head. "No, thanks. I was thinking of the waste. To you, that pile probably doesn't mean much." Meeting his attentive gaze, she smiled. "Just a billion calories."

Rolling up his shirtsleeves on tanned, strong . . . capable looking forearms, he paused. "What does it mean to you?"

She turned to survey the room. "To me, this represents three hundred dollars that could have been spent on meals at the shelter." Turning back, she found him watching her expectantly. "Care to take a guess how many meals that would provide?"

He shrugged. "To be honest— three hundred bucks doesn't sound like much, but when you put it that way-" His expression changed, indicating he was performing some serious mathematical calculations in his head. "I'd guess if you were careful, you could make . . . maybe fifty meals?"

She smiled over the flare of intelligent challenge in beautiful, green eyes. "Actually, we can do a little better than that. With three hundred dollars, the fantastic volunteer chefs at New Beginnings can stretch that to cover closer to two hundred meals."

Jeff emitted a low whistle. "Seriously?" When she nodded, he held up a finger. "Don't move. I'll be right back."

When he disappeared through the double doors once again, she wondered where he possibly derived so much energy. She was leafing through her construction notes when he returned five minutes later— an army of waiters following closely on his heels.

His wink made her stomach flutter. Shocked by her reaction, she schooled her gaze. But his cocky smile told her Jeff had seen it, too. He pointed out the pastry. "I'd like all of this sliced into smaller portions and wrapped so Miss Ortega can take it with her. We'll be leaving in forty minutes."

It was her turn to stare as the waiters scurried to load up the pastries. "Why are you doing this?"

"The money's not totally wasted if everyone at the shelter gets to enjoy dessert, right?"

Why hadn't she thought of it? Jeff Traynor's eyes sparkled when he grinned— reminding her of an overgrown kid who was having way too much fun. He'd taken her lemons and gifted her with lemonade. Mari's smile was genuine when she thanked him. "You're absolutely right."

<hr>

He seriously deserved a medal. Glancing at his watch, Jeff confirmed his award-winning abilities. Yeah. He was damn sure. The last hour and fifteen minutes had been spent inhaling the intoxicating scent of Marisol Ortega. He'd observed at close range— how her eyes changed from one bewitching Caribbean blue to another— depending on her mood and the light in the room. Her hair— long, chocolate strands that whispered for his fingers to run through each curl had remained untouched. He'd noticed— yet miraculously refrained from confirming, what he suspected was the softest, honeyed skin he'd ever seen.

The herculean effort had occurred while he'd been required to speak coherently about the numerous changes she wished to make. She'd hit him with question after intelligent question— how much would this change cost? Would they still have room for another feature? Where would it go? Would it add days to the schedule?

Releasing a frustrated sigh, he watched her gather her briefcase. Marisol had been pleasant. She'd been polite. She'd been persistent— *damn* persistent about what she wanted for her shelter. She'd grilled him steadily— yet by all accounts, she'd been completely unaffected by him. When he'd asked her to lunch, she'd paused for so long, Jeff figured she was trying to think up a polite excuse. When she finally answered, she'd asked if she could decide later. Apparently if their current meeting ran too long, she'd shoot him down again. Not exactly the situation he'd painted for himself.

What the hell was going on? He was charming, damn it. He was persuasive. *Plenty* of women had made it abundantly clear they found him attractive. He worked out. He showered daily. So— what was he doing wrong with her?

"Are you sure you still have time for lunch?" Marisol set her briefcase near the stack of pastry boxes that still needed to be loaded into her car.

His gloom-laden thoughts scattered as his brain skidded back to reality. "Do you?"

"I don't mean to be pushy, but I would have time if you let me pick our lunch spot." She smiled, a question in her mesmerizing eyes. "Would that be okay?"

Hooyah. *Hell, yeah*. He contained his grin with effort. And the high-five. Definitely not cool. "No problem."

"I want to take you to one of my favorite places."

Jeff's stomach tilted. She could choose the most expensive place in town for all he cared. Marisol had offered a genuine smile— the first one directed solely at him. "Lead the way. I'll carry these boxes to your car."

CHAPTER 2

Mari parked in the alley, forced to wedge her car between a delivery truck and a volunteer's sedan. Confirming in her mirror that Jeff was still with her— she crossed her fingers, hoping she wouldn't embarrass herself when she parallel parked in the tight space. With parking at a premium, he definitely had it easier with his motorcycle.

Pulling up next to her, Jeff parked his bike on the sidewalk in an effort to keep the alley clear. She opened the passenger door, intent on hoisting the pastry boxes from her backseat when he approached, concern reflected in his eyes. "What's wrong?"

He scanned the deserted street, frowning. "You shouldn't be parking here— this isn't safe."

She waved a hand to dismiss his worry. "I've parked here before. We'll be fine."

"Where are we? I don't think I've ever been here before."

Before she could respond, he quickly moved in front of her— putting himself and the car door between them. "What are you doing?"

"Stay behind me," he ordered, his voice suddenly tense. "There's a very large, very scary looking guy approaching us. Whatever happens— if I tell you to run— just go."

Mari stole a peek over a broad, solid, and suddenly very tense shoulder and smothered her laughter. Brushing his arm, she felt muscles contract under his shirt. "It's not what you think."

Determined, his unwavering gaze remained on the massive man approaching. "We're *not* about to be attacked by a giant who looks as though he walked off the set of a James Bond movie?"

She tugged his arm, moving into the alley. "Jeff— this is the shelter. We're having lunch at New Beginnings. And this-" She stepped forward to greet the man approaching them with a scowl on his scarred face. "This is Pete Shea." She nodded at the man towering over her. "Pete? I'd like to introduce you to my friend, Jeff Traynor."

To her relief, Jeff immediately relaxed, his guarded expression dissolving in a smile. "Nice to meet you, Pete."

Pete continued to glare down at Jeff from his six foot seven height. His distant expression indicated he'd slipped into his world of military scenarios. She made a mental note to discuss the increasing lapses with his counselor at the VA Center.

Mari sensed Jeff closing the gap between them. "Pete?" She tried again to defuse the tension. "Jeff is building our addition for us. Maybe after lunch— you can walk with us for a few minutes and share your suggestions with him."

Her words had the hoped-for effect. Like a magic charm, Pete's brooding face split with a smile of welcome and he extended his hand. "Nice to meet you. I've got lots of ideas on the addition— lots of stuff that will make the perimeter safer," he explained. "We need to protect the flank. Right now—we're exposed."

"Exposed?" Jeff's questioning gaze shifted to her.

"Yeah, man. It's hard to sleep at night knowing we could be attacked from the south. I don't like it. I don't like it one bit."

Mari ignored the question in Jeff's eyes. "Pete— could you help us carry these pastries inside? If you've already eaten lunch, you could set them out on the dessert table in the back."

"Yes, ma'am. I'll be happy to accept that duty." Passing Jeff without a second glance, Pete gathered the boxes from her seat and headed to the back door of the shelter.

Beautiful eyes reflecting curiosity, Jeff stared at her for a moment before smiling. "I have a feeling this will be the most interesting lunch I've had in a long time."

In a hundred years, Jeff couldn't have guessed how this day would turn out. Marisol had led him through the too-small kitchen to the crowded cafeteria at the front of the building. But not before introducing him to half the staff. He'd met two of New Beginnings' rotating list of chefs who donated their time to help feed the hungry. Some of the finest chefs in northern Virginia volunteered their talents in the tiny, inadequate kitchen of Mari's shelter. *Mari.* He liked the shortened version of her name— wanted to whisper it against her lips when he finally got the chance to kiss her senseless.

Now, as they waited in the line that snaked ever closer to the tantalizing smell of roasting beef, he contented himself with watching her in action. Marisol was animated. She was talkative— to him and everyone who approached her. And she smelled great. While she was busy directing traffic, he resisted the urge to bury his nose in her hair.

"Sorry about scaring you with Pete back there." She turned to speak with him and was jostled into his chest. "Oops."

As his nerve endings scorched in tortured protest, Jeff reached out to steady her and confirmed something he'd already suspected. Mari felt really, really good pressed against him. "For a moment, my life flashed before my eyes."

"Pete has that effect on everyone the first time. I suppose he's a little intimidating, but to us he's always been so sweet and protective."

"He's former military?"

She nodded and took three steps forward. "He's been coming around here for years. He receives great care at the VA center— but there's something about this place that must appeal to him because he shows up every day— wanting to perform sentry duty— guard the perimeter from attack— protect our flank . . . whatever that means."

"Can't blame a guy for wanting to protect a horde of beautiful women."

Instead of taking offense to his compliment as she had earlier in the day— she smiled. "You *would* think of that angle." Reaching the front of the line, she waved to an older woman. "Annie— come meet Jeff."

He shook hands with a woman whose smile, for some reason didn't reach her eyes. "Nice to meet you, Annie." The pale, thin woman appeared worn out— mentally spent.

In comparison, Mari's eyes glowed with enthusiasm. "Annie is another of our devoted volunteers," she praised. "She's here early in the morning and is still here late at night. We couldn't manage this place without her."

 Annie's mouth lifted in a wan smile. "I'm grateful to volunteer my services. New Beginnings means a great deal to me."

"Join us for lunch? Jeff and I are reviewing the plans for the new wing."

Annie darted a knowing glance at him— sizing him up before offering a reluctant smile. "No thanks, Ms. Ortega. We're still pretty busy."

Marisol seemed oblivious to the older woman's appraisal of him, while her staff had made no effort to hide their interest. She worked in a tight-knit and protective group. That could work to his advantage, Jeff acknowledged. If a few of them liked him, they'd lean on Mari to give him a chance. Or they could just as easily close ranks and he'd blow his opportunity.

"Make sure you take your break as soon as the crowd disperses." Mari set her tray on a table near the wall. "I'll be back to help clean up the kitchen in a little bit."

"Honey— you take your time. This place can last a few hours without you." She winked at Jeff before moving swiftly back to the line.

When they were finally alone, he surveyed the crowded hall and smiled. Nearly all the tables were filled with hungry diners. Most appeared to be regulars by the way they chatted with staff and their dining companions.

"So— tell me what you're thinking." Mari passed him the salt and pepper as he cut into savory roasted beef. "Were you surprised when I brought you here?"

Leaning across the table, Jeff closed the distance between them and watched her pupils flare— with awareness of him, he hoped. "I've been surprised by just about everything I've learned today— about you and New Beginnings. This is a special place."

To his amazement, she blushed. "I'm happy you think so. That's how I feel about it, too. I wanted you to see this." She gestured to the crowded room. "So when you look at the plans, you see not only what we're trying to create— but what the obstacles and limitations are."

He took a bite of shockingly tender roast beef and chewed thoughtfully. "That's pretty insightful coming from someone who supposedly doesn't know anything about construction."

Sipping her lemonade, she winced. "We must be getting low on sugar again. You'd be surprised how much you learn about work-arounds when you operate on a budget like ours. We have only eight full-time staffers and we service hundreds of clients each day. That's why we're so grateful to our volunteers. There are at least twenty who show up every day— giving whatever hours they can spare."

"I'm impressed by what you're able to accomplish. You have a skeletal staff and such meager facilities— and still you manage to perform miracles."

"I don't know about miracles." Mari stabbed a carrot with her fork. "But we make a damn fine pot roast."

Hours later, Marisol frowned when she sat down for a brief rest, her thoughts returning to Jeff Traynor. He'd turned out to be nothing like her initial impression. Interested in the shelter, he'd been knowledgeable about the plans after only a brief review— pointing out areas they could sneak in more space for features she hadn't even thought of. He'd spent another two hours after lunch— walking the grounds where the addition was planned. Jeff had even managed Pete's enthusiasm in a kind, thoughtful way, treating him as though his opinion mattered— something she knew Pete didn't experience often.

She threw her pencil on the table. Damn it. By all appearances, he was perfect. Yet she knew that couldn't possibly be true. He was hiding something. They all did. Some huge, terrifying character flaw-

"Who ruined your day? Your scowl is worse than Big Pete's." Sharon Jones grinned as she pulled out the chair across from her.

"It's actually been a fantastic day. The board meeting went better than I hoped," Mari admitted. "I think we've picked up two more corporate donors. I plan to follow up with them next week."

"Honey— fantastic doesn't even begin to describe the hottie you brought here for lunch." The shelter's director fanned herself with exaggerated motions. "Damn, girl— he's fine."

Jeez, not another one. She'd been fielding comments like Sharon's all afternoon. "Jeff is going to be our builder. His father and I have been working on the plans since last spring."

"That fine, young specimen is Linc's son?" Sharon's grin flashed white in her cocoa face. "Hot damn— those are some pretty good genes in that family. And you know he's gonna age well because his daddy sure is hot."

"Sharon— he's at least sixty. And you're married," Mari pointed out the obvious, a reluctant smile twitching her lips.

"Sugar— I ain't dead."

"Regardless of his appearance, this relationship will be strictly business. I don't need another distraction in my life. I've got Hector now— and dealing with his mother is about all I can handle."

"Mari— you're gonna win. You've been fostering him for two years now. How long since his mama last showed up? A year?"

"Eight months," she acknowledged with a troubled sigh. True— custody was strongly leaning in her favor. But she could not risk complacency until Hector was legally hers. Only then would she allow herself the luxury of relaxing her guard.

"No judge is gonna side with the mama when the mama is a drug addict. She's disappeared what? Four times now? In three years of drifting in and out of this shelter?"

"But she's like a bad penny. Just when I start to believe Hector's mine— she shows up again and unravels all the progress I make with him."

Sharon's eyes conveyed sympathy. "I know, baby. But you'll make it. And it will finally be over by the end of the year."

Mari nodded. "But until then-" Her voice trailed off. She didn't want to contemplate anything beyond the court hearing. It made her feel too vulnerable. Experience had taught her not to want anything too badly. Because when it inevitably disappeared, the hurt was twice as painful. "All the more reason I don't need some guy disrupting everything."

"Some hot, sexy, smolderin' stud," Sharon corrected. "Hell— Sugar. You don't have to marry him. Just use him for a little stress relief. Lord knows you could use some relievin'."

Sharon— thirty years married— mother of four kids was giving her advice on her sex life? Had her personal life truly sunk so low? Despite her worries, Mari cracked up. "Am I that bad off?"

"You can't be judgin' every man you meet." Sharon waved an animated hand, jangling an armload of bangles on her wrist. "For one reason or another, you convict them all before you even put 'em on trial." The older woman leveled her with a glare. "No man stands a chance."

She shrugged, knowing it was true. "It's safer that way. Look what happened last-"

"How long you gonna sing that tune?" Sharon interrupted. "Not every man will turn out to be a deadbeat." Her tone was exasperated. "Have you even had a man since Nick?"

Heat crawled into her face. "Not everything is about sex-"

"Mmhmm. Just as I thought," she confirmed. "You haven't been with anyone since that loser. What's that been— two years?"

"Please— I cannot have this conversation with you, Sharon. You're like— my mother."

"So that means I know what's best for you, darlin'. And I think a little bit of attention from that delicious man is exactly what you need."

"I'm sorry to disappoint you— but I can assure you I won't be utilizing Jeff Traynor for 'stress relief'."

Sharon tsked with disappointment. "Well, that's a damn shame. If my baby Latrice didn't already have herself a man— I'd sure as hell be arm-wrestling you for him. That boy has definitely got son-in-law potential— even if he is a little pale."

Her cheeks still warm, Mari rose from the table. Anything to get away from Sharon's knowing cackle. "I think I'll check on Hector. He's probably off the school bus by now."

"Mari?"

"Yes, love?"

"Do you like that man? The one who keeps coming to see you?"

Marisol glanced in the rearview mirror, discovering Hector's earnest brown eyes staring back. "What man?"

Hector smiled. "The one Mama Sharon talks about. She said he was hot and it made you laugh and then your face got red."

Her face heated again— under the scrutiny of a wily five year old. Hector had been grilling her for a week— ever since he'd heard Sharon pestering her about Jeff. "Mama Sharon was teasing.

The man visits the shelter because his company is building the addition."

"Cool! Can I help? I like digging. I could help, Mari." Hector leaned forward in his booster seat. "Can I meet him? I could tell him about how good I dig."

"We'll see, carino." She smiled at his excitement. "He usually comes to the shelter while you're at school."

"Is he hot? Is that why your face is red? Are you hot?"

Dios mio! Did nothing escape his attention? "No, sweetheart. He's just a man. His name is Jeff." A persuasive man. He'd asked her to dinner eight days in a row. And damned if she wasn't weakening toward him. Of all the men she could possibly be attracted to— why did it have to be Jefferson Traynor?

He was a player— just like Nick. A shudder of apprehension trailed down her spine. Nick— first charming . . . then persistent. Then when she'd finally weakened - she'd thrown away all the rules. And it had been the worst mistake of her life. She'd fallen for him— for his illusion— of a loving, helpful man who would stick by her forever. Seven months later— he'd finally shown his true colors. Oh— there had been plenty of signs along the way, but by then it had been too late. Mari had been in love. Why look for signs of trouble when everything feels so good?

But charming had twisted into manipulative and persistent had morphed to controlling. She'd refused to acknowledge any of the warning signs until the day he'd used his fists on her. On that final day, her blackened eye and bruised jaw finally acknowledged what her brain had known all along. And she'd walked away.

Mari had been lucky. She'd filed a restraining order and Nick had given up quietly when she demanded he never contact her again. She knew from experience that wasn't always the case. Heck— Annie was living that very nightmare now. And her ex was proving to be stubborn.

Why was she so willing to chance the same mistake again? Jefferson Traynor wasn't serious— about anything. He'd basically said as much when he asked her out. 'Keep it fun' were his words. He wasn't into commitment. He'd likely never been forced to ask a woman out— and certainly not more than once. The thought made her smile. Soon enough he'd grow bored with the challenge she represented and move on. Guys like him were never alone for long.

"Mama? Can we have macaroni for dinner?"

Mari was relieved to release the bad memories and focus on something lighter. Mac and cheese was Hector's favorite. "Sure, love. It's such a pretty night— maybe we can eat on the porch."

Ten minutes later they were home. In the driveway, she paused to admire the forsythia blooming in the front yard of her bungalow. Her planter boxes were starting to fill in. Soon, the colorful petunias would spill over the sides, creating a riot of pink and purple that would greet them all summer. She nodded approvingly, acknowledging the love and sweat she'd poured into her home.

She'd come a long way. From the pain and humiliation she'd experienced two years earlier, she'd clawed her way back. It had taken a long time to admit that what happened with Nick wasn't her fault. For too long she'd blamed herself— that *she especially*— should have recognized the signs of an abuser. With lots of prodding from Sharon and the other women at New Beginnings, Mari could eventually admit she was not infallible. No woman was. Once she'd finally forgiven herself, she'd thrown herself back into her work. Now, it was finally reaching fruition.

Her dream of the battered women's unit would finally be realized. During that same re-building time, she'd saved every cent for the down payment on the tiny bungalow. It too, was finally hers. And in six months time— she would call Hector her son.

Her life was good. Amazingly good. She sighed as she parked near the garage. Why would she risk ruining that for a man? Even one as appealing as Jefferson Traynor.

⁂

"So— what do you ladies say to the idea of stealing this crawl space?" Nearly a month later, Jeff surveyed the room. They were making remarkable progress, despite the women's desire for reaching consensus on the smallest items. An hour ago, he'd thought they would never move beyond the carpet pattern choices for the waiting room. The thought of talking colors and patterns with five women was daunting. But they'd surprised him— managing to come to agreement on the carpet in only thirty-seven minutes. Pattern only, of course. The color was still up for debate.

Soon he would be forced to concede defeat. Whether he liked it or not, Jeff was going to have to drag his father back into the process— if only to speed along the mind-numbing process of organizing these women into selecting an endless list of colors, patterns, tile— the list went on and on. Linc would be able to charm them into making decisions faster.

Jeff had finally acknowledged over the past week that he desperately needed to get back to work— his *own* work. Projects were beginning to stack up in estimating. As a result, Jake and Harry were not pleased. He'd devoted the better part of a month thinking about New Beginnings. Well— to be honest, he'd spent a helluva lot of that time thinking about Marisol. Her eyes. That smile. Her melodic voice tortured his dreams. He loved her soft, husky accent. He'd noticed it became more pronounced when she argued with him over suggested changes. Since then, he'd done his best to challenge her every chance he got. Of course, thinking about that sexy accent made him fantasize about how she'd sound when he finally managed to steer her into his bed.

Like there was any chance of *that* happening. Mari might be into him— but it was solely because he would make her project happen. The woman possessed a single-mindedness that both frustrated him and forced Jeff to grudgingly admire her. Every time he managed to get close to her— an invisible wall would go up. He'd see it in her eyes. They would be in the middle of a conversation— or more typically— an argument over their design differences— and it would happen. She would morph from animated and enthusiastic to guarded. The shields would go up and the banter was over. Sometimes, he swore it was fear he read in her eyes. As though she'd somehow broken an unspoken rule— as though Mari only allowed herself to behave a certain way.

Jeff had spent the past month coming up with excuses to spend time at the shelter— to spend time with *her*. And she remained completely clueless. No— Mari was too smart for that, he admitted. She was focused solely on New Beginnings. If there was even a flicker of personal interest in him, she wasn't showing her cards.

When he hadn't been thinking about Mari, the remainder of his time had been spent re-drawing several aspects of the project he felt could be better utilized. In the same amount of space— Jeff was able to gain much needed square footage for the antiquated kitchen. Coming up with the extra dollars to afford quality kitchen equipment was a different story. He'd researched lower cost materials so the shelter wouldn't have to sacrifice quality for the cost savings. But he still couldn't shave enough to get the kitchen upgrade into her existing budget.

During this time, Jeff had defended himself to his business partners. His cousin Harry was ticked at him because he'd been late with his project billings. And when it came to money— Specialty's CFO accepted no excuses. His brother Jake was still pissed because he'd missed a project meeting with two subcontractors Specialty wanted to utilize. Jake hadn't appreciated being pulled in at the last minute. But Jeff had been in the middle of a site survey with Big Pete. His brother should try telling Rambo he was needed elsewhere. Instead, Big Pete hadn't allowed him to leave until he'd walked the existing shelter with the giant and then toured the area where the addition would be laid out. That had lead to concerns about parking for staffers since the new design would steal nearly half of the existing parking lot. And there were Pete's concerns about the affordability of the twenty-foot high, military-grade razor-wire fence he wanted installed around the perimeter. That lengthy conversation came after talking Pete out of a gun turret and thirty yard minefield he'd wanted to lay out.

Surveying the room, Jeff sighed. The women had devolved into two separate camps of opinion— over a damned six foot crawl space. His thoughts snapped back to attention when Sharon regained control of the room.

As it quieted down, Sharon nodded. "I say let's do it." She shifted in her chair seeking out Marisol, who, he noted, had chosen the seat farthest from him. Nothing like making a solid impression on the woman of his dreams. "What do you think, Sugar?"

Her cheeks stained pink but her eyes remained wary. Mari had become hyper aware of Sharon's less than subtle efforts to push them together. He'd sensed rather quickly the older woman liked to stir up trouble for her own amusement— and after nearly a month of fruitless pursuit, Jeff wasn't above using her skills in his quest to catch Marisol.

"I think most of these decisions are taking too long. We should allow Mr. Traynor to do his job. He's the expert. That's why we selected Specialty. Without an architect on board, we need to rely on Jeff's recommendations."

Although Mari's backhanded compliment was likely borne of frustration with the pace of the selection process— Jeff was pleased anyway. At this point, he'd lost track of how many times he'd asked her out. Each time she graciously declined. A polite 'no, thank you'. He'd danced around the subject of a boyfriend— just to be sure, even though Sharon had already made it clear Marisol was available. In typical Mari fashion she'd smiled, then asked what that question had to do with the construction process.

He knew what he was up against. When Mari looked at him she saw a guy who was too casual with women. She saw a one and done guy. And—okay, so maybe she wasn't far off the mark. But instead of being put off by her rejection, Jeff was surprised to discover he was enjoying the challenge. The more walls Mari erected, the more determined he became to win her over. Not in a creepy, stalker way. In the way that when she finally said yes— it would be because she wanted him— not because he'd worn her down.

Several decisions later, the meeting adjourned. Jeff was well aware what would happen next. He would be surrounded by a herd of females asking inane questions. While he remained trapped, Marisol would make her escape, giving him a little wave and slipping out the side door.

But not today. He smiled. Today, he had a plan. Thanks to their budding friendship, Big Pete had been happy to assist with a little reconnaissance. Pete had casually positioned himself by the side door so he could slip out after Mari bolted. All Jeff had to do was extract himself from the gaggle of women surrounding him.

"Ladies, I have to step out for a moment. Please hold your questions and I'll be back in ten minutes."

As he bolted for the side door, Sharon gave him a nod of understanding. "Go get her, Stud."

Jeff blew through the door, searching for Big Pete. It was easy enough to spot the giant perched near a mailbox down the street. As he approached, Pete pointed to the corner.

"She just went around the corner," Pete reported. "I think that's where the bus stop is."

"Bus stop?" Jeff hesitated. "Doesn't she drive to work every day?"

Pete nodded, before turning back to the shelter. "Yeah, but that's where Hector's school bus lets him off."

Hector? Understanding dawned. Maybe it was one of the kids from the shelter. It made sense the staff wouldn't allow them to walk unescorted— not in this neighborhood. "Who's Hector?"

The giant didn't miss a step as he turned back to answer. "He's Miss Ortega's kid."

"How was school today, carino?" Mari waited for the bus to pull away before she began their daily ritual. Another bus would come later with the older shelter kids, but this year Hector was the only kindergartener at the stop.

"I got a red star on my math paper. And Billy Stephens had to sit in the corner."

"Again? My goodness. He sounds naughty." Mari hid her smile as she accepted his folder of papers. He slung his nearly empty backpack on his shoulders, still proud that he was old enough to carry one— even if it only contained his lunchbox.

"He's always in trouble," Hector boasted. "He pushes in line and he takes everybody's crayons."

"And what does Mrs. Leonard say about this?" She slipped his fingers through hers as they rounded the corner, loving the feel of his sturdy little hand in hers.

"She says if he doesn't quit disrupting us she's sending him to the office." Hector stopped dead in the middle of the pavement, causing a mini traffic jam as pedestrians swerved around him. "Mama— what's disruppin'?"

Mari gently tugged him out of the line of foot traffic to explain. "It's disrupt. There's a 't' on the end. Disrupt. Por favor, repita," she directed. Once she'd discovered his unusual fascination with words, she'd created games to encourage his curiosity.

His eyes gleeful, he repeated, choosing to spit the 't' on the end. "Disrupt."

"Okay- that's enough." She smiled in spite of herself. Though Hector was intrigued by words, the five-year-old was even more fascinated with typical little boy antics.

"What does it mean?"

They began moving down the street once again. "It means to cause trouble, sometimes because you are bored or because you can't sit still."

"And sometimes it's because you're a born troublemaker," announced a familiar voice.

Startled, she glanced up. "Jeff— what are you doing here? Did I leave the meeting too soon? I had to meet the bus."

Jeff shook his head. "I was heading out and I saw you down the street. Just thought I'd introduce myself to your friend here."

Hector sidled closer to her but kept his gaze on him. "Who're you?"

"I'm Jeff. My company is building the addition on the shelter." He fell into step with them as they retraced their path to the shelter.

"I'm Hector. I live with Mari." Hector stopped dead in his tracks once again, his brown eyes widening with recognition. "Are you the man Mama Sharon talks about?"

Mari braced herself, not wanting to contemplate what secrets would tumble from his mouth over the next half a block. "Let's keep moving, Hector. We're blocking traffic."

"Mari— is this him?"

Ruffling his hair, she smiled. "Is this who, love?"

"The hot guy— you know— the one Mama Sharon says you should date."

"Dios Mio," she muttered as her face began flaming its way to incineration. If one could die of embarrassment, her moment had come. She knew without looking that Jeff was grinning. If only the pavement could open up and swallow her whole.

"I sure hope she was talking about me." Jeff caught her gaze over Hector's head. "You're even prettier when you blush like that."

"Did Mari tell you about me? Did she tell you I like to dig? Did she tell you I can help?"

Promptly forgetting his shyness, Hector fell into step with Jeff. She ignored the twinge of hurt when he shook his fingers free of hers. More than anything, Hector wanted to be a big boy. And big boys didn't hold hands with their wanna-be mothers.

"Really— when you start diggin' I can be your helper. I'm real good at paying attention— Mrs. Leonard gave me a gold star for listenin'."

To his credit, Jeff didn't smile— or worse— laugh. His expression was one of thoughtfulness, as though seriously considering the little boy's request. "Well, thanks buddy. I appreciate your offer to help. I'll talk it over with our superintendent, Hank— he's the guy who will be in charge of the construction. I'm sure he'll agree to let you help us out, but we're not going to start digging for another month. So, in the meantime, you keep up the good work in school and we'll talk then, okay?"

Hector's eyes grew huge. "You mean it?"

Jeff nodded. "But the listening part is very important when you build stuff— because you can get hurt if you don't listen. So, I want to see that you're still getting gold stars before I can agree to let you help us. I'm going to check with Miss Ortega to make sure you haven't slipped up. Do we have a deal?"

"Yes, sir. We got a deal."

By the time they reached the shelter, Hector had insisted on shaking hands over their pact. Mari was simply relieved they'd finally arrived without any further embarrassing revelations. "Okay, carino— go inside and get your snack. I'll check on you in two minutes."

"Mama— when will I get to see Jeff again? I want to hear about the digging."

She studiously avoided Jeff's inquiring eyes. "We'll talk about it tonight, okay? Miss Robin is waiting for you in the daycare."

Clearly sensing her discomfort, Jeff winked. "Now that I know what time you get back from school, I'll try to come by to see you on my next visit. Maybe we can all go out for pizza one night."

"Awesome! That would be so cool, Jeff."

She bit back a squeak of surprise. "P-perhaps." With relief, she watched Hector walk through the double doors, before she turned to face him. "You're not playing fair, Mr. Traynor."

"When I'm dealing with someone as stubborn as you, I'm forced to use every weapon at my disposal." Jeff shrugged, not at all put off by her frown. "Besides, Hector seems like a great kid. I like his enthusiasm."

"He's a wonderful boy but he tends to talk your ear off when he meets someone new. I'm sorry if we delayed you."

"I don't remember you mentioning having a son."

Mari hesitated several seconds, unsure how or even *if* she should answer his roundabout question. In a way, it was the perfect thing to put him off. Guys like Jeff were into easy, laid-back, no-strings relationships. Hector was not easy, nor was he no-strings. "I didn't realize Hector factored into our business relationship."

"Well played, Miss Ortega." He accepted her jab gracefully. "I deserved that. I just assumed we were becoming friends."

Grinning, she decided to let him off the hook. "I believe we are friends, Mr. Traynor. And as friends, I will tell you that Hector is my foster son. I hope he will be my *real* son by the end of this year."

"That's pretty cool." He smiled. "I'm sure making that decision wasn't the easiest one in the world."

But it had been the *only* decision Mari could have lived with. "Not easy, but definitely the right one for me. He's a great little boy who's had a rough couple years. We've been together on and off for more than two years."

"Why on and off?"

She winced, unsure she wished to voice the worries that kept her awake at night. "His mother still pops in from time to time. She's an addict. She makes it very difficult for Hector— to settle down in his new life."

"She stops by just often enough to fill him with false expectations." His eyes flashed with sudden understanding. "And what does that do to you?"

Mari was caught completely off guard by the lump in her throat. "I— I don't—"

She had not expected insight from a man like him. As she searched for words that would not start tears flowing, Jeff gave her hand a squeeze, seeming to know instinctively that she was suddenly floundering on emotional thin ice.

"Let's just say I'll be relieved when he's legally mine."

"I'm glad you finally told me about him. He seems like a great kid."

Jeff smiled and turned toward the parking lot, squinting in the afternoon sun. It was almost as though he sensed she needed to gather herself. Mari was left to ponder whether she'd been too harsh in her judgment.

"And just so we're clear-" He turned back to face her. "I'm serious about the invitation but not the way I said it."

"What do you mean?"

"As much as I really want to go out with you— I was joking when I said I would use Hector." He released her hand reluctantly. "I love kids. I have three nieces and a nephew who's only a little older than Hector. I would sincerely like to take you both out for pizza. Why don't you check your schedule for tomorrow night? I'll give you a call and you can let me know."

Mari watched him round the building to the parking lot before she finally took a step toward the front door. Could Sharon be right about her? Maybe she *was* too cynical. It was growing increasingly difficult to resist the magnetic pull of his smile— to resist that can-do attitude. Or his thoughtful way of interacting with the shelter staff. She recalled how he'd dealt with the horde of women taking such a ridiculous amount of time to make decisions; never once had he shown signs of impatience. She liked and appreciated how he always made time to discuss things with Big Pete.

Startled, she realized maybe she didn't want to scare Jefferson away after all.

CHAPTER 3

"Jake—it's one damned addition. What the hell is taking Jeff so long?" Harrison Traynor leaned forward in his chair, his expression disgruntled.

"Chill, Harry. It's a little more complicated than that. The shelter has funding issues. We have to squeeze every dime or they won't have enough money to start— let alone finish." Jake leaned back in the old, leather chair, wincing when the springs squealed in protest. One of these days, he'd lean back and the damn thing was gonna keep on going. "In his defense— this project was dumped into his lap when Linc decided to take a month off without warning any of us. What's Jeffie late on now?"

Harry sighed. "It's his billings again."

"Anything I need to worry about?"

"No— it's more annoying than anything," he admitted. "Instead of waiting on Jeff, I've just been going around him and getting the numbers from the project managers. What's the deal with him lately?"

Jake stared at his cousin. He'd been wondering the same thing. His brother was distracted. *Big time* distracted. And there was no way a relatively small project like the homeless shelter could be the reason. "It's probably a woman."

Harry's eyes narrowed. "Get serious. He's never let his women get in the way of Specialty business before. How many girlfriends cycle through Jeff's revolving doors each year?"

"Maybe this one is different."

"You're kidding, right? He doesn't have to do anything and they fall into his lap."

He shrugged. "Maybe this girl is making him work for it."

Harry shook his head. "It's gotta be something else. Maybe the project?"

"Hank says everything is on schedule. They've got enough money to get rolling. He's starting out there next week with the sitework." The more Jake thought it over, the more certain he became. His brother's behavior suddenly made sense. The absentmindedness— the disappearing act. The homeless shelter did not require his presence on site three days a week. "No— it's a woman."

"How can you be sure?"

"Don't you remember how you were? C'mon Harry, it was only a year ago."

"I'm not following you." He frowned. "Who was Jeff seeing back then?"

"Not Jeff, dummy." Jake worked to contain his smile. Harry was so damned focused all the time. "I seem to remember you doing a pretty good impression of Jeff. You were distracted. You disappeared for days at a time." He ticked off the evidence. "You were completely focused on a certain site contractor. Does Adams and Rey ring any bells?"

"Okay— I get it." His cousin reluctantly smiled. "Although I don't think 'disappearing' is quite an accurate description. I was protecting our investment."

"And trying to score with that cute girl from A & R. What was her name again?"

"Kendall was not the sole reason I was distracted-"

Jake held up a hand. "Yeah— whatever. How's she feeling, by the way?"

"Pretty queasy the past few weeks but I think it's easing up. The past two days I haven't had to run downstairs at dawn for crackers." He smiled. "And Ken's a little less cranky."

"Dude— consider yourself lucky. Jen hurled every day for three months with the twins." Mention of his wife made Jake smile. No way could he have predicted how great his life would turn out. In a year's time he'd gone from being completely alone to landing his beautiful wife and her two kids. Two months earlier, they'd been gifted with the twins. His life had been truly blessed.

When someone tapped on the office door, Harry rose from his chair, using it as his signal to leave. "So— I assume we're cutting Jeff some slack until his love life is back in order?"

Not too much slack. Specialty was getting busy. He couldn't afford to let projects stack up in estimating. Jake sighed. "I'll talk to him."

Jenna's head appeared around the door. "Whose love life are we discussing?"

"Hey Jen! When are you coming back to work?" Harry leaned in to brush her cheek. "We miss you around here. Your husband is making Mrs. Reilly crazy."

Jenna smiled. "That started long before my time here."

"You realize I'm sitting right here?" Jake tried for a solemn expression. "I used to command respect around here."

After Harry left, she crossed the room to his desk. "So— whose love life are we discussing?"

Jake pulled her into his arms. "Ours. When are those babies going to sleep through the night?"

She dropped a kiss on his chin, laughing over his disgruntled expression. "They're only eight weeks, Jackson. Give it some time."

"It feels like forever since we've been alone," he confessed as he drew in a satisfying breath of her scent. "I miss us."

Jen pulled back to stare at him. "Well— I have this idea I wanted to run past you."

His pulse notched higher over her secretive expression. Something was up. Please God, let it involve some alone time. "I'm all ears."

Her shoulders shook with laughter. "Judging by your hold on me, I can feel there's a great deal more to you than just ears."

He hauled her back against him. "That's entirely your fault. Tell me this idea."

"Well— your mom is already babysitting the kids. I thought maybe— we could have dinner somewhere romantic."

His beautiful wife was blushing crimson. There had to be more to her plan— and he was dying to hear it. "Is there something you're not telling me?" When Jenna leaned in to whisper in his ear and he had to fight the urge to kiss her senseless.

"I had my doctor's appointment today and she said— you know . . . we could-"

Relief and lust roared through him. "Thank God."

Jen suddenly looked troubled. "I still have seventeen pounds to-"

"Don't even go there," he warned, cutting her off. "You're beautiful. You're the sexiest woman in the world to me."

Despite his assurance, her expression didn't change. "This body is *not* beautiful. Stretch marks. No sleep. Nursing every two hours . . ."

"Listen to me." He pulled her against him, loving the feel of her in his arms. "This body has given me everything I'll ever want." She stilled against him, waiting for his next words. He dropped a kiss along her ear. "This *amazing* body gave me a family."

"Jake-"

He kissed her again. "Think about it, Jen. You gave me Megan and Alex. And now you've given me the twins. Everything important in my life . . . you created."

Her eyes suddenly glistening, she nodded.

"Do you know how long it's been?"

"Well, yeah. It's-"

He trailed a kiss along her jaw, interrupting the math in her head. Making her shiver. "Ten weeks, three days-" He checked his watch. "Fourteen hours and nine minutes."

Her eyes widened, her reluctant smile telling him he'd said the right thing . "You've kept track?"

"Hell, yes."

"Just to let you know, you had me at *'you're beautiful'*." Shifting in his arms, amusement shimmered in her eyes. "I just wanted to see what you'd do with a challenge."

Nearly groaning in anticipation, Jake released her carefully. When he groped for the desk phone, his hand was unsteady. "Mrs. Reilly— please cancel my appointments for the rest of the day." He hung up with a smile. "I'm ready to leave now."

"Jake! It's only two," she stammered. "The only dinner we could have now is at a drive-thru." She rested her hands against his chest. "I feel guilty. You shouldn't cancel-"

"You like a challenge? How's this?" He leaned in, bewitched by her expressive eyes. "There aren't enough hours left in the day for what I'm planning." If it were possible, her fiery blush deepened as she stared at him. "Trust me, love. I'll find a hotel that serves *very* romantic room service."

Mona had just settled Rosie for her nap when she heard a tap at the front door. Hoisting Rosie's still alert twin to her shoulder, she wandered through her son's expansive home to see who was waiting. Smiling when she recognized her former husband through the frosted glass, she opened the door. "Linc— what are you doing here?

"Thought I'd drop by for a visit." He smiled as he leaned in to kiss her cheek in greeting. "I stopped at the office to see Jackson earlier today and he mentioned you were babysitting for Jen's appointment."

She smiled. "Actually, I'm here for the evening now. Jake just called. He wants a child-free dinner date with his wife, so they won't be home until nine."

"You need some help?"

Pleasure heated her smile. "I'd love your company. Megan and Alex will be home from school soon. Maybe we can order pizza."

"Sounds good. If you'd like, I'll walk down to the bus stop."

Mona shifted the baby on her shoulder. "How have you been? I haven't seen you in a few weeks. You must be busy."

"Which one is this? Roosevelt or Madison?" Linc made a funny face at the infant and was rewarded with a wide-eyed stare. He opened his arms in a wordless offer to take the baby from her.

Mona inhaled his outdoorsy cologne and bit back a sigh when she transferred Maddie to his arms. Damn the man. He still smelled great. "When are you going to learn to tell them apart, Grampa? This is Madison. Rosie just went down for a nap."

Linc chuckled. "When they're together I can sorta tell. Maddie's got a little heft to her." He gazed at Madison, a smile on his face. "How about you two beauties grow some hair? That would help your old gramps tell you apart."

"Want a cup of tea?" Mona drifted into the kitchen. "I was just about to put the kettle on."

He followed her, taking a chair at the table. The baby's eyes had started to droop, so he hoisted her to his shoulder, gently stroking her back. "Make mine with a splash of Jameson and I'm in."

"I thought Jefferson said you were out of town?" Mona moved briskly around the airy kitchen. "We had dinner two nights ago."

"Yeah— that's what I told him. I needed a reasonable excuse to get him involved on the New Beginnings Shelter." Linc grinned when she paused at the counter. "Now, I'm just trying to stay out of the way for another couple weeks."

"Uh-oh. I know that expression. What are you scheming now?"

"Nothing— not much, anyway," he backpedalled. "I'm testing a theory."

She set a mug of steaming tea on the table before him, ignoring his request for whiskey. "And what would that theory be?"

"That the beautiful woman managing the homeless shelter fundraising campaign would be absolutely perfect for him."

"Who— Omigosh— not Marisol?" Her mouth dropped open. "Linc— are you crazy? How can you— of all people— think about matchmaking?" Mona bit her lip to keep from laughing. "You have a new girlfriend every month."

"Which makes me somewhat of an expert— wouldn't you say?"

The sparkle in his eyes was the very same she'd fallen for nearly thirty-five years earlier. His zest for living, his boundless enthusiasm. His glass-half-full outlook on life. She'd often noticed similar qualities in their youngest son. For as serious as Jake was— Jefferson was the complete opposite. Mona shook her head. "Well, you've certainly got my attention. What's your plan?"

"Well - you know how involved I've been in designing the new wing, right?" He waited for her nod. "I've really gotten to know Marisol. She's smart and tough and sassy. She's kind and giving. What's not to like, right?"

Mona didn't disagree with his assessment. She was a passionate, committed woman who gave of herself to benefit others. But Jefferson? Her youngest son was a wonderful man— but he wasn't ready for any sort of serious relationship. "Linc— you know Jeff. He's more love 'em and leave 'em at this stage of his life. He falls in love with someone new about as often as you do."

Linc cracked up. "I won't argue the point, Moe. But people change. I can already see subtle signs of maturity in our Jeffie."

"Does Marisol have anything to say about this? Has Jeff figured out what you're doing?"

34

LAUREN GIORDANO

"Hell no! All I've done is set it up so he's taking responsibility for the addition. As far as he's concerned— she's just another client— an incredibly attractive client. He's probably feelin' like the luckiest guy on earth."

"Mmm." She set her spoon on the table. "This project is on deadline, right? Is he going to step up to the plate and make the job happen— or is he going to spend all his time trying to score with her?"

"That's the beauty of it," Linc crowed. His voice startled Madison who released a faint whimper of protest. "That's the beauty," he whispered. "Marisol is all business. She wants that shelter done and she wants it now. He'll tow the line— or he'll face her wrath."

"And exactly where do you fit into the scheme?"

"I'm staying out of the picture for another week or two. The rest is up to him. I've just thrown them together— two people I believe could have a strong relationship— with a great deal of sparks."

"Sparks also cause wildfires," Mona muttered. "I think you're way over your head, darling."

"He wants more responsibility," he reminded. "Jeff sees what Jackson has— and now Harry. They're both happy— in love. And he loves kids. Between Jenna's kids and the twins— he adores all of them. Now Harry and Kendall are having a baby-"

"It doesn't mean Jeff is *ready* for all that," she protested. "He may want it— and someday he'll make a wonderful husband. But that doesn't mean he'd make a good husband right now."

"But Marisol is perfect for him," he insisted. "She'd balance him out— make him stronger and more grounded."

Staring at him, Mona wondered where this sudden interest in Jeff's life was coming from. Linc had never been one to meddle in his kids' lives. In fact— he'd been so busy building his business, he'd barely had *time* for their children while they were growing up. Too many times to count, she'd played the role of both mother and father. And she— more than anyone, knew the cost of marrying someone who was more enamored with his work than his wife or family. "What's this really about, Linc?"

He hesitated. "I see what a wonderful girl Mari is— and I want that for Jeff. Good women don't come along every day. Guys always think they will— hell— we *assume* they will. We assume if we lose one— it's not a huge deal. The next one's around the corner. When you're young, you think you have all the time in the world." He paused— suddenly seeming to choose his words carefully. "But then you round that corner— and she's not there. So you round the next corner— still hopeful. I mean— how hard can it be, really?"

Her heart pounding, Mona's hand shook when she raised the teacup to her lips. Linc was talking about her— *about them*— their life together. She wondered if he even realized what he was saying. She cradled the cup in both hands so she wouldn't drop it.

"By the time you realize your mistake— you've trudged twenty blocks in the wrong direction." He swallowed hard. "Even if you go back to that first corner— everything's changed. The traffic pattern is different. That girl you were crazy for— she's moved on. She found someone else— someone who was ready. Someone who wanted the same things. And the worst part— the very worst part is— you've finally realized you wanted those same things all along— and you wanted them with her. But you're too late."

His voice trailed off and the silence lengthened— a ribbon of guilt. Regret. Pain. Swirling around them. Mona couldn't speak— couldn't breathe. For perhaps the first time in her adult life— she had absolutely no clue what to say. Little Madison's snuffly breathing broke the awkward silence and they both smiled. Linc's shoulders shook with silent laughter as he glanced at the angel sleeping on his shoulder. Mona finally summoned the courage to meet his gaze.

"I understand, Linc." Releasing a shuddering breath, she reached across the table to squeeze his hand. "But relationships don't always work out the way we choose. Sometimes you can do everything right— and it still doesn't work. People make decisions based on the information available at a given moment. It's impossible to see around that next corner."

Her silver-haired husband smiled awkwardly, realizing he'd revealed far more than he'd perhaps intended. "I don't want that for Jefferson. He really likes her— and I think she likes him. If I can somehow help it along-"

"Liking and loving are very different emotions, dear."

He shrugged, his smile impish. Linc was back on solid emotional ground. "I'm banking on Jeffie. My boys go after what they want."

She raised an eyebrow in mocking disapproval. "Does Mari have any say in this matter?"

"If she puts him through the ringer— even better. Jeff's had it too easy with women for too long. He needs to suffer."

"You make her sound like a battle you're strategizing. It's a little insulting."

"He'll appreciate the reward because he had to fight for it," Linc defended, the smile on his face one of merriment. "Jeff is a man who likes a challenge. You can't fault him for that."

Sitting there, plotting strategy— it was hard to believe they'd been divorced for a decade. She leaned forward in her chair. "Okay— you've convinced me. What can I do to help?"

"Take it easy, Sport. If you eat too fast, you'll get sick." Jeff eyed Hector as he inhaled a third slice of pizza. He still couldn't believe he'd managed to pull it off.

Marisol Ortega. With him. On a date.

With Hector playing chaperone. . . But why get caught up in details? Technically— it was still a date.

"I won gek sif."

"Finish chewing before you speak. Where are your manners, tonight?" Mari reminded. "Jeff can wait to hear your answer. He doesn't need to see all that pizza rolling around in your mouth."

Hiding his smile, Jeff wasn't surprised when Hector cracked up. Reminding the little boy of the mess in his mouth would only entice him to show it again. Her lecture would have the opposite effect of what she hoped for.

"She's right. A gentleman keeps his mouth shut when he's eating— especially when it's pizza." He softened his words with a wink. "We don't want Mari getting sick all over the place, do we? Then we wouldn't be able to stop at the park after dinner."

As expected, Hector took immediate notice and sat up straight. His mouth slammed shut. Hearing her exasperated sigh from across the table, Jeff tried not to gloat. "Something wrong, Miss Ortega?"

"That's much better, Hector." Ignoring him, she acknowledged the little boy's efforts before reluctantly meeting his gaze. The luscious mouth he'd spent weeks considering, twitched with the effort not to smile.

"Thank you for your assistance, Mr. Traynor. You've been very helpful this evening. I'd planned to ask you back to our home later, but since I might get sick all over the place . . . I wouldn't want to burden you with that possibility."

You had to appreciate a woman who thought on her feet. "I am willing to assume that risk."

Hector's eyes widened as he tried to follow their conversation. "Are you sick, mama? Can we still go to the park?"

"I'm fine, love. We're only joking." Her beautiful eyes remained locked on him when she tousled Hector's curly hair. "Remember the dessert we made earlier? Didn't you want to ask Jeff something?"

Hector's fork clattered to the table as he bolted up in his seat. "Oh, yeah. I forgot." He turned, big, brown eyes suddenly serious. "Jeff— we made brownies after school today. Before you gots us-"

"I love brownies." He couldn't help smiling over the little guy's excitement.

Hector's face lit up. "Mari said you would. She says all boys like chocolate. We want you to come inside and have brownies with us— after the park." He turned to check with her. "And maybe we can have ice cream with them?"

She nodded. "If you're a good listener at the park."

Jeff relaxed in his chair. So far, the evening was progressing perfectly. He'd been surprised earlier to acknowledge he was nervous. All day, he'd been eager for this night to arrive. Not wanting to be late, he'd allowed extra time. But her directions had been spot on.

Yet when he'd pulled into her driveway, he'd hesitated. Convincing Marisol had taken twenty-nine days. Jeff had lost track of how many times he'd officially asked her— but it was easily a dozen. He didn't want to blow a month of effort with a mistake. His heart had actually been pounding when he rang the bell. But then she'd opened the door— gorgeous, sea blue eyes welcoming. And here they were. A fun dinner with a sweet little boy and a beautiful woman who was slowly, cautiously starting to lower her guard.

Jeff couldn't remember ever experiencing this level of uncertainty before. Part of him resented feeling this way. Obviously— it was the part that had always taken anything he ever wanted from the opposite sex. But the rest of him was enjoying the hell out of the challenge. The rush of uncertainty would definitely keep him fully engaged. There was no danger of complacency with Mari. There would be no games— not that he'd ever really been into that. But he also knew she wouldn't put up with them.

He'd already sensed she wouldn't tolerate a slacker, but he was absolutely certain she wouldn't risk exposing Hector to getting his feelings hurt. He'd met up with Hector accidentally— but staying on the fringes of his life would be solely up to Marisol. That made this date— and any he might be fortunate enough to secure in the future— high stakes. The way he viewed it— he had two choices. He was either all in and betting with confidence or he should fold his hand and get out tonight.

"Can we go to the park soon, Jeff? It's gonna get dark."

"Hang in there, Sport. We have plenty of time." He smiled over Hector's worried expression. "Let's make sure your mom has finished dinner."

"Mari, pleee-ze? Are you done?"

She hid her chuckle behind her napkin. "When you ask so nicely, how can I possibly refuse?"

"Okay, Hec. Lead the way." Jeff caught her glance and winked, hoping to provoke another blush. She'd done it all evening. For someone so tightly in command of her emotions, it was perhaps the one thing Marisol couldn't control. It probably drove her crazy— that a purely physical response could reveal all sorts of secrets she didn't wish to share. Did she blush like that around every guy? Or was her reaction reserved solely for him? Was it possible he made her nervous? The thought made him smile.

He'd thought of no one else this past month. From the moment he'd set eyes on her— she'd been it. Until she trusted him enough to let the wall down, her blush was one of the few signals he had to gauge her thoughts. And before they were through, that wall was gonna tumble.

Oh, yeah. He was all in.

Marisol blew the wayward curls out of her face. Still flushed from the heat in the bathroom during Hector's bath, she was supremely conscious of the fact that she was completely disheveled. If her son hadn't insisted on Jefferson tucking him into bed, she wouldn't have cared so much about her appearance. But he was still here— waiting patiently to tuck him in. Then they would finally head downstairs together— alone for the first time. And she was a straggly mess.

She chewed her lip in frustration. Why did it matter how she looked? She wasn't getting involved with anyone— remember? Just because Jeff was stunningly gorgeous— even after a sixty minute stint in the park chasing her son— even after another hour spent crawling on the living room rug playing trucks.

"Mama— come on! I'm dry. Let's get out there."

She finished buttoning his pajamas, her frazzled thoughts calming with the basic task. "Jeff is waiting, carino. He won't leave without saying goodnight."

The moment she finished, Hector bolted for the door. She surveyed the damp towels near the tub before deciding the mess could be cleaned later. She'd stalled long enough. Avoiding the mirror, she turned off the fan and headed to her son's room.

To her surprise, Hector was already under the covers when she entered his room. Jeff sat perched on the end of the bed, absorbed in talk of baseball.

"Mari— Jeff likes baseball, too. He said his nephew plays tee-ball. And he's my age." Hector's eyes were wide. "Can I do that?"

She glanced from one to the other. "If you'd like to try it, I'll call the parks department to see if there's a program here."

A flash of worry crossed Jeff's face. "Even if there isn't a program, Hec . . . you can still learn to play and then join a league next year."

"But I want to play," he protested.

"I promise to call for you," she repeated. "Now— isn't there something you'd like to say to Jeff?" His suddenly confused expression made her smile.

"I wanna play tee-ball?"

Jeff's chuckle made her sigh. "To thank him for dinner," she prompted. "And for taking us to the park?"

"Oh, yeah. Thanks, Jeff." He beamed at his new best friend. "I had fun playin' with you. I think you should come over again tomorrow."

Jeff's expression was solemn. "I had a great time, too. And we definitely should do it again soon. I promise I'll talk with your mom before I leave."

"Okay." His eyelids were already drooping when he yawned. "Goodnight, Jeff."

"Sleep tight, buddy."

She watched from the doorway when he rose from the bed and straightened the blanket around Hector's slender shoulders. She tried not to read too much into his actions— tried to stop the visions scrolling through her brain. Tucking in children, walks in the park . . . with the person who would know you best in the world— who you could rely on, no matter what the situation-

What was wrong with her? They'd had one date— a few hours together— a mere blip in the span of a lifetime. Just because Jeff had been amazing tonight didn't mean she could simply insert him into her fantasy of the perfect family. She couldn't afford to allow fantasies to rule her head. She'd made that mistake before. And where had it gotten her? Emotionally shattered— and in need of a restraining order.

She drew in a shaky breath when Jeff turned and smiled. No doubt about it— he was beautiful. And thoughtful. He'd been kind and patient with her son. For those reasons, he scored extra points. Beyond that— she barely knew him. All men were capable of appearing interested for brief periods. It was the long haul that usually revealed their commitment problems.

They didn't speak until they were downstairs. Despite her unease, Mari's pulse tripped with anticipation. She feigned normalcy as she headed for the kitchen— as though the presence of gorgeous, attentive men were a commonplace occurrence at her dining table. "Can I get you a beer?"

"That sounds great. I don't suppose I could negotiate for another brownie?"

Pausing in the hallway, she studied his hopeful expression before bursting into laughter, her tension dissolving.

"What?" He shrugged. "They were really good."

"My mother will be pleased to hear. I made them from her recipe." The realization that Jeff possessed a sweet tooth like Hector made her smile.

"Do your parents live close by?"

She shook her head. "Near Baltimore. We try to get everyone together at least once a month for family dinner."

"Sounds like a big family. Brothers or sisters?" Jeff seemed to fill the doorway when he leaned against the frame and she took a tiny step backward into the kitchen.

"I have two sisters and one brother. My older brother, Manuel and an older sister, Caridad." She ticked them off on her fingers. "Then I'm in the middle and finally, my baby sister, Serafina."

"Pretty names," he acknowledged. "I'm one of three. Andrea is the oldest, then Jake, then me. And my cousin Harrison is like a brother to us. He basically grew up in our house."

"Does everyone work for Specialty?"

"Jake runs the show. Harrison manages accounting and I head up estimating."

"And Andrea?"

"She works in marketing, but only part-time. Her girls are teenagers now, but she always wanted to be there when they got off the bus." Jeff took a step into her kitchen and she took another step back. "Tell me about your parents. Where is Ortega from?"

She smiled. "We are the definition of an American family. My father is Cuban, but born here— in Miami. He works for a defense contractor near D.C."

"And your mom?"

"My mother is Bridget. They met at Florida State. She has flaming red hair and blue eyes. We're all a weird blend of Cuban and Scottish."

He grinned over her word choice. "What's weird about that?"

"Well, I have a sister with strawberry blond hair, a brother who looks Hispanic like me— except for our eyes and a sister with red hair and dark eyes like Dad. You should see the family portrait."

He took a step closer. "The way I see it— you get that beautiful, golden skin from your dad and your amazing eyes from your mom."

"I . . . thank you. I-I guess so." Mari drew in a steadying breath, the compliment sending a jolt through her system. When it came to flirting, she was seriously out of practice. "Why— don't I get our drinks? We can sit in the living room. It's just down the hall." She ducked into the pantry, suddenly in serious need of regrouping.

"Why don't I help?"

To her dismay, Jeff followed her into the tiny space. Great— now she had a large, attractive man crowding the suddenly claustrophobic room. She adored her cottage and all of its charming nooks, but her pantry left much to be desired.

Again, she wondered why she was so thrown off balance by a few compliments. Lord knew she'd heard it all before— from guys just like him. Only this wasn't just another guy. This was the man she'd been thinking about— for weeks. Against her will. His smile— and that dimple— had slipped into her subconscious and wormed their way into her brain.

Scooping a few brownies onto a plate, Mari was supremely conscious of him watching her actions. Her pulse skittered with anticipation— or perhaps it was fear. This date had been a big step. One she'd been nervous to take. Out of habit, she licked the chocolate crumbs from her fingers.

"You can take these into the living room. I'll be there in a moment." She spoke over her shoulder as she opened the refrigerator to retrieve a beer. She'd already decided on water for herself. *Cold* water. With lots of ice.

When she extracted herself from the fridge, she discovered him standing right behind her. She was good and wedged— the counter at her back and Jefferson standing before her. "What are you doing?"

His gaze locked with hers, Jeff carefully set the plate on the counter and took a step closer. "The way I figure it— we're both wondering what it will be like when I finally kiss you. I thought maybe . . . we should just get it out of the way now."

Her breath caught in her throat. It was suddenly overly warm in her too small kitchen. "Actually, I-I'm not wondering at all," she lied. Her face heated with embarrassment.

Jeff's eyes snapped with humor as he examined her face before slowly grinning. "I'm gonna call liar on that statement. Possibly even 'pants on fire'."

"I do not lie." Except perhaps to herself. Because kissing him sounded like an amazing idea. A spectacular idea. He took a step closer and Mari's pulse ricocheted. "I don't think this is-" He reached out, gently tucking a strand of seriously out-of-control hair behind her ear. She gulped in a breath of air. "-a good idea."

"Soft and beautiful." Jeff acted as though he hadn't heard her. His hand slid around to cradle her head, his fingers tugging through the weight of her curls before they paused to massage her nape. Mari had to bite back a groan over the sensual touch.

"I've been imagining this for at least a month," he muttered.

"Y-you have?" It took real effort not to lean into his hand. As she stood between his feet, his free hand traced lightly down her arm. His fingers trailed a shivery path along her skin. The sensation of those large, capable hands on her body was making it difficult to remember what she wanted to say.

"This is your fault, you know," he said absently as his fingers left her hair to feather along her jaw.

"What's my fault?" Her heart was beating so loud Mari could barely hear him. She should have been panicking . . . yet she was honest enough to admit that all she could think about was how very much she wanted to kiss him.

"You said it earlier— all boys like chocolate." Leaning in, his beautiful eyes were sober as they watched her— giving her every opportunity to stop him if she desired. "Let's see if I can taste it on you."

"Jefferson, please-" she whispered against his lips before they brushed against hers. Marisol knew her plea was futile. She'd been fighting her attraction to him for weeks. His mouth was slow and deliberate— almost teasing her with his control. And she grew hypnotized by the sensation building within her. A blend of frustration and need and wanting.

The very moment he deepened the kiss, a shudder tore through her. He felt so good— so incredible that she forgot all about her initial reservations. With a heady sense of wonder, Mari realized she had never experienced anything like this before. When his arms tightened around her, she forgot everything except the amazing man— kissing her as though his life depended on it.

Jeff nudged her back against the counter, his mouth insistent. And when his tongue swept inside in search of hers, Mari met him eagerly. In the back of her brain, she heard him groan as she tasted him. When his lips left hers, she felt immediately bereft, until he trailed kisses down the side of her face. Shivering when his mouth found a sensitive spot on her throat, she cried out when his hand brushed against her breast through her suddenly constricting blouse.

Jeff believed he might actually be in shock— for there was no rational explanation for the mind-blowing sensation of kissing Marisol. It was unlike anything he'd ever experienced before. He was gentle at first, almost afraid he would scare her— afraid his passion would overwhelm her and then he'd never get the opportunity again. He'd known she would be amazing— if only because he'd fantasized about this moment for the past month. He'd memorized every nuance of her face and now he was finally touching the soft skin he'd dreamed of.

When she'd challenged him, he'd been determined to seduce her slowly, to tease her and drive her as crazy as he'd begun to feel whenever he was near her. Her blush had told him everything her words denied. Though her beautiful eyes had flared with panic, they'd also revealed passion she wanted badly to hide.

His experiment had worked perfectly— until the moment she began to respond. And *whoa*— did she respond. Trouble was— he hadn't counted on going a little crazy himself. His control was something of a matter of pride. Countless women before Mari had left him unscathed. While he'd always enjoyed himself, he'd never experienced a need that couldn't be quenched rather quickly.

Until now. Awareness surged around them in a force field of sexual energy. He deepened the kiss, thrilled when Mari's arms crept up around his neck. She was actually trembling with need. Or hell— maybe that was him. Her soft whimper only pushed him closer to the precipice, imagining what it would be like when he finally made love to the beautiful woman in his arms. When she pressed herself against him, he nearly staggered over the sensation of her lush, perfect curves molded to him. Her warm, scented skin surrounded him, making him burn for more.

He'd never wanted a woman the way he wanted Marisol Ortega. As though it were a hunger. As though she'd somehow taken over a part of him. Jeff wanted to hold her and touch her until she melted against him and then he wanted to do it all over again.

When he found the sensitized skin of her throat, she shivered and clung to him- her hands everywhere. Jeff discovered he wanted her touch— needed it desperately. He knew he should stop, but hell if he wanted to. The soft throaty sound she made nearly sent him over the edge. He wanted to keep kissing her until-

Before she completely lost her mind, Marisol broke free of the force field. She wrenched from the embrace before realizing her arms were still locked around him. She used the last of her strength to push away from him. They were both breathing as though they'd run a marathon. It was a terribly small consolation that Jeff appeared to be equally shell-shocked.

"Jefferson-" Her voice held a frisson of pure panic Mari couldn't begin to hide. She slid away from him, the counter at her back to support still shaky legs, her heart racing. Dios— what could she be thinking? It had been so long since she'd allowed herself to feel anything for a man— and Jeff was an incredible man. But she was in danger of forgetting herself.

"I know." His voice was still whisper soft. "I should probably go."

She raised her fingers to swollen, sensitized lips. "I— I don't know what to say."

Jeff smiled over the croaking sound of her voice. "Don't say anything, sweetheart. I'll take a rain check on those brownies. I think I've had all the sweetness I can handle for one evening."

"I— I'll see you out." She bolted for the door, praying he would follow. If he kissed her again, Mari wasn't sure she would have the strength to resist.

"I'll call you tomorrow," he promised. She nodded, too afraid to say anything while she still felt so out of control of careening emotions. When he leaned in, she went completely still— until she saw his satisfied grin. Then she remembered to breathe.

"Good night, Mr. Traynor."

Before she could pull away, he brushed her lips once more before he reluctantly drew back. "Goodnight, Miss Ortega. I greatly enjoyed kissing you and I hope to do it again— very soon."

He was rewarded with a crimson blush.

CHAPTER 4

Jeff checked his watch for the fifth time and groaned. Tossing his pencil on the unread specifications, he rose from his chair and stretched. So much for getting a jump on the week ahead. Instead, his Sunday was melting away. He should have accepted the invitation to Jake's to watch the ball game.

Instead— he'd driven to the office, sat down at his desk and proceeded to dissect his weekend with Mari. After a futile Friday night spent reliving each bone-melting kiss, he'd virtually guaranteed himself a sleepless night. And after imagining his hands on her amazing body, he'd required an icy blast in the shower to rein in his short-circuiting brain. By mid-morning Saturday, he'd been unable to suppress the urge to call her.

All his old rules— his modus operandi for nearly a decade— his guidelines for a pleasurable life— had gone up in smoke. Before Mari— as he was starting to view time— he never, *ever* would have called a woman the next day. Yesterday he hadn't even waited twelve hours. His friends would be so disappointed. Hell— he'd thrown the bro handbook out the window.

And he'd been grateful, damn it. Because thankfully, she'd picked up the phone. And then, as time stood suspended— she'd agreed to see him again. But he'd heard the reluctance in her voice. Jeff had the sneaking suspicion she'd only agreed because of Hector. Apparently, the little boy had pestered her from the moment he'd awakened Saturday morning. He'd be sure to thank Hector for that.

They'd spent several hours together in the park while he'd taught Hector the basics of baseball. Mari had packed a picnic lunch they'd enjoyed before the little guy had made a run for the swing set. Jeff had wasted no time closing the distance between them on the picnic blanket. With Hector in plain view, Mari had protested vigorously. Luckily, he'd persisted— but only in driving them both to the brink of sanity. As they'd both watched Hector, he'd stroked her back. He'd caressed the amazingly soft skin at the nape of her neck. He'd absorbed each shudder she experienced at his touch . . . heard each indrawn breath . . . watched sensual pink lips part . . . seen ocean blue eyes turn stormy with passion. And then they'd been interrupted by a sweet, energetic five-year old wanting a push on the swings. Mari had recovered quickly, laughter bubbling from her throat as he'd risen reluctantly from the blanket. But he'd needed the fifteen minutes with Hector to cool down.

Mari was definitely interested. That kiss in her kitchen Friday night had confirmed the attraction was not one-sided. Hell- he'd known he would go up in flames the moment he touched her. But he'd been relieved she'd felt the same. They'd been maddeningly close to the edge again Saturday. Jeff had held off for as long as— any normal human could deny himself something he wanted desperately. But even holding her hand as they strolled through the park had set his pulse thumping erratically. By the time he was finally able to kiss her, his gut had been knotted with anticipation.

And it had been fireworks all over again. He was honestly beginning to feel as though he'd never get enough of her. And what the hell did that mean? What was so special about her? His chair squeaked in protest when Jeff rose to stretch, giving in to sudden agitation. She'd become like a damned drug he couldn't get enough of. When they'd said goodnight on her doorstep, Mari had looked almost— afraid. As though she felt it, too. And was absolutely terrified by the chemistry between them. Not exactly a vote of confidence.

You should end it. Jeff paced the length of his office. Twenty paces. He nodded. It was the sensible solution. They were in a working relationship. It had been a mistake— a huge mistake on his part. Twenty paces back. Mari was beautiful. She was gorgeous. Smart. Funny— He would like nothing more than to get her into bed-

Hell— that was the completely wrong visual to be scrolling through his brain now. Pivoting, Jeff paced to the far side of his office once again. But he absolutely, positively was *not* interested in getting serious. He wasn't even thirty yet. Despite their chemistry, Mari was the last woman he should be pursuing. She was dedicated to the shelter and her clients— bordering on workaholic, now that he thought about it.

Ironically, her work ethic was one of the things he admired about her. But that didn't make her right for him. Marisol wasn't like anyone he'd dated before. She had serious commitments. Which left little time for fun— with him. Jeff nodded. A relationship with her would be too much work. Too much planning. Releasing a deep breath, he felt his resolve return. He strolled back to his desk, feeling more in control. He had his answer. He should end it.

The women he usually settled for were ready for anything. It left Jeff free to plan or not plan. It left him free to call at the last minute— making certain nothing better came up that might be more fun. It left him free to decide whether he was even interested in putting out the effort— going through the motions— enduring an endless night of chick banter just to get laid.

Between their two schedules, he'd probably never see Marisol— even if he wanted to. Another reason she was wrong for him. His chair squeaked when he sat down, then protested when he bolted up again. He strode in the opposite direction - giving in to the restless impulse to move. He needed his freedom— his ability to pick up and go— to ride his motorcycle whenever he felt the urge. Not that he got the chance very often anymore. Work was usually too crazy for much time off.

Jeff paced a bit more. On top of that— she'd voluntarily accepted the burden of fostering Hector. Mari was what— twenty-seven, maybe? She had her whole life to tie herself down with a family. Why would she end her freedom so soon?

Although— her choosing to foster Hector made him like her even more. She was protective of those who couldn't protect themselves. She was passionate and dedicated. Unafraid of a challenge. She would gain custody of Hector because his drug addicted mother couldn't provide the environment he deserved. Mari would give him everything he needed and more. Jeff skidded to a stop. She would value him.

A relationship with her would never work. Jeff contemplated banging his head against the wall. Yeah— she was beautiful, passionate, dedicated and giving. *Who the hell wants a woman like that?* Feeling like an idiot, he stomped back to his desk and sat down.Retrieving a pencil from the plans he should have been reviewing, Jeff drummed it absently. Since Hector seemed to be fascinated by excavation, he'd managed to track down a kid sized hardhat for him to wear once they began construction at the shelter. They'd break ground in a few days-

A chill jagged down his spine. What the hell was he thinking? He'd only known Hector for a week. What was he doing— making plans for him? As though he had the right to. As though he'd be hanging out with the kid indefinitely. Jeff laid his head on the contracts he'd been reviewing and groaned. What was happening to him?

When his phone rang, he was almost relieved. "Traynor."

He smiled when he recognized his father's voice. It was about friggin' time. "Where have you been? I'm up to my eyes with your homeless shelter project." He jotted a few notes on the dog-eared pad on the corner of his desk. This was his chance— to extricate himself from the project. And from Mari's tempting clutches. "You're at Jake's? Yeah— I can make it. I'll be there in thirty minutes."

"What are all those deep thoughts making you scowl, mi hija dulce?"

Mari smiled. Even after all these years, she couldn't get used to her fiery-haired, freckle-faced, blue-eyed mother speaking Spanish. It always seemed so laughably out of context. "*My sweet daughter*? I sense serious prying coming my way."

"Joke if you want, but I know that expression." Bridget paused in setting the table. "Something is distracting you, and I don't think it's our Sunday afternoon pork roast."

Sighing, Mari passed her mother another place setting. Perhaps it was for the best she didn't see her family as often as she wished. It was easy to forget how well they all could read her. She'd accepted the invitation to dinner thinking the long drive to Baltimore would be a good way to take her mind off her problem. Yet even in the safe cocoon of her parents' home, she could not escape thinking about Jefferson. About how good it felt to be in his arms. About how wonderful he was with Hector. About how much she already wanted to see him again. How if he'd called today—she would have said yes. And she wouldn't have tried to talk herself out of it.

And how utterly terrifying it was to realize that.

Her mother eyed her skeptically. "Something is bothering you, carina."

Why was she fantasizing about a relationship with a man who didn't 'do' relationships? She'd already run the gauntlet with Caridad. Thank goodness, Serafina hadn't arrived yet. "It's not important, Mom. You know me— I'm dwelling on something I can't control."

Panic flared in the older woman's eyes as she grabbed Mari's arm. "Lord— it's not Nick? He's not back— is he?" Her mother appeared ready to bolt into the living room and jerk her father from his armchair.

"Mom, calm down. I haven't heard from him— not in two years. It's all over." Guilt lanced her over the terror in her mother's voice.

Her mother released a steadying breath. It was several seconds before the fear dissolved from her eyes. Mari experienced a wash of shame. She'd forgotten how much her volatile relationship with Nick had affected her family. As the person who lived it, she'd borne the brunt of his abuse. But her mother— her sisters— had been victims as well. From witnessing the physical damage he'd inflicted, to dealing with her emotional baggage in the aftermath.

Her sisters had also paid a price in their parents' hyper vigilance. Their dating lives had been shoved under a microscope. Between Manuel and her father— no Ortega girl in the dating pool had left their apartments without the distinct possibility of being tailed. The sisters held strong suspicions their father had called in favors to have background checks performed on one of Caridad's boyfriends and several of Serafina's dates.

"Is it Hector's mother? We'll all be there for you, carina. Whatever you need."

Relieved, Mari took the easy way out. "Yes," she lied. Under no circumstances did she want to discuss Jeff. Her feelings were too new— too strange. "Just nervous about the hearing."

"But that's months away, love. Shelve your worries until the time gets closer."

She leaned in to kiss her mother's cheek. "You're right, Mom. I'll try. Is Sera showing up today? I'm starving."

Thankfully, Bridget Ortega's scattered thoughts turned to her youngest. "You know Fifi— she'll bolt in at the last minute claiming one distraction or another. She's always late."

"Mari, I'm hungry." Hector chose that moment to bound into the dining room. "When is supper?"

Bridget mussed his hair, smiling when he protested. "Your aunt is late again, querido."

Hector frowned. "Serafina is always late. I think we should eat without her." He peeked into the kitchen. "I want to have cake and I can't have it 'til I eat the vegetables. I need to get started."

Bridget chuckled as she reached into her pocket to retrieve her phone. "Here, love. Call your auntie and tell her she needs to get here, pronto."

⁘

Mari rinsed the last dish and placed it in the dishwasher. It had been a perfect day. A loud, delicious dinner with her family, Caridad's fabulous cake and Hector nearly droopy with fatigue after playing in the yard with Manny and her father. Hopefully, he would sleep most of the way home. She was just about to rap on the window to signal it was time to leave when they came storming through the screen door.

Manuel dropped a kiss on top of her head. "So, little sister— what's this I'm hearing about the new man in your life? Do I need to schedule a trip to Arlington to check him out?"

She drew in a startled breath as the after dinner racket died away. She turned in the sudden stillness to face the stunned expressions of her mother and sisters— and the quiet intensity of her father. Silverware stopped clanging into the drawer. Caridad stopped tickling Serafina. Her mother froze, dish towel in hand, an expression of horror on her face— as though Manny's announcement had been about her posing for a men's magazine instead of about a pizza date.

Before she found her voice, Hector piped in. "He's Jeff. He's really good at baseball . . . an' he promised to teach me. An' he's buildin' Mari's addition. He even said I could help."

Caridad was the first to recover. With ginger hair like their mom, her eyes were a copy of her father's serious brown ones. A conversation with her was like tackling both parents at once. "Oh, really? Tell us more, Hec. Your mommy has been here all day but she somehow forgot to mention him to us."

Hector innocently obliged. "He took us for pizza on our first date. And then he took us to the park. And then he took us to the park again yesterday. We had a picnic and I went on the swings."

Mari finally found her voice. "Hector, please go get your backpack ready. We're leaving in ten minutes to drive home."

Serafina waited for him to leave the room before she pounced. "Ooh— sissy's got a boyfriend."

"He's not my-"

"What's he look like? Is he cute? Tall?" Her sister's eyes lit up. "Is he rich?" Her younger sister scarcely came up for breath. Painfully aware of her father's suddenly intense interest, she answered carefully. "His name is Jeff-"

She caught herself before she revealed his last name. Her father would be on the phone with his mysterious connections before she left the driveway. And Jefferson would wind up on the receiving end of an income tax audit. Or possibly a cattle prod. "He's— he works for the company building our addition at the shelter."

"What was that company?" Luis whispered, nudging her mother. "Bridgie— do you remember?"

Mari paused when her mother shushed him. "We've only known each other a month-"

"You've been dating him a month and you didn't tell us?" Serafina flounced into one of the dining room chairs.

"I *met* him a month ago and we've had two dates," she corrected. "And you just swung your hair into the mashed potatoes," she pointed out to her pouting sister.

Sera frowned as she removed her ponytail from the bowl on the table. The long, strawberry blonde curls that were her pride and joy held a glob of cold potato. "Dammit."

When her sister rose from the table and stomped to the bathroom, her older sister slid into the chair. "But that's big news for you, kiddo. You haven't dated anyone since Ni-" Caridad's voice halted mid-sentence when she realized where she was steering the conversation. No one wanted to be the one who riled up Luis Ortega. She quickly glanced at their father.

"That's right," she quickly confirmed. "I wasn't sure how I felt about dating— and I'm still not sure." She aimed the last comment at her father. It would be safer to acknowledge the elephant in the room and move on before Papi started stewing. Two years earlier, she'd feared her father would actually hunt Nick down and hurt him. Thankfully, her ex had proved to be more of a wimp than a bully. He'd bolted for parts unknown, saving her father . . . and probably her brother, now that she thought of it, from being brought up on assault charges.

"I'm taking things very slow." Hector reappeared with his backpack and jacket. Mari took the opportunity to edge closer to the hallway— only steps to her escape. "I would appreciate all of you remaining calm while I do this."

"Once we meet him— we'll be calm." Manny rounded the kitchen counter, his eyes intent. "Papi— I can take a few days off work-"

To her chagrin, her father actually nodded at her knucklehead brother. She glared at him and straightened to her full height. "I will do this on my own. Translated, that means *without* help from you." She waved off her brother when he would have interrupted. "And when I use the word help— I'm just trying to be nice. What I really mean is I don't want interference— no background checks. No stakeouts. No tailing me on dates. No GPS locator secretly installed on my car."

Caridad smirked. "Oh, Mariboo— just wait. You have no idea what they're capable of."

⚬⚬⚬

"So, how's the shelter progressing?"

Jeff set his beer on the coffee table and reluctantly turned his attention from the game on his brother's giant screen television. The last thing he wanted to think about was the shelter. Because that made him think of Marisol. And when he thought of her— it made him want to call. But he couldn't call because he'd sworn not to.

"We received the permits Friday, which frees up Hank to head down there Tuesday. Groundbreaking is Monday— if Dad can squeeze it into his busy schedule." It was pathetic to want to hear her voice when he'd just seen her the day before. Especially since he'd decided it might be best not to see her again.

"They've secured all the financing?" Jake grinned when his son Alex threw himself onto his shoulders. "Careful, there kid. You're getting heavy."

"And your old man is out of shape." Jeff smiled when Alex cracked up. At age seven they were so easy to impress. All it took to be awarded favorite uncle status were knock-knock jokes and pizza. Even Hector had practically made him out to be a superhero because he'd tossed the kid a few baseballs.

"Yeah- Mari— the shelter," he corrected, "has secured enough to get us through to the finishes. So that gives us at least six or seven months of work before they run out of money."

"And the way Mari secures donations, they'll be in fine shape by then." Linc entered the room, a drooling infant in his arms. His mom followed with the other twin. Jeff still couldn't tell the girls apart yet. They were both adorable. And terrifying.

Glancing at his brother, he wondered how the hell Jake managed to do it. In just shy of two years, Jake had gone from an unmarried, bad-tempered workaholic to a seriously married, slightly less cranky father of four. Frankly, when it came to his wife and their kids, he'd turned into a friggin' marshmallow.

His totally awesome sister-in-law was whipping up something fantastic in the kitchen. The smell made his stomach growl in anticipation while he watched Jenna's son scramble over his brother's shoulder to plop into his lap. His brother loved Jen's two kids as though they were his own. Their daughter Megan was the spitting image of her mother. And now they'd added the twins.

Jake's laughter filled the room. He'd never seen his brother happier. What Jeff had trouble imagining was ever wanting that scene for himself. Settling down. The words seemed so foreign. And so— final. Yet seeing what his brother had achieved sort of made him start thinking. Not any time soon- But . . . someday. Maybe.

"What do you think of her, son?"

Huh? His thoughts scattered when his dad spoke. "Think of who?"

"Marisol. Isn't she fantastic?"

"Yeah. She's great." Why did his old man have to keep bringing her up? He'd been trying to go more than thirty minutes without thinking about her. "They're all great," he was careful to add. "But

I seriously could've used your help over the past few weeks. Getting those ladies to make decisions requires a charm I seem to lack."

"Don't be silly. I knew you'd do a bang-up job, Jeffie."

"When are you coming back, Dad? I need your help sorting out the decorating issues. Some of the finishes have a pretty long lead time and those women are feisty. I need to get the colors selected and get the damn order placed."

"I don't know, exactly. I've still got a couple irons in the fire. Might be a few weeks."

"*Weeks*? I'm starting to get stacked up in estimating." That caught his brother's attention.

"How stacked up?" Jake stopped tickling Alex long enough to shoot him a look.

"Not that bad," he admitted. What the hell was going on with the old man? It was only a few years ago that Linc Traynor lived, breathed and bled for Specialty. To the tune of his marriage, his family— his everything . . . Now, Jeff couldn't get him to commit an hour? "Is there a new lady in your life, Dad?"

"Is there one in yours?" His mother chimed in from her corner of the couch.

"Yeah— no. I mean— no one . . . special." Liar. Jeff felt the urge to pace again. What was with the sudden interest in his love life? Was there no one else they could focus their attention on? "So, Alex— how's school?"

Linc shifted his grandbaby to the opposite shoulder. "I woulda thought you'd like Mari. She's a beautiful woman."

His mother jabbed Linc with her elbow. If he'd blinked, he would have missed it. His dad grunted before he turned to scowl at her. What the heck was going on between those two? Despite their divorce, his parents had been getting along pretty well the past two years. He shot a glance at Jake.

His brother shrugged. He'd seen it too. "How's the budget looking?"

"We're over by about seventy-five grand, but that's my fault. I added in some high end kitchen equipment. They feed so many people each day— and their equipment is crap. I just wanted to see if I could make it happen for them."

"What happens if we get to the end and Mari-the-amazing-fundraiser doesn't secure enough donations?"

Jeff grinned. "You know me. Somehow I'll make it work."

"That's what I was afraid of." Jake sighed. "Try to remember I have four kids to put through college."

Jenna appeared in the doorway. "Dinner in five. Can I borrow someone tall to help with the serving dishes?"

He rose before his brother could dislodge Alex. "Let me do the honors. I'm the only one not wrestling a kid."

Jake waited for his brother to leave the room before he caught his father's attention. "Hey— break it up, you two."

His parents stopped squabbling long enough to turn their attention to their eldest son. If he wasn't mistaken, Jake could've sworn he'd seen sparks flying between them. But that wasn't possible— was it? They'd been apart for a decade. He made a mental note to discuss the subject with Jenna. His wife had an uncanny knack for picking up on vibes that usually went completely over his head.

"What's goin' on with you, Dad?"

Before his father spoke a word, Jake knew he'd hit on something. Linc was guilty. It was written all over his face. But— of what? "Come on— give. Is this about Jeff?"

His mother looked horrified as she raised a finger to her lips. *Sweet*. The plot grew more interesting by the second. She rose from the couch, still clutching Madison to her shoulder and hurried over to sit beside him. "Not so loud."

He winked at Alex, who until now, had been getting bored with the conversation. But any mention of a secret meant he would be all over it. "Okay— we promise not to tell, right Sport?"

"Uh-huh. I promise."

Mona heard his dad snicker and paused to glare at him. "Your father's trying to set Jeffie up with the woman from the shelter. That's why he bailed on helping him."

"What woman?"

Alex snorted and gave him a poke. "Jeez, Dad— pay attention. Even I picked up on that one. It's the girl Mari-somethin', right?"

Mona rewarded her supremely intelligent grandson with a smile. "It's Marisol," she whispered. "Grampy thinks they're meant to be together."

"Lord help us."

Jenna appeared once again in the doorway. "Come on, everyone. Let's eat."

Jake hoisted his son from his lap and plopped him on his feet. "Mark my words, Alex— this might feel like the longest dinner of your life."

Alex ran three steps before whirling around. "Yeah, but then we get to have Grandma's brownies."

She was a big chicken.

It had been four days. Mari threw her pencil down and rubbed her eyes. Four endless days since she'd seen him Saturday. She'd somehow managed to live twenty-six years and four months without ever knowing Jefferson Traynor *existed.* Then a month ago, it had all blown up. Her perfectly safe, moderately exciting— but definitely adequate life had ceased.

She'd known Jeff was trouble the moment she'd spotted him ogling her in the parking lot. But he'd been so persistent and sweet and so damned attractive that she'd caved. And look where it had gotten her. She was smiling . . . hopeful . . . pathetic. Wanting desperately to see him again— and never wanting to see him again. When she could have seen him Monday— she'd gone out of her way to avoid him. All day long, she'd both dreaded and anticipated his arrival. How would he act toward her? Would he take one look at her and know she was seriously losing it for him? What if he'd changed his mind? Would she be able to resist throwing herself at him and kissing him senseless?

In the end— she'd chickened out. Oh— it had started out innocently. She'd taken a call from a former client— a woman who was out of the shelter and living on her own. A success story who'd needed a little advice. But as the call ran longer, Mari started thinking how much safer it would be to just avoid the meeting altogether. Perhaps she should take a few days to think. Being in close proximity to Jeff was the last thing she wanted when trying to think clearly.

As she'd driven home that night, she'd been forced to admit she'd deliberately made herself scarce for the ground breaking ceremony. *Her project*— her dream. And she'd lacked the courage to show up. Even worse, she'd been forced to suffer the knowing glances she received from Sharon and the others. And there was no better tormentor in the building than Sharon.

"Did I mention he asked for you specifically?"

"I was on the phone, Sharon." Two days later— she was still bringing it up.

Her boss grinned. "That he stayed late— hopin' you'd show up?"

"If it was urgent, he knows where my office is." Mari sighed as she reviewed her monthly donation goals. A few of her old standbys were late with checks again. She'd have to pencil in a few visits on her calendar.

"You look tired. You sleeping okay, Sugar? The nightmares aren't back, are they?"

"I'm fine," she reassured her work mom and tormentor. "Just a little concerned about Annie's problem." Her 'problem' being that her ex had shown up again last night— just as Mari was leaving for the day with Hector. Phil had been drunk— again. And making threats. Poor Annie had taken it hard. All the strides she'd taken in therapy— all the confidence she'd begun to build had been knocked to the ground again. It was to the point where Sharon and the other administrators weren't sure they could continue to keep Annie and her boys safe. New Beginnings was the third shelter they'd lived in. Each time, Phil found them. Now Annie was afraid to leave the grounds, for fear her ex would be waiting.

Mari sighed. She knew what that fear felt like. She'd experienced the same terror after Nick's assault. Of not knowing where he was— wondering whether he watched her, whether he was following her, plotting his next attack. . . She scrubbed at the sudden goose bumps on her arms. "What's our plan?"

If left to fester, Annie's fear would take on a life of its own. It would manifest itself and grow larger than the actual threat Phil posed. But what to do about it?

"Hell if I know. I thought it might be best to move her to another shelter . . . but no one's got space for her and the two kids. And we sure as hell can't split them up."

She frowned. "You think he poses that great a threat? I think it's mostly talk— don't you?"

Sharon's bracelets jangled against the desk every time she moved her wrist. "I'm worried that he always seems to show up when our staffing is light. I don't want him slippin' in here simply because we didn't have enough volunteers on duty. I wonder whether he's been watching enough to know that— or if he's just getting lucky."

"I'll be glad when we get the new card access system installed." It would be worth the huge expense to have peace of mind. But that installation was months away.

"Sugar— we need that system now. And just look at what it's gonna be like for the next several months during construction." She waved her arms around, bracelets clanging. "There's people walking around all over the place."

"They've all had background checks. I made sure that was in our contract." Biting her lip, Mari wondered how hard it would be for someone to slip into the building while they were under construction. The shelter had been noticeably more chaotic since they broke ground two days earlier. At least twenty new faces— moving in and outside. Multiple entrances to the building.

Awareness crackled through her. "Damn, we should have thought of this during the pre-construction. All the systems we have in place to protect ourselves-"

"All gone," Sharon completed her thought. "For the next seven months we ain't gonna know who the hell is inside this building. And that goes for all the serving times during the day, too. The way we contain the homeless clientele to the vestibule, the cafeteria and the bathrooms. In a month or so— we won't be able to even do that. This place is gonna be Grand Central."

"We need a meeting with Specialty."

Sharon nodded. "My thoughts exactly. I'll go talk to Hank outside and have him call Stud Muffin. We need to see if they're available for a conference call. You go round up the staff."

⌇⌇

"Good morning, Annie." Jeff offered a smile and wave as he passed through the cafeteria. Since he'd started visiting the shelter, he'd made a special effort to greet the older woman each time he ran into her. "Expecting a big crowd today?"

"Good morning, Mr. Traynor." She moved her set-up cart to another table. The shelter staff was between mealtimes so the pace, while steady, was not as frenetic. "If it is, we'll be ready."

"Annie, do you think maybe by the end of this project, you'll be calling me Jeff?" She was so damn shy. He'd watched her in action. She was quiet and efficient and very dedicated. Annie had to be volunteering an easy fifty hours a week at New Beginnings. But she was painfully withdrawn.

She offered a rare smile. "We'll have to wait and see."

He smiled and headed toward the office wing, his mind shifting to Sharon's call. It was never good to receive an urgent call from the client on Day Three. Hank had simply told him to get his ass down there as quick as possible. Hank had already expressed his concerns about dealing with so many women 'changin' their minds every five seconds'. As a retired Army sniper, Hank wasn't exactly schooled in the art of finesse. His style was blunt. Their compromise had been that Jeff would handle the 'finessing' and Hank would 'build the damn job'.

Though he probably should have been more worried, Jeff couldn't contain his eagerness. Mari would be there. It was a full staff meeting— so she couldn't pull a disappearing act like she had Monday. It had taken every ounce of willpower not to seek her out. Then it had taken restraint not to call her that night. And the next day. But damn it, he'd wanted to. And what the hell did that say about him?

That he was head over heels in lust with a beautiful woman? There was nothing wrong with that. The problem was his suspicion that it might be *more* than lust. The month that she'd refused to date him had made him try harder. And by trying harder, he'd gotten to know her. And now that Jeff knew her— he liked her. A lot. Drawing a steadying breath, he released it. Mari wouldn't hide from him today. They were going to talk. What the hell he would say— he had no idea. But he wasn't wasting any more time pretending not to think about her. He was going to act.

He entered the conference room with a renewed sense of purpose. "Sorry to hold everyone up. I got here as fast as I could. What's our issue?"

Nodding at the chorus of hellos from the group, a quick glance around the room acknowledged Sharon and Hank, already in discussions over a set of plans. The rest of the administrative staff was huddled in groups of two and three. Mari glanced up from the notes she was taking, a frown marring her honeyed skin. She acknowledged his presence as neutrally as possible before averting her eyes.

His stupid heartbeat accelerated anyway. The atmosphere around him became charged the moment he saw her. Jeff wondered if anyone else could feel it. Damn— he'd missed her. As soon as he made the admission, he frowned. What the hell was happening to him? It had only been since Saturday. Four days and he was acting like a lovesick moron.

"We've got security issues." Hank looked up from the drawings, a frown in his eyes. "We may need to reconfigure some of the schedule to make sure we can button up the building."

Relieved to set aside his pathetic thoughts, Jeff mentally calculated the production schedule. "Can you be more specific?"

"We have clients here who are at risk— of being exposed to family members they don't wish to see."

His gaze shifted back to Mari, relieved he had a legitimate reason to catch her glance. "You're referring to the overnight guests, I assume? Women on the run?"

"That's correct." Her beautiful eyes held his, her expression grave. "But we're also concerned about the volunteers' safety during the day. While we feed a tremendous volume of people each day, we have systems in place to make sure the homeless population is contained to specific areas. They are not allowed to roam free in this building."

"We realized yesterday that with the chaos of the construction, we may have a breach in security." Sharon's usually gregarious personality was subdued, her chocolate eyes reflecting concern. "There were unfamiliar faces wandering in and out— and we haven't even begun work on the interior."

"Maybe we should badge all the contractors?" He glanced at Hank. "Everyone's had a background check, right?"

Hank nodded. "Trouble is— the doors that are usually locked during the day— some of them are gonna have to remain open. I can see at least four times in the schedule where there might be an exposure."

"We're not as worried about your subcontractors," Mari admitted. "Our concern is more about potentially violent behavior from the people in our client's former lives." Her husky voice crawled through Jeff's system while he diligently tried to ignore the impact.

"Meaning what specifically?"

"Meaning these women have escaped a known episode of violence against them or their children." Her tone indicated a weary familiarity with her topic. "The abuser is not pleased his victim has escaped. All too often, the abuser will seek a way to re-engage-"

A light bulb went off in his head and he interrupted. "Are you saying he comes here to get another shot at her?"

"That's exactly what we're saying." Sharon's mocha voice held a thread of steel. "We've had periodic attempts to break in— to kidnap the woman or her children. He knows if he can get to the kids— his threats will bring her back. It's not an uncommon occurrence."

"Sick bastards." Jeff was silent for several moments. "Okay— we've got two issues here. The first being our ability to keep the shelter on lock-down during the construction so everyone is safe." He directed his comment at Hank. "The second is projecting the exposure during each phase of construction and then coming up with appropriate work-arounds."

He shifted his attention to the group. "Hank and I will run through the plans and the schedule today and make a list of what we need to account for and what we think it will cost to implement each measure."

Sharon grimaced. "How much do you think this will add?"

Jeff knew them well enough by now to anticipate cost would be their first concern. He would have to calculate carefully. Knowing this group, if the price was too high, they'd sacrifice their own safety.

"Maybe we can steal from other areas?" Mari's expression was determined. Several others nodded in agreement. "We could select cheaper tile? Less expensive carpet, maybe? Perhaps we can pare down the size of the new bathrooms. That part of the budget is a big chunk of what we have to spend."

Jeff was impressed by her near photographic memory of the detailed renovation budget. This project had been near and dear to her heart for a long time. "Don't worry yet. Let me work up a revised budget and we'll review each measure before we implement anything."

"We may be able to find cost savings on items that were already budgeted," Hank reminded. "The new security features may not be entirely add-on cost."

"You mean like substitutes?" Sharon brightened considerably. "Hank Freeman, you may be my new best friend. I believe I'll be buying you lunch today."

Specialty's normally reserved foreman actually grinned. "Ma'am, I'll look forward to that."

The collective mood was a little deflated as they adjourned, but overall, Jeff felt the meeting went well. His client was worried about budget, but still confident in Specialty's ability to resolve the problem. The most important aspect of the client relationship— almost more than the actual building— was keeping their faith. That Specialty would do what they promised. Anticipating several hours of number-crunching, he spread out the plans on the conference table, rather than load everything up to take back to his office.

His staying had absolutely nothing to do with Mari. At least— that's what he told himself. Jeff mentally repeated the lie as he traced the steps down the hall to her office. And again as he rapped on the doorframe. What was it about her that had him absolutely tied in knots?

She glanced up, her expressive blue eyes startled. "Jefferson? Do you have everything you need?"

"I'm fine. I just wanted—" To take her in his arms. To kiss her until she was so out of her mind for him they'd contemplate locking the door and- He dragged in a deep breath. "I wanted to say hello and see how you and Hector were doing."

"I— we're . . . fine. We went to visit my parents Sunday. And now— it's just . . . work."

Forcibly reining in his thoughts, Jeff took stock of the situation. Marisol was clearly nervous, her tension palpable. She'd blown off the meeting Monday. And she was avoiding him now. If he wasn't careful, she'd convince herself the sexual fireworks they experienced every time he touched her were not something she cared to explore again.

"I have a few questions from the meeting. I asked Sharon and she suggested I talk with you."

Mari chewed her bottom lip, drawing his gaze in a way he wished he had the discipline to ignore. "Of course. I thought-" Whatever she was about to say would remain a mystery. "Please have a seat."

He exhaled slowly. Crisis averted. For the moment. "Can you give me some specifics on the types of threats you receive here?"

Mari steadied her nerves. She was acting like an imbecile. Everything was *not* about her. Jefferson had a job to do. They had to be able to work together. Especially since Sharon would keep throwing them together no matter how she tried to avoid him. She also had to face facts. Whether she liked it or not— she felt something for him. A ridiculously strong something.

"At our current size, we don't experience a great deal of violence. But there are always cases where the potential is there and we prepare for that possibility. Once we complete the addition and we fill to capacity, I can estimate we will experience several episodes per month."

"How often now?"

Jeff stared at her with serious hazel eyes that were thinking through a problem. Despite knowing that, Mari had trouble maintaining her focus. She remembered how his eyes heated when he'd kissed her. How they'd seemed to drink her in— as though she were the most beautiful woman he'd ever seen. Even now— with him seated across her desk— his mind on work— Mari felt the crazy, urgent need to touch him. To be touched by him. To see his control slip. The impulse was so strong it felt like a magnetic pull.

"Marisol?"

"Yes?" Embarrassed, she forcibly shook off the images crowding her brain.

"Does this door have a lock?"

Huh? She jerked herself from the self-induced haze. "Excuse me?"

His eyes darkened as his gaze swept over her. "Honey, if you keep looking at me like that— I'm going to lock that door and have my way with you."

Mortified, she pushed back in her chair, swallowing hard. "I-I'm so sorry. I don't know what's wrong with me."

"There's a lot of that going around." Sitting back in his chair, Jeff grinned, enjoying her confusion. "Okay— let's try again. Approximately how many times per month does an incident occur?"

She took a deep breath and regained her footing. "Probably three times a month for the overnight guests." She mentally reviewed kitchen incidents over the past month. "And another ten times per month with feeding clients. But those occur during the day when we have a large staff to handle them."

He scribbled something on his pad. "So, it's a bigger problem at night because you have less resources to deal with it."

She nodded. "And because the abuser is so invested in his victim. During the day we mostly deal with drunks and addicts, mental illness— sometimes violent, but usually just belligerent."

Jeff focused his attention on her and her pulse jumped in response. "Give me an example— when was the last time?"

She tried and failed to hold his gaze. "Um— actually it was last night."

His entire body stilled. "*Last night*? There was violence here last night?"

"Yes. An ex-spouse showed up-"

"Did he get inside?" Jeff's stunned expression betrayed the reaction most people probably felt when they heard something so completely foreign to their existence.

Mari nodded. "I was leaving with Hector-" Apprehension sizzled up her spine when he sprang from his chair.

"Dammit— you were in the middle of it?"

"It's fine, Jeff. We were able to stop it before it escalated."

"It's *not* fine."

Before she could react, he'd rounded her desk, concern flaring in his beautiful eyes.

"Mari— are you-" His voice worried, he gently tugged her from her chair. "Is Hector okay? Were you in danger?" He ran his hands down her arms before he pulled her roughly against him in a quick hug.

Still bewildered that she was experiencing the fantasy she'd imagined moments earlier, Mari hugged him back. "We're both fine, Jefferson. Nothing happened." When he didn't speak, she pulled away from him. "Are you angry?"

"No." His mouth brushed her forehead before he reluctantly released her. "I can't seem to think straight when I'm around you," he admitted. "When we started this conversation, I never imagined thinking about the security issues with you in mind."

"My being here doesn't make a difference. It's our clients who need protection."

"It matters to me." His expression was grim as he took a step back. Jeff hesitated several seconds, his eyes uncertain. Mari realized it was the very first time she'd ever seen him appear less than sure of himself. "It's become much more personal to me."

Part of her wanted to cheer over his admission. They were obviously attracted to each other— but it appeared he may actually like her, too. In a short period of time, he'd become important to her. And how she'd allowed that to happen, Marisol wasn't quite sure. But she was startled to realize Jeff's concern felt— good. The thought that he might worry about her had warmth coursing through her heart.

"I appreciate that you've grown to like the staff here," she said, intent on placating him to allay his fears. Working in this environment had risks. But, so did every job. Working at New Beginnings meant something different but no less important to each person who chose to accept the challenge. "We all know the risks when we take this job— the volunteers, too."

"If that's supposed to reassure me, it's not working."

She tried again, intent on softening his suddenly hard, determined features. "We're trained to deal with violent confrontations."

"Seriously? Now you're just making it worse." Jeff's eyes darkened as he closed the gap between them. As her heart began a free-fall to her stomach, he tipped her chin up. "Just so we're totally clear— I don't want to think about anyone getting close enough to hurt you or Hector."

"I understand-"

"Damn it— I don't think you do." His muttered oath was whispered against her lips before he tugged her against him. His kiss was undemanding at first— until Mari met him eagerly, more than willing to admit she'd missed him. His large, capable hands stroked down her arms before coming to rest on her hips. And the strength in them, the weight of them anchoring her to him did strange things to her heart.

She wound her arms around his neck, suddenly needing him closer. When he took the kiss deeper, her shudder rippled through them. Mari went under— adrift in sensation as his hands stroked her, then cupped her bottom to pull her closer still.

She was vaguely aware of Jeff moving— toward the door to push it closed. *Dios*- She'd completely forgotten where she was. The next thing she knew, she was leaning back against it as Jeff nuzzled her throat. His tongue discovered the sensitized spot on her collarbone and her knees buckled when the incredible rocket of sensation sapped her strength. No one— *no one*— had ever made her feel as wild as she felt every time she was with Jeff. He only had to look at her and she was his for the taking. The mere thought of him— naked— over her— in her bed made her crazy with need.

When he staggered back, she offered a half-hearted protest. His eyes glowed with frustration— and something else. Shock. Confusion.

"Jeff?" The regret in his eyes had an icy knot of worry seeping into her chest.

"Sweet Jesus, Mari." His voice hoarse, he jammed shaking fingers through his hair. "Another minute and I would have stripped you out of your clothes."

His confession melted the chill that had begun to swirl around her. "At least you remembered the door."

Dragging in an unsteady breath, he managed a smile. "I think we'd better create some distance or we'll be in trouble." When Jeff returned to his chair, she had a fleeting sense of disappointment. Straightening her blouse, she retreated to her chair— safely behind her desk— as she dealt with the slow cooling of her raging hormones. As Sharon had been so quick to remind her . . . it had been far too long since she'd-

Though she knew her face was staining pink with embarrassment, Mari could only hope her eyes didn't convey the desperation she felt. How could she want him so badly? When she barely knew him? She prayed for strength— to get through the rest of this conversation without making the situation more awkward. "We should get back to— our discussion." She swallowed around the sudden dryness in her throat. "The shelter . . . security-"

His expression turned immediately somber. "At the meeting this morning-" Jeff hesitated as though searching for the right words. "When we were discussing violence— you were the furthest thing from my mind."

"I don't understand."

"You and Hector have opened my eyes to something I'd never really given much consideration." His beautiful eyes turned thoughtful. "I know you work here . . . but I viewed this renovation— these security measures as being important for the residents." His gaze was troubled. "Don't get me wrong— I want to protect your clients."

"Then what's your concern?"

He was quiet for several seconds. "I don't like thinking that you or Hector could ever be in danger here."

If he only knew. Her heartbeat accelerated over that truth. It wasn't only their clients who experienced violence at the hands of someone they believed loved them. Mari drew in a steadying breath. Now would probably be a good time to share her past- Yet— it felt way too soon. She wasn't ready. What happened was too personal— too horrifying to share with someone who might not be around in a month's time.

Instead, she shut her mind to the wayward thoughts. It could wait until later. Much later. Until she knew for sure what he meant to her. And to discover whether she meant anything to him.

CHAPTER 5

To say Jeff was floored would have been an understatement. Overwhelmed was more accurate. Staring at the plans on the conference table, he scribbled notes with Hank, but all he could see were images of Mari and Hector. In danger.

An hour later, he couldn't shake the worry disrupting his concentration. Couldn't understand why he was so edgy over the danger she'd casually dismissed. About the possibility of angry ex-partners showing up at New Beginnings. She'd worked there for years, Jeff reminded himself. Marisol was accustomed to dealing with their clientele. She knew what to expect and how to handle serious situations. So, why the hell was he freaking out about it? Why did he suddenly care so damn much?

All the benevolent thoughts about New Beginnings and the volunteers who worked there had to be rearranged. Suddenly, the women who lived there— who'd run there to hide— had become painfully real to him. Hyper aware of how fragile their existence was, Jeff realized he'd been deluding himself. Each and every change they discussed now held new meaning. Every lock— every bolt was significant. Because some irate nutcase could show up at the shelter and-

The cold knot in his stomach cinched tighter. Jeff swallowed around the lump of panic clogging his throat. All he could think about was what he might— God forbid— *be feeling* . . . for Mari. And the helpless, queasy sensation wasn't settling well with him. The acknowledgment sent jagged shards of dread slicing through his gut. Who the hell would choose to spend their life feeling like this? Only to have it end when you least expect it. Like his parents-

"Jeff? You in there?"

Words were erupting from Hank Freeman's mouth. He just couldn't seem to wrap his brain around them. His foreman tossed his hardhat on the table with a resounding clatter.

"Son— are you listenin' to me? Or is it time to change the light bulb in that head of yours?"

Blinking, Jeff turned to acknowledge his irritated foreman. Hank's insistence on maintaining a military crewcut for his salt and pepper hair meant his face tended to crinkle up like a raisin when he scowled. Consequently, he always looked more ticked off than he actually was. "Cool your jets, Colonel Cranky. I'm thinking about too many things at once."

His friend grinned. "I'll wager one of them is the hot tamale down the hall."

He glared at the older man before retrieving his pen. That Hank was right only served to piss him off. It would be a long friggin' afternoon. "That obvious?"

"Yup."

He released a frustrated sigh. Relieved to shelve the disturbing thoughts cluttering his brain, he attempted to refocus. "Okay— where were we?"

"I was reminding you that you wanted to give Miss Ortega's son a tour of the site today." Hank checked his watch. "We got thirty minutes before he'll be out of school. You want me to handle the show? Or you wanna do it?"

Jeff smiled when he remembered the child-sized hard hat sitting in his jeep. "I will. I promised Hector." He pointed to the plan of the interior hallways. "What do you think about card access for these corridors that lead to the dorm? That would eliminate any worry of outsiders getting into the living spaces."

"That could work." Hank leaned across the conference table, his brow furrowed in thought. He dragged his finger along the hallway. "If we spend the money here . . . and here, we can recoup it with good, solid locks on the rest of the doors— but save the expensive card access for where they really need it." He glanced up. "Damn, Jeffie— you're not as vacant as you look."

"And you're not as big an ass as people say." He returned the shot with easy familiarity. They worked on the logistics of several more issues before wrapping up the meeting. While he loaded his briefcase, Hank picked up his hardhat. "I'll make sure there's some earthmoving going on when you get out there with Hector. No sense in putting on half a show."

"Great. Hector will love it. He's convinced we need his help."

Hank's face split with a rare smile. "He's probably right."

His friend continued to linger while he rolled up the plans and threw them over his shoulder. "We all set?"

"Uh— one more thing." The older man suddenly looked flustered. That rarity caught Jeff's attention right away. "Um— I was noticin' a woman in the kitchen. She seems to work every day . . . cute little thing but kinda quiet? Blonde? She doesn't wear a ring."

Jeff set his briefcase down and grinned. "Makin' fun of me, are you? And all the while, you've been scoping out the ladies."

"This is different," he protested. "I'm not lookin' for a quick score."

Like him. Hank left the obvious words unspoken. Hell— they'd always been true in the past. Against his will, Jeff's thoughts circled back to Marisol. Was this time really any different? If the panicky feeling he'd experienced earlier was any indication of what it felt like to be in a relationship— then there was no way on earth he'd allow this thing with Mari to get out of control. Relationships didn't last anyway. What would be the point in even trying? Once they finally slept together, the picture would become clear.

Sex was always the beginning of the end— where wants and needs went to die. Sure— he could last a few weeks beyond that. In truth, that was when his dating efforts paid dividends. The payoff— weeks before everything turned to crap. Before she started expecting him to check in. Before she began making demands on his time. Soon enough, it always became crystal clear when it was time to get out. "What *are* you looking for?"

"What everyone wants— someone to talk to . . . someone to have dinner with— to make it worth the bother of makin' dinner." Hank scratched the whiskers on his chin, warming to his topic and apparently forgetting to whom he was talking. "I miss the noise— of having someone in your life. Maybe if Gayle and I'd had kids— then the past few years might a' been easier. And harder," he amended. "But, at least I'd have had something to focus on."

To Jeff's knowledge, this was the first time Hank had shown interest in another woman. Since his wife's death four years earlier, he'd become a hermit. Except for working ridiculously long hours, Hank retreated to his farm each evening. Alone. "I think you're describing Annie. She practically lives here. But I should warn you— she's not much for small talk. Even my legendary Traynor charm hasn't worked."

 He rolled his eyes. "I'm just askin'— she seems nice, that's all. I've been eating lunch here every day— not because 'a her," he hastily added. "There's no sense in packing my lunch or taking the time to run offsite when they've got great food here."

"Makes sense to me." At least Hank had a legitimate reason for being there. He'd been spending way too much time at New Beginnings himself lately. Jake hadn't lectured him yet over his disappearing act, but Jeff knew he was on borrowed time.

Hank shrugged. "I feel a little guilty— like I'm taking food from someone who really needs it."

"I think the kitchen is open to everyone. Mari says they get lots of regulars."

He looked relieved. "Well, I make sure to stuff money in the jar on the counter. I don't want them to think I'm mooching."

Jeff retrieved his briefcase. "You want me to say something to Mari or Sharon? Maybe find out what Annie's story is?"

Hank thought about it for several seconds then finally shook his head. "Nah. I'll handle it. I need to take it real slow because I'm twenty-two years out of practice." He jerked his head down the hall. "Besides, you'd better concentrate on your own situation. It appears you've got your hands full."

Hector was wiggling with excitement. Mari couldn't contain her smile as she tried to zip his jacket. "Hold still, pequena."

"Hurry, Mari." He paused to frown at her. "If I'm not ready Jeff might change his mind."

Her heart sank. After all this time, that's what everything boiled down to with Hector. Disappointment. His young life had been filled with empty promises— that his mother would stay. When she appeared sporadically, she promised the moon. Then withdrawal would kick in and she'd disappear again, the need for drugs trumping everything else. Weeks later, she'd return, acting as though it had only been hours she'd missed— instead of days— unaware her son had spent hours each day . . . waiting. For his mother to return. For her to keep the promises he'd held close to his heart as though each was a talisman. Promises she'd never intended to keep. As Mari's journey with Hector had progressed, his mother's visits became less frequent. But they were no less destabilizing to him when she did show up. Each visit renewed hope that maybe this time, she'd stay.

Blinking back the burn of tears, Mari squatted to the ground, pretending to work on his zipper so she could see his eyes. "Has Jeff made a promise he hasn't kept?"

Hector cast his worried gaze to the ground. "No. But he might . . . get sick 'a me— or he might have work stuff."

"He is *not* sick of you."

"But I'm annoyin'-"

"Who would dare call you annoying? They will answer to me." She forced a smile into her voice as she made a production of smooching his cheek.

"Stop, Maaari— that tickles."

His reluctant giggles made her feel marginally better. Not for the first time, Marisol wondered how long it would take before the ugly voices of doubt in his head would clam up and go away.

She tipped his chin up. "I spoke with Jeff just a little while ago. He'll be here soon. And he has a special present for you." Her spirits lifted when she read the excitement in his eyes.

"What is it?"

"She can't tell you— because it's a three-part surprise."

They both turned at the sound of Jeff's voice. She wondered how long he'd been standing there. Though he wore his usual smile, his eyes were somber, making her suspect he'd overheard them.

Racing over, Hector gave him a hug. She slowly stood, watching Jeff's expression change— from the guarded glance he shot over Hector's head to his delight over the little boy's exuberant hug. Mari smiled— knowing exactly how it felt to experience both despair over his innocent comments and the swelling of love each time he made new strides away from his former life.

"Dude— you're getting strong. You practically knocked me over." When he winked at her, she felt the telltale blush stealing into her face. The expression in his eyes had heat igniting in the pit of her stomach. How could a mere glance make her heartbeat accelerate?

"A three part surprise? That sounds complicated." She knew about the hard hat, but he'd obviously cooked up something else to surprise Hector.

"Yeah— what's my surprise, Jeff?"

"First is this." He showed Hector his own hard hat, before reaching inside and revealing the little one he'd brought for him.

"Cool— is this mine?"

Jeff set the hat on his head, testing the fit. "Yup. See here? It's got your name on it. Whenever you step outside you have to wear your hardhat. It's a rule."

"Like if a buildin' tipped over on me? This would keep me safe?"

He shuddered over Hector's bloodthirsty imagination. "Let's hope there will be no buildings tipping over."

Hector's eyes were huge. "This is— like one of the coolest thing I ever got." He shook his head, testing the tightness. "I can't wait to show Tommy and Jason."

"You ready? Because the next surprise is outside with Hank." Jeff checked his watch before he caught her gaze. "We'll be back in about twenty minutes. And the third part of my surprise includes you— so you'd better stick around."

"C'mon— let's go." Hector was pulling Jeff's hand toward the door.

"Alright. I'll be waiting." Mari acknowledged the flutter of excitement dancing through her. It grew increasingly difficult to reign in her feelings when Jeff was casting a spell over both of them.

If she didn't watch out, she could get her heart broken. And this time, it would affect Hector as well. She shivered as they walked out side by side, a growing sense of unease encroaching on the starry-eyed feeling. What would she do when he grew tired of them?

"That was awesome. I can't believe I got to ride the steamroller with Lefty. Is that really his name? Can we do that again?"

"We'll have to check with Hank. We might be pouring concrete by next week. We have to get your new addition up fast." Jeff scooped Hector into his arms to cross the mud pit that the newly excavated foundation had morphed into as a result of an overnight thunderstorm. Sharon probably wouldn't appreciate them tracking mud back into the building. The site crew was already afraid of incurring her wrath. They'd laid down an intricate series of mats outside the door so they could scrape their feet off before entering her building— something of a rarity on a project this size.

He nodded to Big Pete, who was still standing sentry duty, despite it being after four o'clock. Usually he was gone by now. "Got a status report for me?"

Pete's gaze remained rooted to the street beyond the construction area. "Been watching a red pickup. He's been out there since lunch time. Keeps circling the block."

"Maybe it's one of the crew?"

"Maybe." Pete didn't sound convinced. "I'll keep my eye on him for a little while longer."

Jeff patted his beefy arm. "Thanks, Buddy. But don't work too late. We need you bright and early tomorrow."

"I got your six when you and Miss Ortega leave. I don't want any incidents like last night."

Jeff froze in his tracks. *With Mari and Hector.* Her explanation had lacked detail. He'd gotten the sense she was hesitant to discuss it with him. But asking in front of the little guy was not cool.

Nodding to Hector squirming against his shoulder, he signaled Pete that he didn't want to discuss the incident in front of him. "How about I meet you here for coffee tomorrow morning? We can talk then?"

Catching the look in his eyes, the giant nodded. "Affirmative. See you at 0700." He held the door for them before closing it behind them.

"Can I ask you something?" The muffled question came from his shoulder.

"You can ask me anything, Hec and I'll do my best to answer." Jeff discovered he liked the feeling of the little boy's arms wrapped around his neck. It was nice— sort of protective and powerful at the same time. And where the hell had that thought come from?

"I gots a question about bullies."

Damn— his first real test and it might be a difficult one. Though he could have set Hector down, Jeff continued to hold him as they passed through the quiet corridors leading to the cafeteria. "Okay. Lay it on me."

Hector lifted his head to stare at him. "Well— it's sorta for my friend. He needs to know what to do when someone bullies him."

"My advice depends on where the bullying happens. Can you tell me more about it?"

When they reached the cafeteria, Jeff could see it filling with the dinner crowd. Not only that, but he was surprised to see Hank— making time with Annie at the counter. Even more shocking— she was smiling. Though her face was flushed crimson from the attention, there was a spark in her eyes he hadn't ever seen before. Way to go, Hank.

"What do you mean?" Hector stretched away from him to stare into his eyes.

"Like— is it happening at school?" Not wanting to derail his conversation with Hector, he turned down the hallway to the conference room. Once there, he set him on the edge of the table and closed the door. "Because if that's the case then I would say your friend should talk to his teacher first. And his mom. Then she could work with the school to fix-"

He shook his head. "It's not happenin' at school."

The worry visible in the little boy's knowing brown eyes sent a frisson of warning through his system. "What is it, Hec? An older brother? A playground thing?"

"He might— get in trouble-"

Jeff squatted before the little boy, his heart sinking over his troubled expression. "I promise he won't."

"He's worried 'cuz . . ." Hector glanced over his shoulder at the door, then dropped his voice to a whisper. "He's worried because it's . . . his daddy."

Jeff rocked back on his heels, his mind reeling. Sweet God— he was five. Hector was five friggin' years old. He should be worrying about his baseball card collection— or what healthy snack he had to trade from his lunchbox to get something good. But he sure as hell shouldn't be worried about child abuse. Taking a deep breath, Jeff released it slowly.

He chose his words cautiously, making sure his voice betrayed none of the fury coursing through him. Stay calm. "His dad . . . is . . . hurting your friend?"

When Hector nodded matter-of-factly, Jeff's gut clenched as though blindsided with a sucker punch. Between the conversation he'd overheard earlier with Mari and now this— he was suddenly at a loss. Hell— the more he thought about it, he was in way over his head— with both of them. He had no more business pretending he knew how to help this sweet kid— than he did getting involved with Marisol.

Because she was different. From anyone he'd ever met. Not that he would have acknowledged it to Hank, but she was special— in a way he grew more sharply aware each day. And he— was a flight risk. Increasingly, he didn't want to risk taking advantage of her.

"And their mommy. So— he wants to protec' her— but he's sorta . . . not big enough."

And their mommy. Their. It was more than one friend. Brothers? His ears roared with the surreal buzz of shock over what he was hearing. "Does your friend live here? At the shelter?"

Hector paused, his sad, puppy eyes gauging whether he could trust him. "Yes."

"Then— aren't they safe here? At least for now?"

His eyes filled with tears then, his brave, sweet face crumpling under the weight of a worry too big for his slender shoulders to carry. "He k-keeps f-findin' them. And I h-heard Mama Sharon tell Mari they might have to m-move again. But . . . they're my friends."

Hector's sobs tore at him— exposing a gaping wound in himself that Jeff didn't know how to fix. How the hell did Mari and the staff do this job? How did they not allow anger and sadness to win? He scooped him up again, needing to hold the little boy probably as much as Hector needed to be held. "It's okay, buddy. We're going to fix it. We'll help him. I promise-"

"You promise?" Hector's tear-stained face pulled back from his shoulder to stare at him.

Oh God. *What was he doing?* The little guy had a thing about promises. And now, here he was— guaranteeing something he had absolutely no idea he could deliver. What the sweet hell was he doing? What if he screwed up? "I want you to promise *me* something, Hector."

"What?" The little guy was stoic as he dried his eyes on his sleeve.

"I've made you a promise— that I will do everything I can to help. Now you have to promise me you won't worry about this anymore. Do we have a deal?"

Marisol. He could discuss the issue with her. She knew what she was doing. She had parenting skills. She'd know best. Together, they would develop a plan. Hector trusted her. And he did, too, Jeff realized. She would help him keep the promise he'd just made. Releasing the breath he didn't realize he'd been holding, Jeff forced himself to calm.

"You really mean it?" Hector's mouth slowly lifted in a smile as the worry cleared from his eyes. He stuck out a sturdy, little hand. "It's a deal."

Mari found them in the conference room, deep in discussion. She cracked the door open with a smile. "Are you boys lost?"

Hector glanced up, his eyes brimming with excitement. "Mari— guess what?"

"What, carino?"

"The third surprise— Jeff's takin' us out for supper. And I get to pick where."

She raised an eyebrow in question and Jeff shrugged. "If you don't already have plans."

"I picked tacos." Hector's expression was jubilant.

She smiled as a wave of eager expectation washed over her. "We don't have plans."

She was giddy, damn it. This crazy attraction had to stop. She could not go on feeling so ridiculously happy over spending time with him. It was dangerous to feel this way. So lighthearted. So— hopeful. Because feeling this good meant the only way left to go was down. Mari didn't want to take that plunge. And she sure as hell didn't want to take a soul-sucking dive with Hector in tow.

"Are you ready?" Jeff's appealing voice broke into her thoughts— dispelling all those resembling rational ones. Was she ready? Not really. Falling in love was not on her agenda. Now— or a year from now. She had— plans. For herself and Hector. In half a year's time, with any luck— with the gods shining down on her, he would be legally hers. She had real-life decisions to make.

Jefferson was a distraction— a gorgeous, sexy distraction. But the timing-

Aware he awaited her answer, Mari nodded. Even if Jefferson turned out to be only a distraction— she had to deal with it. She couldn't continue avoiding decisions just because it was easier. Eventually, everything either blew up or worked out. And winging it just wasn't her style. She could face her fears head-on or she could be burdened with them subconsciously. Either way— her feelings for Jeff weren't going away.

"Great. I know the perfect place."

One way or another, she would have to give him a test drive. "I'm ready."

Do you have a few minutes to talk?"

Mari turned her key in the lock and pushed the door open. Hector stampeded past her in his rush to get to the bathroom, leaving Jeff standing in his wake behind her on the porch. "Sure— I have to get Hector squared away. It's a school night and he still needs a bath."

"I'm sorry. I forgot about that. It can wait until tomorrow."

She sensed his hesitation . . . had sensed all evening he was only partially with them. Jeff had been brooding about something. If he was contemplating dumping them, it would be better to get it over with— before she made the mistake of letting him get too close. "No— please come in. I could tell there was something on your mind."

He frowned as he stepped into her foyer. "How'd you know?"

"I guess I picked up on the vibe." There'd been a wariness to his eyes all evening. Probably because after nearly eight weeks, he'd concluded she was too much damned effort. Perhaps he'd finally realized what the term 'single mother' entailed. She and Hector were a package deal which meant Jeff was probably getting bored. They were never alone for long— not the way they would be if they were really dating.

There was certainly no way Jeff could have failed to pick up on the stares he'd received from virtually *every* female in the restaurant. Single, beautiful women who didn't have children to bathe— who could linger over margaritas before taking him home for wild, uncomplicated sex. Mari dropped her keys in the bowl and hung her jacket in the closet. "What's on your mind?"

He followed her into the living room. "This should probably wait until Hector goes to bed. I don't want him to overhear us."

"Okay." Great— he was definitely dumping them. Her heart dropped to the pit of her stomach. She'd known it couldn't last. So, why the hell had she allowed herself to hope? Why had she let down her guard? Damn it— she knew better. Guys like Jeff didn't end up with women like her.

Steeling herself against the pain knotting her chest, Mari prayed her expression was more serene than her churning stomach felt. This time around, she may not leave the relationship battered— but the time she'd spent with Jefferson would certainly leave her bruised.

"That won't be for an hour or so." She sighed. Why couldn't he have just left her alone? "I don't want to hold you here. Why don't we talk on the porch?"

"I'm not in a hurry. I mean— it's no rush." Confusion flashed in his eyes. "Is something wrong?"

Clearly she wasn't delivering on the calm, collected expression she'd been striving for. Getting dumped was one thing— but she still had to work with the guy for the next several months. There was no way in hell she'd leave him with the impression that she was broken up over losing him to some sexy, tequila-shooting twenty-year-old.

"No— but I get the feeling this is important." Mari moved quickly for the safety of the kitchen. "I'll just make sure Hector's cartoon is on and then meet you there in a minute."

It was more like five minutes by the time she assured herself Hector was settled before the TV, that he possessed none of the implements necessary to burn the house down, nor could he overdose on chocolate or cookies while she was outside breaking up with the man of her dreams. Mari paused for several deep breaths in the kitchen. "Let's get this over with."

God was allowing for small favors this evening, she acknowledged as she closed the door behind her. Twilight had arrived while she'd been inside hyperventilating. Without the porch light on, Jeff wouldn't be able to see her lips trembling. She'd be able to hold it together long enough to slip back inside. A sense of calm settled over her. It was the calm of despair, but she was grateful for it nonetheless.

"It's gorgeous out here tonight." Jeff was already sitting on the top step. "What's that smell?"

"I planted jasmine last fall." The perfumed breeze wafted over her like a shawl. It was a beautiful, sultry night— the kind meant for porch swings and holding hands. For sipping wine and stealing kisses before you crept inside and fumbled your way to a darkened bedroom-

"It's fantastic. We should sit out here more often." He patted the top step beside him. "Come sit down. I'll try to be quick, so you can get back inside to Hector."

Huh? Was this how Jeff broke up with women? Why was he being so pleasant? Maybe with his experience, he'd become professional at it. Maybe— they'd end up friends. It would be just like him to dump her so skillfully that she still found him irresistible after it was over. Bracing herself, Mari dropped down beside him.

"What did you want to tell me?" *Just do it*. Rip it off. Like a bandage.

He shifted toward her, their knees touching. When he scooped up her hand in his, she startled. "Wow— your hand is like ice." Tugging her closer, he kissed her knuckles. "Are you warm enough?"

Mari shivered over the exquisite sensation before nodding— now completely at a loss as to what would happen next. "I-I'm fine."

His smile was a brief flash of white in the growing darkness. "Okay— here goes. . . Hector sort of . . . confided in me earlier today-"

Oh God— Hector must have told Jeff he liked him. Or loved him. It had to be something big to scare him off this quickly.

"One of his friends— a boy at the shelter— he said the boy's father was beating them." His grip on her hand tightened convulsively. "I didn't know what to do. Hector started crying— he said he'd overheard you and Sharon." Jeff finally glanced at her. "He's terrified he'll lose his friend if you move them to another shelter."

Understanding crashed over her, leaving her stunned and nearly drowning with relief. *He was concerned for Hector*. Marisol nearly trembled with the realization that she'd been entirely wrong. Lord— what was wrong with her? Why couldn't she trust anyone? She'd completely jumped to conclusions over his motives— and she hadn't been close.

All this time, Mari had been feeling sorry for herself— and her little boy was suffering. She was being selfish— and ridiculous. Despite her desire to remain cool and unflappable— she simply couldn't maintain her composure when it came to Hector hurting.

Her throat filled with tears. "I know— he's w-worried. He's talking about the dad who came by two nights ago." Annie's ex-husband.

Jeff halved the distance between them and pulled her closer. Clearly he'd heard the impending meltdown in her voice. "The guy you tangled with? The one who threatened you?"

She nodded. "It was unusual for Hector to witness something like that. I hate that he's worried for his friends." Feeling him tense next to her, Mari glanced away, upset that Hector had overheard her conversation with Sharon. He had enough worries to deal with.

"Try not to be angry with me," Jeff asked. "I promised Hector I'd help him— help *them*. I'm so sorry, Marisol. I know I overstepped my bounds— but he was crying— and I felt . . . helpless. I've never felt that way before."

Her eyes widened. "Why would I be angry with you? I think it's sweet that you care so much. Parenting kids like Hector— who've endured so many— terrible things . . . it makes you want to protect them from everything bad. Like— they've suffered enough and you can't bear to see anyone else hurt them."

"I know this will sound naive to someone like you— but I really want to help. What can I do? How can we help this kid?"

Marisol found her first smile in several hours. *We*. He'd said 'we'. Whether Jeff liked it, they were all growing on him. Their little family at New Beginnings. When he was done building their shelter— whether he cared about her or not— Jeff would take a piece of them with him.

Damn, it would be so *easy* to love him. She was dangerously close to falling for him. Maybe she already had. Her heart thudded in a quick, painful flash of panic. She'd thought she loved Nick, too. She pushed the terrifying thought from her mind, unwilling to even contemplate the possibility of another disaster. There would be time later to lie awake wondering how she'd let it happen.

She forced her mind back to their conversation. "We're trying not to move them again. Frankly— there's nowhere for them to go. The other shelters are full."

"Are they safe? Can you get a restraining order?"

"We take precautions. But a restraining order is only effective if the abuser honors it."

Jeff had begun massaging the knot between her shoulder blades— as though he'd figured out where she carried all her stress. Biting back a sigh, she allowed herself to enjoy the languid feeling for a moment longer. But his long, amazing fingers paused. "My sister Andrea's husband is a state trooper. What if I get him to come by and talk with the staff about extra safety measures?"

She mulled over his suggestion, flattered that he cared enough to offer his assistance. They'd all had training in safety precautions, managing potentially violent situations . . . but Jeff's offer was so kind, Mari hated to shoot down his idea when he was being so thoughtful about trying to protect them all. And they could always use a refresher course. "I think that's a wonderful idea— if you're sure it wouldn't be any trouble."

"I'll call Charlie tomorrow. When is the best time to get your staff together for training?" His fingers paused their magical massage and she nearly groaned.

"Between meals— probably after lunch. That's when we have the most staffers on site."

His eyes lit with satisfaction. She'd forgotten that sensation— of feeling able to help. It was easy to feel helpless in trying to solve the overwhelming problems faced by the homeless, the hungry. All a person could really do was try to make a difference. Jeff would feel good about his actions— and perhaps would replicate them when given the opportunity to help later. "How're your donations looking? Did you finish off the building campaign?"

She frowned. "Not great. I've got a few stragglers who haven't honored their commitments. I have to track them down. And I'm meeting with another promising group tomorrow. If we can secure funding from them, I'll have enough to get Specialty through nearly to the end." She glanced at him, a sudden smile on her lips. "Are you worried about getting paid?"

His eyes warmed as he leaned in to whisper. "I know where you live."

"So, this is all part of your strategy?" Jeff's eyes had the most amazing flecks of gold in the iris. It was sinful, really. That he could be so impossibly attractive without even trying.

"You're on to me," he confessed. "I'm wooing you so when I hit you with a giant change-order you won't be able to resist. I plan to ensnare you with my charm. You'll be so captivated that when the price doubles, you'll just smile and write a bigger check."

"Is that how it works?" Marisol was having trouble keeping up with the thread of their conversation. The closer his lips moved to hers, the faster her heart began beating, and the louder the rush in her ears grew. "And here I thought if I seduced you— I might get you to throw in the fancy tile in the girls' communal bathroom."

His lips were smiling against hers when they met. The first contact was a tentative brush over her mouth— not so much testing, as it was teasing. Because they both knew exactly how explosive it would be. She shuddered anyway. The merest touch from him made her pulse race crazily. The second kiss was almost painful in its sweetness. Jeff leaned in, his hands still not touching her, his mouth covering hers in a leisurely, sensual way that left her nearly bereft when he drew back. His steady gaze locked with hers for several moments, neither of them speaking. She wondered fleetingly what thoughts were racing through his head before he leaned in again, this time cupping her face in his hands. When he covered her lips this time, it was in an explosion of heat, of desire, of a fierce aching need that made her want to climb into his skin.

When they finally broke apart, it was with painful reluctance. Marisol had never, *ever* not wanted Hector in her life. But for a fleeting moment of insanity, she wished with all her might that she could stumble into the house with Jeff, kissing and caressing him all the way up the stairs to her bedroom. Hell— if Hector wasn't home, they wouldn't even *make it* to the stairs. She'd strip him in the hallway and take him on the kitchen floor.

Jeff leaned back on his hands, his breathing ragged. "Mari, honey— you're killing me." He turned to her in the growing darkness. "I can't seem to keep my hands off you."

"Me too."

"I want you so much. Hell— the only thing saving you right now is that I can't quite see your eyes. Because if you're looking at me like you were this afternoon-"

"Worse than this afternoon," she confirmed, smiling when he groaned. "And we have Hector," she reminded softly.

Startled, he glanced at his cell phone. "Damn— we've been out here fifteen minutes. I should probably go."

Reluctantly, they rose to their feet. Mari's blood was still singing with unspent passion as she embraced him. Which lead to another round of frantic kissing that left her hormones screeching with frustration. It was then she decided to throw her normal, cautious, conservative outlook to the wind. As Jeff took his first reluctant step down the porch steps, she blurted out an invitation. "How about dinner tomorrow night? We could grill out back?"

He hesitated only a moment. "That would be great. Can I bring anything? Maybe something Hector likes?"

She enjoyed the heat in his tortured eyes— heat meant solely for her. In spite of the edgy need wrapped around them, Jeff still managed to think first of her little boy. Her heart stuttered and softened another notch. He was making it nearly impossible not to love him. Even frustrated, he looked amazing, beautiful. "Why don't you bring wine instead?"

That got his attention. "Are you sure?"

The anticipation was almost too much to bear. Unable to wait a moment longer for his reaction, Mari smiled. "Hector has a birthday party tomorrow night."

Jeff froze mid-step. "H-how long do we have?"

Enjoying the way his voice had gone raspy in seconds, she took a step closer. Her smile was one of smug satisfaction. Take that— beautiful, unattached women. This single mom was still capable of doing something crazy. "Did I forget to mention this is a *sleepover* party?"

"Mari-"

She would remember forever the way he released her name on a raw groan, the rough silk of his voice cutting through the darkness. Anticipation hung in the air, clouded in the heady scent of jasmine— of what might prove to be the most amazing night of her life. "He's spending the night at his friend's house. I'm dropping him off at five."

Jeff recovered long enough to flash his patented smile. "I'll be here at five-thirty."

Flicking a glance at his watch, Jeff sighed. Ten hours, forty-five minutes to go. Blinking the exhaustion from his eyes, he attempted to focus. It was a very good thing he'd be slugging back coffee with Gigantor in a few minutes. After lying awake half the night, he was in serious need of a caffeine boost. And he had Marisol Ortega to thank for that.

Hell— he'd dreamed of getting her naked from practically the first moment he'd seen her. *Tonight* it would finally happen. But how the hell had she expected him to sleep after receiving news like that? When the alarm chirped that morning, his bed had looked like a warzone. The sheets had been thrashed from the mattress and his pillow had been punched so many times during the night it looked as though it required first aid. He'd lain awake all night— thinking of Mari, dreaming of her. Imagining the gorgeous curves he would discover when he stripped her out of those clothes and finally got his hands on her. Checking his watch again, he pulled into a parking space near the shelter. Ten hours, forty-*two* minutes.

Damm— this would be the longest day of his life.

A few minutes later, caffeine trickling into his system, he started feeling human as he sat through Big Pete's situation report. In Pete-speak, it was a sit-rep. No matter how quiet the site appeared to be when Jeff left for the evening, Pete would produce a list of potential 'issues' that somehow accumulated overnight. For the past two days, it was his insistence that New Beginnings was quite possibly under siege. Their commando-in-chief was adamant they were being 'staked out' by a man in a big, red truck. His eyes held a faraway look Jeff had learned to respect, if only because he knew Pete would eventually get around to telling him what he wanted to know. As long as it was according to his timetable.

"Okay, I'll ask Hank to look into that truck for you. It's probably nothing to worry about, but I appreciate you being so observant." It was hard to remain sluggish around Big Pete. The Iraq war vet was nearly always on high alert. Jeff downed the rest of his coffee, patiently awaiting his opportunity to steer the conversation back to what he *really* wanted to know— the disturbance earlier in the week.

When his friend's eyes lost their cloudy sheen, he knew it was time. "Now that Hector's not around, why don't you tell me what happened Tuesday night."

Pete's eyes scrunched as he mentally switched gears. The pencil in his gigantic fist stopped scratching notes in his log book. "I was still here which was unusual— but I like when they serve meatloaf for supper. So— sometimes I stay late."

"How was it?"

"The meatloaf?" When he nodded, Pete's mouth lifted in a smile. "It was damn good."

"Did the ex-husband show up before or after dinner?"

"Before." When he scowled it reminded Jeff how fortunate they were that Pete was on their side. The giant would be a formidable opponent for anyone unlucky enough to cross him. "Yeah— Miss Ortega was leavin' with Hector. I saw them, so I got out of line . . . so I could hold the door for her. She had a bunch 'a files and her briefcase and she was tryin' to hold Hector's hand but he wasn't listening to her." He picked up his to-go cup and took a long pull. "Coffee's still hot. That's nice."

Jeff resisted the urge to nudge him along. Whatever demons the poor guy continued to wrestle with since his return, Pete had learned he could keep them at bay with orderly, methodical conduct. Consequently, the vet's helpfulness had to be achieved on his terms.

"So I'm walkin' over to the door to help Miss Ortega when this guy bursts through the side door— right next to her." Pete's gaze left the ragged list on the table and focused on the door, as though seeing the incident replay in his head. "Miss Ortega musta recognized him cuz she shoves Hector behind her and tells him to go to the kitchen."

"The man— his name is Phil, I think. He takes a step toward Miss Ortega . . . like he wants to talk to her." Pete's gaze shifted again and he frowned. "But I knew he didn't wanna talk."

A visceral warning jagged down Jeff's spine. He wasn't going to like what the giant said next. "How did you know?"

Pete hesitated. "I did a few tours in Iraq before I finally came home. I got the same feelin' about Phil I had when we were clearing houses in those little villages. After a while, you just sorta knew which house was booby-trapped. You'd get that feelin' in your gut— and you learned to pay attention to it. Or you got waxed."

"What did Phil want?" Jeff was wide awake now. Damn. His heart was in friggin' overdrive. He knew it was going to be worse than what Mari had made it out to be.

Big Pete shifted his gaze back to him. "We won't know for sure cuz Miss Marisol got away from him. I walked over there and put myself between him and her while Miss Sharon called the cops."

"But you know . . . right, Pete?" A cold, dangerous flame ignited in his chest.

The giant nodded. "That guy is a whole lot more dangerous than they want to admit. I been watchin' for him ever since."

Lowering his voice, Jeff leaned across the table. "What was he going to do?"

Pete leaned back in his chair and drained the rest of his coffee. He took his time setting the empty cup on the table before he finally leveled his gaze at him. "He was gonna use Miss Ortega to get to his ex. He was gonna take her hostage."

CHAPTER 6

"Yes, Mom." Mari leaned an elbow on her desk and absently rubbed her forehead as the day from hell just kept getting worse. "No . . . we're not remotely close to where I'd inflict a family interrogation on Jeff."

She heard Sharon smother a chuckle at her desk across the way. "Don't *'carida'* me. That won't work. No family dinner. Not yet. Not a month from now."

She shot a baleful glance at Sharon who tried to fake being busy with the unread reports on her desk, before groping for the aspirin bottle in her drawer. "Ok— I have to go, Mom. Sharon is standing here-" She sighed and held the phone away from her ear.

"Be nice," Sharon whispered before she leaned in closer to hear her mother's side of the conversation. "What's she sayin'?"

Mari covered the mouthpiece with her free hand. "She's probably checking availability at the Wedding Palace-" She frowned as she sifted through the babble. What had her mother just said? "Hold on— say that again?"

She stared at Sharon, who raised her brows. "I didn't hear nothin'."

"Mom— what about Dad and Manny?" Her heart began thudding with warning when her outgoing, talk-a-blue-streak mother began backpedaling. Damn. Something was up. Her mother totally sucked at lying. "No, you said . . . Manny told Dad what?"

She listened as her mother attempted to stutter and stammer her way out of the hole she'd dug for herself. "Never mind. I'm late for a meeting."

"What was that all about?" Sharon's over-eager eyes were wide with curiosity.

Mari sighed. "Hell if I know." She'd have to remember to call Caridad. Since their father's attempts to control her sister's life two years earlier, Cari had made it her business to always know what was going on with their parents. She'd become a rather adept spy herself— a chip off the old block. If her father had any clue, he likely would've been proud.

"Knowing my parents . . . it can't be good."

Her boss chuckled. "They mean right, Sugar. Speaking as a parent— we tend to worry."

She glanced at her friend. "Would you hide a tracking device on your daughters' vehicles? Would you perform background checks on their dates? Would you force your son to follow his sisters around like a Neanderthal thug?"

Sharon's eyes widened in disbelief. "While he may be going a bit overboard— you know your daddy has good reason. After what happened to you— I could justify their becoming a bit overprotective. Can't you?"

Mari gritted her teeth. "It's been two years. And my poor sisters never had an incident like what happened to me. They're paying the price for my mistake."

"Honey— how many times do you have to be reminded it wasn't a mistake? You did nothing wrong."

She reached across the desk and gave her friend's hand a squeeze. "I know, Sharon. I'm not blaming myself. I haven't started slipping," she reminded gently. "But my parents need to let it go."

Her bangle bracelets clanged against her desk. "Maybe your mama was just making conversation."

"No— they're up to something." Damn. It probably meant her family would descend like locusts this weekend— a surprise attack meant to catch her off guard. She made a mental note to bolt the doors tonight. It would be just like her family to arrive unannounced and completely ruin her evening with Jeff.

Lord— *Jeff.* Mari gulped in a suddenly shaky breath as the previous evening came tumbling back. She'd succeeded in shoving her lapse in sanity to the back of her brain— but only temporarily. Every few hours, it charged back— taking center stage and setting her heart pounding. While a part of her was completely exhilarated and nearly trembling with eagerness for her date with Jeff— the rest of her pulsed with a racing sense of terror. As though she'd fallen into the deep end of the pool and suddenly forgotten how to swim.

"Sugar— you okay? You're lookin' a little green around the edges."

"I-I'm fine." Sharon's motherly voice intruded on her panic attack. No way in hell could she handle her friend's sudden interest. All Sharon knew was she and Jeff had been to dinner with Hector a few times. That's all she wanted anyone to know. Mari was nervous enough. If everyone at work started discussing their relationship, she wouldn't be able to think clearly.

It was definitely time to change the subject. "We should run down this list of late donations. Some of them are starting to worry me."

Her friend's no-nonsense cocoa eyes stared at her for a beat longer than necessary and she crossed her fingers. That I'm-on-to-you look. The I've-caught-your-scent-of-fear expression.

"Seriously, Sharon— aren't you concerned? I'm off budget by thirty thousand in donations this month. With the new card access system, we need to come up with *more* money, not less."

"Okay, we'll play by your rules. But if you think I don't know that you're head over heels for our friend, Mr. Stud Muffin . . . then Sugar, you don't know Miss Sharon very well."

Her face in flames, she dropped her head into her hands. "Is it that obvious?"

Her friend's rich chuckle filled the tiny office. "Only to me, sweetie. Oh— and Annie suspects . . . and Miss Robin mentioned something yesterday. And the Tuesday chef squad-"

She peeked at her friend through her fingers. "Seriously?"

"We're happy for you, darlin'. You deserve some fun. And you deserve to have it with that hot, sexy man."

"I don't know if I'm ready for this." Despite her misgivings, Mari blurted out her biggest fear to the woman who knew her nearly as well as her own mother. "I think we're moving too fast-"

"Now, Sugar . . . the only thing movin' too fast is that brain of yours. You need to let it rest. Shut it down for a couple days. Don't think about anything. And see where it takes you."

She raised a brow. "Would you be giving this advice to your own daughter?"

Her friend stifled a chuckle. "I promise you, if my Latrice had scooped up a man who looked like Stud Muffin— I'd a told her to go for it weeks ago."

She raised her gaze to the ceiling. "I don't know who's worse. Me— for contemplating a relationship with someone like Jeff or you, for egging me on."

"What do you mean *someone* like Jeff? From what I've seen, he's not only one fine lookin' specimen, but he's kind . . . thoughtful. He makes a steady paycheck. He's responsible. He gets on with Hector like his long-lost big brother." The older woman scrunched her nose in confusion. "Mercy Sugar, what the hell else are you lookin' for?"

Assurance he'd never hurt her. Faith he'd stick around? Who the hell offered that sort of ironclad guarantee? And why did she suddenly think she needed one? Mari chewed her lower lip. Was she using an impossible set of standards to keep him at arm's length? "When you say it like that— I guess I don't know what I want."

"You want to know for sure he ain't Nick. I can sit here all day long and tell you Jeff isn't like that. He's not the kind of man who needs to beat up on a woman to feel powerful. He doesn't strike me as the sort who takes out his anger on others. But until you see it for yourself . . . what anyone else says really doesn't matter."

She nodded slowly, confirming what she'd already been thinking . . . what she'd been hoping. Mari smiled, sensing some of her restless panic ease. She couldn't control every damn thing. "You're right. I'm gonna stop over-thinking this and just . . . try to enjoy it."

"*Try*?" Sharon cracked up. "Sugar, if you don't enjoy it with him— then there's no hope for the rest of us."

Jeff was still brooding when he pulled into her driveway that evening. He'd tried all day to forget what Big Pete had said— to discount his story as being over the top. But Pete babbling about the mysterious truck of the day or a teen graffiti artist on the loose didn't come close to hearing Marisol might be in danger. No way would he discount a story like that.

Suspecting the confrontation was worse than she'd claimed, he'd sensed a strum of anxiety when she'd discussed the incident earlier in the week. Instinctively, he'd known Mari wasn't telling him everything. She'd been placating him, or worse— trying to convince herself the Phil problem would go away on its own.

They needed to have a serious discussion, but tonight wasn't the time. He'd waited too long to risk ticking her off over an issue that was technically none of his business. Even though Jeff planned to insert himself squarely in the middle of it, he was smart enough to choose a different time to address the touchy subject and the role he planned to play.

His smile returned when he climbed the porch steps and a waft of jasmine hit him square in the face. The subtly erotic scent took him straight back to the previous evening. The memory of Mari in his arms— her beautiful eyes torturing him in the sweet, scented night— had been scorched into his brain. He would never smell jasmine again without thinking of her and remembering the exultant feeling he'd experienced when she'd shyly invited him over tonight.

A sense of victory and a feeling of rightness— all rolled up in his finely tuned awareness of her. There was no mistaking the attraction. Hell— it had been there all along, fisted in his stomach, strumming along his nerves and poking him in the chest for nearly two months. More confusing was the crazy way she drifted through his thoughts. When he wasn't even with her. Or the unease he felt over this problem with Phil. Or the way he wanted to find that expensive kitchen equipment for her— for the shelter. Just because it would please her.

And what about the way he was feeling toward Hector? How much he enjoyed being around him— how much he liked teaching him stuff like baseball. With alarming frequency, Jeff was able to imagine taking Hector to a ball game with his brother and nephew or out to the farm for a Traynor family celebration.

All of those *feelings*— were highly irregular for him. He should be worried . . . and he *was* a little. But he wasn't panicking— and that made this experience different from the past.

Drawing in a deep breath, Jeff rang the buzzer. Tonight, there would be no worries. There would just be time. Hours and hours alone with Marisol. Getting to know her— what she was really like. Not the devoted mom, not the dedicated helper of those less fortunate. But the fiery, passionate, strong-willed woman he'd caught only glimpses of.

When Mari opened the door, his breath caught. Something about her made him want to forget the social niceties and just kiss her senseless. Her long, wild hair hung loose at her shoulders. Jeff wanted nothing more than to run his fingers through it and pull her closer. Her beautiful eyes were welcoming and unfathomably blue. Her creamy olive skin beckoned to be touched.

"Hi— you're right on time."

"You look beautiful." He leaned in for a kiss and heard her breath hitch in anticipation. "I knew you wouldn't cut me any slack if I was late."

"For you— I'm starting to think maybe I can make exceptions."

His mouth lingered over the task of kissing the smile from her gorgeous, full mouth. Jeff hoped this evening he would begin chipping away at the impenetrable wall she seemed to surround herself with. If not, he was sure as hell scaling over it— for tonight.

"Don't cut me any slack," he warned as she closed the door behind him. "It keeps me on my toes."

"You want me to be hard on you?" Marisol smiled over his confession before twining her fingers through his and retracing her steps through the hallway. He loved the affectionate gesture of possession— even more so because she probably wasn't aware of it.

"I like that you have expectations," Jeff admitted, shocking himself with the honesty of his answer. Another first. He should have been hearing alarms sounding at this point— or that voice in his head reminding him *'dude— no promises'*.

Over her shoulder, she threw him a beguiling smile that made his body tighten with anticipation. Instead of warnings, his brain flashed to an image of them stumbling through this hallway on the way to her bedroom, clothes scattering along the way. He wondered if they'd even make it up the stairs. "Okay— remember that tonight when it's time to wash dishes."

Mari was completely different from the women he'd dated previously. In so many ways. For one— she hadn't wanted him. She'd made him work for it. She'd challenged him— against his will, Jeff readily admitted, to get to know her. Even now— when he'd been intrigued by what he'd learned, she still allowed only glimpses. Something— or someone in her life had taught her caution. Probably a 'someone' very much like him.

Instead of his usual tactic of disarming a woman with charm so he could speed up the process— he'd been surprised to realize that with Marisol, he was willing to wait. Not that he'd been completely in control of their situation— another big difference. In spite of her calling the shots, he'd discovered he was enjoying the process, probably as much as he typically enjoyed the end result.

In the past, Jeff had avoided any appearance of emotional entanglement. No sleeping over. No breakfast the next day. No expectations of a repeat performance unless they were both still game. Women knew up front what he wanted. Though some might consider him a player, he wasn't about leading women on. They knew exactly what they were getting when they jumped into bed with him. No commitments. No promises. The only time things got ugly was when someone tried to change the rules.

Because of Hector, Jeff had known this time would be different. He'd accepted the change and respected Mari more because of her refusal to yield. Despite her no nonsense approach— despite how guarded she was, he'd willingly stayed in the game. Hell— he'd been eager for more. He hadn't begun to scratch the surface on who Marisol really was.

"I thought we could have dinner outside tonight." Mari's heart was thumping a pleasantly erratic beat as she led him through the kitchen and out onto the deck. A waft of jasmine hit her nose and she inhaled the intoxicating scent. It was just breezy enough tonight to have dinner outside without risk of mosquitoes.

"Wow. This is amazing." Jeff admired the view before stepping off the deck to wander through the small backyard. "You've really transformed the yard. It's so private."

"I imagined turning it into a secret garden," she admitted. "I knew it wasn't large enough for Hector to really play, so I went for peaceful and secluded instead." Admiring the pretty table she'd set for two, Mari enjoyed the idea that tonight would be for her and Jeff. The thought of Hector caused a quick pang of missing him, but she set it aside as she remembered his excited face as he'd leaped from her car earlier this evening. He would have as much fun at his sleepover as she would hopefully be having with Jeff.

"Did you do all this work yourself?" Retracing his steps, Jeff joined her on the deck.

She offered him a beer before pouring herself a glass of sparkling wine from the cooler. "I did. I had no idea how much work I was undertaking. My brother Manny did some of the digging for me, but if I'd known how hard it was going to be— I might've had second thoughts."

Jeff smiled over her confession. "But your end result is incredible." He leaned over the side for another look. "Most of this stuff will take care of itself except for watering. You planned really well."

"Thanks. I'm still glad the work is done." Joining him at the railing, Mari's pulse skittered when he slung his arm around her, drawing her closer. She loved the lean, tough feel of his body next to hers, loved the quiet strength he exuded without trying. The clean, heady scent of skin and aftershave surrounded her. Despite her jangled nerves over the evening ahead, everything about being with Jeff was easy. There were no moods, no games.

"Are we grilling tonight— because I think you should know I'm pretty awesome."

She nodded, mesmerized by the expression in his eyes. "I— I have shrimp and vegetable kabobs marinating. Whenever you want to fire it up— I will defer to your expertise."

"I'm already fired up. I've been thinking about you all day," he added, his voice dropping to a whisper as he skimmed a kiss along her jaw. "And I was awake half the night imagining what tonight would be like."

Her heart lurched into her throat as his mouth travelled there, too, pulling gently, caressing her skin. "I— me too," she admitted. Dios, if he kept that up, she would take him right there on the deck. Her pulse in overdrive, she knew her face was stained pink when she risked a glance into his amazing eyes. Tongue-tied, she blurted out the thought she'd been wondering all day. "Is this s-something else you feel we should get out of the way first?"

Beautiful green eyes heated before his mouth curved in a slow, sure grin. "I think we should take our time tonight. I've wanted you from the day we met. Tonight— I'm going to torture you with just a fraction of what I've been feeling for the past seven weeks, six days and-" Jeff glanced at his watch. "Ten hours."

She startled over the admission. Suddenly, Marisol felt more relaxed— more certain of herself than she'd felt in weeks. This night with Jeff would be memorable. And more than that— it would be fun. For once, she was going to loosen up and enjoy herself and not care where it led. "In that case, I hope you don't mind a little spice."

His breathing quickened, making her smile. "The marinade— it's a Cuban recipe from my dad. The heat builds slowly, but if you're not careful . . . you can go up in flames."

"Mari-" When his gaze locked with hers, she couldn't look away. His beautiful eyes promised the world.

"When the spice overwhelms you, I have just the right treat to cool you down— your palate, I mean. When things get fiery . . . we have an icy sorbet and a sweet fruit salad to slow the heat before we let it build again." Marisol resisted the urge to smile as she saw the effect her words had on him.

He pulled her against him and she felt the hard length of him against her stomach. The way he held her, the way he held *himself* indicated a taut control that would hopefully end tonight. Mari shivered in anticipation. Lowering his head, Jeff's mouth was a mere whisper from hers.

"I'm supposed to be torturing *you*— not the other way around," he rasped before he nibbled at the corner of her mouth. His lips, warm and insistent against hers, moved methodically against hers, never staying in one place. The grazing bites made her heart pitch crazily in her chest. When he traced her lower lip with his tongue, her knees buckled.

"It's w-working." Her breath hitched in her throat as she tugged his head down to hers. It was almost a relief from the exquisite torture when he finally kissed her full on, his tongue thrusting inside seeking hers. She clung to him, grateful for the support of the rough wooden deck rails against her back.

When they broke free several moments later, they were both breathing heavily. When Jeff's head dipped to the hollow of her throat, she shuddered, nearly dizzy with wanting him. His fingers were shaking when he undid the top button on her blouse. When his mouth covered the skin above her lacy bra, she tipped her head back, allowing him better access. A murmur of pleasure caught in her throat. Who was this woman she'd become? No one had ever made her feel this crazy— out of control— alive.

"Jefferson— please," she whispered. The plea ended on a gasp as his mouth latched onto the satin covering her breast. His tongue flicked over her sensitized breast and it was all she could do to prevent herself from screaming. No one had ever touched her this way. No one had ever made her lose control the way she was about to with him.

Buen Dios— if she let this continue, she would take him right here on the deck. And not give a damn if anyone heard them. With the little strength she had remaining, Mari shoved him away, regaining much needed distance. For a moment, his eyes registered shock— as though he truly believed she wanted to stop. In a tiny recess in her brain, she noted how he immediately backed away. Without anger. Another difference from what she had been used to.

"You make me feel dangerous," she admitted, her voice trembling. Not wanting the misunderstanding to lengthen, she smiled. "It's a little scary."

"Now you know how I've felt since we met." His hoarse voice scraped over her like sandpaper, leaving her tingling.

She extended her hand, wanting desperately to feel the warmth of his again. When his fingers tightened around hers, she continued. "I don't want our first time to be on this deck but if you do that again I can't be held responsible for my actions."

Jeff's eyes widened before he recovered enough to smile, though it was definitely not his usual self-assured grin. "On a deck at twilight? That would be a first for me."

She smiled— and damn it— began blushing. Would she ever learn to control it? "Maybe once it's really dark we could try something like that-"

"With you, I'm game for anything," he admitted. "But if you want to slow things down, then we slow down."

"If we take this inside right now— we might just make it upstairs to my bedroom." Marisol dragged in a much needed breath of oxygen, not caring that she probably sounded completely desperate. "But I don't hold out much hope of making it that far."

Jeff gathered her into his arms and carried her the few steps to the French doors. He set her down only briefly— to make sure the doors were locked. His gaze still locked on hers, she heard his breath hitch as she slowly undid the remaining buttons on her blouse. She watched it flutter to the floor. When she unclasped the front hook of her bra, her nerve endings were on sensory overload with the need to be touched.

On a groan, he released the breath he'd been holding. "Mari— you are so beautiful. You're perfect."

Taking a step back through the kitchen, she smiled. "I think you should know if you don't touch me soon, I'm going to scream."

He caught up to her in one step, pulling her back against him before dropping a kiss on her shoulder. His mouth was warm and insistent, sending shivers of exquisite sensation down her spine. Slowly, he wrapped his arms around her, capturing her breasts in his hands. As he began to stroke them, she moaned, the ragged, needy sound breaking the silence in the room. "Like this?"

Her head rested back against his shoulder. Standing there with him felt so right. Absorbing some of the powerful strength he exuded. His warm, wet tongue nuzzled the sensitized spot on her nape, his erection pressed hard against her back as he fondled her. She sagged against him. "Dios, Jefferson. Forget the bed. This hallway will work just fine."

Slowly turning her around to face him, he smiled that sexy, arrogant smile she'd grown to love. "Do you know what I like most about you?"

Intent on unbuttoning his shirt, she shook her head. "My wanton lack of control?" Mari sighed as she finally slid her hands inside his shirt, her fingers colliding with warm skin. His ropey muscles contracted under her touch. "Let's get this off."

Jeff groaned as she pressed herself against him. The skin on skin contact was almost too much to bear. She went to work on his belt, only pausing when he tipped her chin up so she was forced to stop what she was doing and look at him. "Why aren't you helping me? Is this what you mean by torture?"

He laughed as he bent to kiss her. "The thing I like *most* about you," he reminded, "is this incredible blush." When he caressed her cheeks with calloused thumbs, she shivered as sensation swept through her.

Despite the whirlwind of heat swirling around them, despite her need for more— more kisses, more touching, more everything—

Mari frowned. "I'm standing here half naked, begging you to make love to me . . . and the thing you like is my blush?"

He nodded, his gaze never leaving her face. "All those weeks when I didn't know where I stood with you— I concentrated on what you were thinking, instead of what you said." Jeff brushed her cheeks again. "This always gave you away— and gave me hope."

If possible, her face heated even more. "So— I have no secrets from you?"

"I wouldn't go that far." He kissed the scowl from between her eyes. "But at least I knew to keep trying."

She pulled his head down for a long, wet, slightly frantic kiss. Her body was on auto-pilot now— and it was begging for relief from the slow, sweet torture Jefferson was putting her through. She felt him tighten as her nails scratched lightly over his sinewy biceps and she slid his shirt from his shoulders.

"Mari, love— we still have the stairs to get up."

"Later." She rained kisses on his face before she buried hers into his chest. "You smell so good. I promise we can go slow later."

Jeff staggered back a step, seeming dazed for a moment before twin flames ignited in his eyes and he accepted the challenge she'd thrown down. He made quick work of her shorts, taking a horrifically long time to tease them down her hips. His hands slid across overheated skin, dipping into her panties to torture her before retreating to tease her again. He actually grinned when her legs sagged against him.

"So beautiful. So sweet," he whispered, his voice growing more edgy with need as he touched her. His fingers danced between her legs yet again. "So wet for me."

"Please." She was panting now, needing Jeff Traynor more than any other thing on the planet. Needing him— all of him thrusting inside of her or she would not live another moment. If she'd been capable of thinking rationally, she would have wondered what had become of Marisol Ortega— the woman she had been before Jeff. Because that woman had never, ever before begged for sex. She'd had it, she'd enjoyed it, she'd even initiated it. But she'd never *needed* it— as though struggling for her next breath. That Marisol would have believed the desperate woman in this hallway was seriously loco.

⟨✂⟩

"Easy, sweet." Jeff held her up as he unbuttoned his jeans, grateful he was able to kick them free as quickly as she demanded. He smiled over her husky plea to hurry, and again as she helped him tear open the condom. But his knees buckled when she took him in her hands to finish the job for him.

If it hadn't been so painful, Jeff wished he could freeze this moment and just spend it staring at her. Feasting on her. The gorgeous, sexy, amazing woman in his arms was close to coming undone and he hadn't really touched her yet. But he was damn sure going to be touching her all night. She'd been right about the first time— about not making it upstairs. He would explode if he didn't get inside her this very moment. "Mari, love— are you sure?"

"Maldita sea! I've been sure for days."

"I'll take that as a 'yes'." Grinning, he propped her against the wall near the stairs. She was kissing him with reckless abandon. He sunk in even deeper, satisfied when her groan of need matched his own. When he sucked on her tongue, her whimper of pleasure was a visceral hit straight to his gut. Her beautiful, perfect breasts swelled in his hands, the tight nub sensitized beyond reason to his touch. He wanted more. More everything. More Mari.

Heat swept over him in a way he'd never experienced before. One tiny brain cell wanted to analyze the wildfire, out-of-control feeling. But it was quickly overruled by the rest of him. The rest of him was prepared to be scorched. He'd never had to wait this long before— never had to earn the right to sleep with a woman. The wait was a perfectly logical reason why he was ready to leap into the deep end. Any guy who waited for a gorgeous, totally hot woman like Mari would be a little crazy when he finally got her.

When he couldn't bear the building pressure for another moment, he lifted her gently, pinning her back to the wall. He took one perfect breast into his mouth and was rewarded with a sob of pleasure. Her midnight hair was curly and untamed, her eyes unfathomably blue— and burning with passion for him. She was the most beautiful woman he'd ever seen.

Mari was out of control now, as wild and close to the edge as he felt. When he could stand it no longer, he entered her swiftly. Her low, satisfied groan was the sweetest sound he'd ever heard. Unable to resist touching her, he pulled her from the wall, cupping her sweet butt in his hands. She locked her legs around him and it was the most powerful feeling he'd ever experienced. He wanted all of her. Thrusting into her again and again, each time she took him deeper. Jeff wished like hell he could make it last forever.

When her release swept over him, it was cataclysmic, rocking him to the core. She cried out his name, muttering in Spanish in that husky, sexy accent. She tightened around him, squeezing him, kissing him, gifting him with the most powerful orgasm he'd ever experienced. Her name was torn from his throat as he let himself rocket away from earth.

It took several minutes for her to stop trembling and for Jeff to reattach himself to his brain. When he regained consciousness, he opened his eyes. "Mari, sweet— are you alright?"

She released a shaky sigh, her body still slack in his arms. "Never better."

He buried his face in her throat and inhaled the sweet, spicy scent of her fragrance mingled with the heady scent of their joined bodies. The lethal combination was burned into his brain— like the jasmine in her yard. Her eyes were dazed and slumberous with satisfaction. Her overwhelmed expression was enough to make him hard again. Somewhere deep inside, he experienced a primitive stab of possessiveness. That expression— belonged to him.

Unsure what to make of the foreign feeling, Jeff shoved it aside. There would be plenty of time later for Monday morning quarterbacking. Much later. For now, he was going to enjoy every single moment of his time in paradise.

"You were right about us not making it upstairs." He released her gently, setting her back on her feet, waiting for her to stop swaying before he let go.

She smiled. "I knew exactly how I was feeling. I'm just glad you felt it, too." Without pausing to retrieve their clothes, she roped her fingers through his. "Come on. I'll show you the upstairs. Perhaps after the tour we can try to make it back down for dinner before midnight."

He watched her gorgeous butt sway up the stairs in front of him and felt himself tighten all over again. Blazing hot sex halfway up the stairs was increasingly likely. But dinner before midnight? Highly questionable.

Several hours later, Jeff's stomach growled as he was propped up on one elbow watching her. Even as she slept, Mari was beautiful. Sifting silky, dark chocolate curls through his fingers, he admired the cute sprinkle of freckles fanned across her nose, guessing she got those from her mother's side of the family.

Her bedroom, like the rest of her house was sparse, functional, yet still warm and feminine. There was no clutter on the bureau, no piles of clothes or messy jewelry boxes. Her room reminded him of an oasis— her bed was comfortable, the pillows even more so, the colors soothing and somewhat tropical. Jeff liked being there. Though he probably wouldn't spend the night, he didn't think he'd *mind* sleeping there— should he ever decide to bend one of his rules.

That alone was revelation enough to accelerate his heartbeat from its deeply relaxed state. Just because he'd enjoyed several rounds of the most amazing sex of his life wasn't reason enough to start randomly chucking rules out the window.

"Has a ferocious beast taken up residence?" Turning her head on the pillow, Mari opened her eyes. "Or could that possibly be your stomach?"

He felt a punch of heat when her gorgeous turquoise eyes locked with his. Not for the first time tonight, he wondered what the hell was happening to him. Unlike most dates, he didn't feel restless— as though the evening was pretty much over and it was time to head home. Usually, Jeff couldn't wait to get back to his place where he could collapse in his own bed and not worry whether he was hogging the sheets or taking too much space. Where he could wake up the next morning satisfied from decent sex, yet refreshed because he was finally alone again.

He'd always viewed it as his way of beating the system. Because he didn't have to make small talk. He didn't have to shower in a strange bathroom that was cluttered with makeup and stupid girly soaps and female junk that took up way too much space.

"Does this mean you're finally ready for the spice part of the evening?"

Sliding back under the covers, he kissed every one of the cute freckles he'd been admiring. "I thought we'd been experiencing the spice part— for the last four hours."

Her eyes widened in mock innocence. "You haven't experienced anything yet. We need to fire up the grill before we starve to death up here."

He raised an eyebrow. "It *is* dark enough now for us to spend some quality time out on that deck." Recalling her suggestion that they make love out there, he hoped for another fiery blush as a reward.

Her sweet, talented mouth split with a smile, revealing even, white teeth that appeared more so against her soft, honeyed skin. Even now, Jeff found himself a little dazzled by her beauty. Mari didn't even have to try hard and she stole his breath.

"Well, what are we waiting for?" She pushed back the covers and stretched. "I'm starving."

He watched her cross the room, her naked body lithe and golden in the light spilling in from the hallway. And grew hard as he watched her slip on a tee shirt. Seriously? What was it about this woman that made him so crazy— so desperate for more?

"I'm going to take a quick shower. Then we can light the grill and finally cook our dinner." Crossing to the doorway, Marisol was oblivious to his suddenly red alert body.

Jeff rose from the bed in search of his clothes, finally remembering how they'd been urgently discarded at the bottom of the stairs. Hearing the shower start as he entered the hallway, he paused on the top step. The water changed patterns as it connected with all that gorgeous skin. Hesitating only a moment, he turned in the opposite direction and made his way to the bathroom.

Admiring her through the frosted glass of the shower stall, his heart flipped over in his chest as she soaped the curviest body he'd ever seen. When Mari noticed him standing there, she opened the shower door, a beguiling smile on her face.

"Mind if I join you? I'm suddenly very hot again."

She smiled again as water splashed over them, her eyelashes spiked together as though she'd been caught in a summer rainstorm. "It will be a tight fit. Old houses like this don't offer much assistance."

"We'll make it work." Crowding into the space with her, Jeff couldn't wait to kiss her senseless. The hitch in Mari's breath stole his own. The feel of her slippery body gliding against his was impossibly, amazingly good. "God— you feel unbelievable."

The fleeting worry he'd experienced in the hallway left him. This thing with Mari was a novelty. Once the magnetic attraction wore off— once the sex settled into a more predictable pattern— he'd be fine. He'd be back in control. He'd be able to resist her. Hell- he'd probably grow bored, as he always did.

The only real difference with Marisol was that he liked her. A lot. They'd become friends. And he liked Hector.

But as he lifted her beautiful body, as he anchored her against the shower wall, the water beat down on them in a relentless, crashing wave. Jeff entered her with a groan of pure male satisfaction. As he thrust into her in a mindless haze of raw pleasure, a tiny fraction of his brain grew more alarmed. As her nails scored his shoulders, his eyes sought hers— wanting more than anything to see what he did to her— wanting her to know what she was doing to him. When her release contracted around him, Jeff could only mutter her name, coming with a fierce violence he'd never experienced before.

And he knew.

This was dangerously different. *Marisol* was different.

While part of him wanted to shout with pleasure over the new, exciting feeling— another part wanted to run for cover. Because the overwhelming mess of feelings— uncertainty— confusion would swamp him. Expose him. Leaving him vulnerable in a way he'd sworn never to allow.

Jeff didn't want the perfect relationship. He didn't want to meet the love of his life. He'd never wanted anything that came close to mimicking his parents' relationship. He didn't want a woman who would become his best friend . . . his lifeline. Or the years spent together raising a family. And he sure as hell didn't want the wrenching, horrible end to all that happiness. The end that would occur for no discernible reason. An end that would roar upon him like a locomotive and flatten him. As his parents' marriage had.

As he held her, Mari shuddered in his arms, her eyes revealing satisfaction . . . and something else. Vulnerability? Confusion? He kissed her gently as they both recovered, his soap-slicked hands still trembling as he stroked the length of her magnificent spine. And he tried like hell not to be terrified by what was happening to him.

Jefferson was already different. Mari stole another glance at him while he sipped his beer and gazed out at the night sky. They'd eaten grilled shrimp by the dozen, laughing over their ferocious hunger. They'd drunk wine, they'd talked about everything and nothing. To an untrained eye, his smile was still cocky, his words still light. But he was different.

She didn't know whether to be upset by the change or relieved. For she had gone into the evening with eyes wide open. Between her pep talk with Sharon and her own raging desire to finally take the next step with him, Marisol had prepared herself for better or worse— mostly for worse. She had tried to set her expectations as low as possible so she wouldn't be disappointed.

She smiled over the revelation. Her expectation had been for one amazing night with Jefferson Traynor. And she'd received it.

"What are you smiling about?" Jeff had lowered his gaze from the sky to stare at her.

"You. This incredible night." She could afford to be honest with him. Unlike Nick— at least Jeff's behavior was predictable. Could she truly fault him for acting the way she'd known he would? "I've had a great time with you, Jeff. Probably the best date ever."

"Let's do it again sometime," he suggested, beautiful eyes heating. "I know with Hector in the picture, you probably don't get the chance to go a little crazy very often. So, I'm glad it was with me."

"Me, too." Despite her desire for a playful facade, her heart beat a little faster. This was the hard part— the 'after', when he would turn polite . . . acting as though what they'd shared had just been a typical Friday night. Hell— for him, it probably had.

Maybe for him it hadn't been amazing. Maybe he hadn't felt the earth shift. It probably wouldn't occur to Jeff they were two people incredibly in sync with each other. Or perhaps, Mari realized, it was only she who felt that. He was so incredibly different from Nick— so much more likeable and open. She felt in balance with Jeff in a way she'd never experienced with her former boyfriend. Tonight had been effortless— being with him, talking with him.

Even before the violence that had destroyed her relationship—
that had nearly destroyed her spirit— she'd never felt close to
Nick. He'd always held himself apart. Brooding, quiet, moody. Her
twenty-four year old self had naively viewed those qualities as a
challenge— as a prize to be won. The bad boy who could be
tamed. She'd believed if he only trusted her, if he relied on her, she
would love and protect him. Mari would 'fix' the dark, dangerous
parts of him as only she could. And when that hadn't happened—
because it could *never* happen, she was honest enough to admit
now— she'd felt failure. He'd bruised not only her body, but her
spirit.

But tonight was different for Jeff. For him, it was just a date . . .
an evening of casual sex with a woman who intrigued him. She
was one in a probable long line of amazing sexual experiences.
Because that's who Jeff was. She couldn't act hurt by this
revelation— because it wasn't a surprise. Her twenty-seven year
old self had accepted his terms when she'd agreed to keep seeing
him. And she couldn't try to change them because he'd never
painted himself as someone different. Despite knowing what
Jefferson was about, she liked him.

"As much as I would love more nights like tonight. . . I wouldn't
change my life. I love that Hector is part of it. I could never give
that up." Marisol discovered she was grateful for the darkness. At
least he wouldn't see the heat of embarrassment crawling up her
face. "But I'm glad tonight was with you."

While she would love the chance to continue this dance with
him— she knew it likely wasn't in the cards. Jeff would grow
bored, moving on to the *next* big challenge. Since she no longer
held that appeal for him, he would find it easy to walk away. There
was no sense getting worked up over it.

"I promised I'd help him work on his swing tomorrow." Jeff's
gaze followed her as she shifted in her chair. "When do his
practices start?"

Unlike her time with Nick, when she'd foolishly fallen in love
way too fast— this time Mari would be careful. This time she
would maintain an emotional distance. Keep it light and friendly.
She would not dream of him, she would not make plans for him.
She would appreciate this evening for what it was. And move on.

"Peewee league practice starts next week." She sipped her wine, hoping to cover the sudden hoarseness revealed in her voice. She'd promised to keep her emotions under tight control. But the thought of him spending more time with Hector filled her with trepidation. And longing.

It wasn't fair. That he could be so in tune with her son— yet already distancing himself from *her*. Mari was suddenly unsure whether she should allow their friendship to continue when she knew how it would end. Why should Hector have his heart broken, too?

"What time are you picking him up in the morning from his party?"

"Around nine. What time did you want-" As the silence lengthened, Marisol hesitated. For the first time all evening, she felt awkward, sensing the charmed atmosphere surrounding them begin to fade. How could something so magical turn out to be so fleeting? "I guess I can take him to the park to meet you. Are you sure you want to do this?"

"Absolutely. I promised." Stifling a yawn, Jeff grinned as he rose from the table. "Not only have you completely exhausted me tonight, but I barely got any sleep last night either."

Her heart stuttered in spite of her resolve. "Why?"

Leaning over her chair, he brushed his mouth against the rocketing pulse in her throat. "After last night on your front porch? How can you even ask?"

The heat in Jeff's eyes made her feel slightly better. At least that, she recognized. But . . . was heat all there was? Marisol wondered whether he even knew what he wanted. Between his ambivalence toward her— toward any woman, probably— and her mounting confusion, they made quite a pair. She began gathering their glasses. Her beautiful, magical evening was quickly morphing into a pumpkin.

"This won't take long to clean up."

"I promised to help with the dishes-"

"If you need to leave-" Her words, spoken over his, sounded as awkward as they felt. Offering him a weak smile, her words trailed off.

He stared at her for several seconds, his eyes unreadable in the flickering candlelight. "Right— of course. I should go."

"So, you want to meet us there— at the park?"

"Uh— yeah. That'll work." Jeff carried several dishes in, placing them on the counter before making an elaborate show of searching for his keys. Her temper flaring, Mari schooled herself against it. She couldn't control *his* desire to place distance between them. Even if it was foolish. He would flee— when they could have left the dishes on the counter, turned out the lights and headed upstairs. Together.

Damn it, what was wrong with him? What was he so afraid of? If anyone had a right to be terrified— it was her. Yet, there she stood, willing to toss aside her good sense. And how stupid was that?

"I'll walk you out." Rather than drag out their awkward goodbyes under the harsh and unforgiving foyer lights, Marisol slipped out the front door to the darkened porch where jasmine danced on the breeze.

"Mari— I had a great time. I don't want to leave with you thinking otherwise."

She placed a hand on his arm, her touch light . . . again grateful for the darkness closing in around them. "I did, too. We both got what we wanted tonight. Let's not read too much into it."

Jeff stiffened as her words hit home. "What does that mean?"

"You wanted to sleep with me and I wanted the same. For you, it was a challenge. For me— it had been awhile . . . and I— needed to feel wanted again." Leaning in, she brushed his cheek with her lips, but his jaw had suddenly become as unyielding as the rest of him.

"That's not-" His usually confident voice faltered. "Marisol. . . I care about you."

"And I like you, too." She kept her voice light, though her heart sank like lead in her chest. She wasn't very skilled at subterfuge. Desperate for the safety of her darkened house, Mari wanted to burrow under the covers and release the scalding tears that were suddenly burning the back of her throat.

"Good night, Jeff. We'll see you at the park." Once inside, she resisted the impulse to peek out the window. Watching him leave would only bury under a pile of sadness the evening that had started with such promise.

CHAPTER 7

How in hell had the best night of his life suddenly gone so wrong? Jeff stood on the darkened walkway, his feet unwilling to move toward the driveway. Like a car missing the bend in the road, his conversation with Marisol had just careened through a guardrail into a darkened forest. And the way his body was still tightened like a fist— he knew he'd just crashed into a big, friggin' tree.

His feet finally moving, he closed the gap to his car, his brain incapable— or unwilling— to digest what had just occurred. For unknown reasons, Jeff was hyper aware of his own breathing— the angry rasps he dragged in and released. *Angry?* Why the hell should he be upset? In the bro playbook he'd been the recipient of the textbook *perfect* evening. Great food. Fantastic sex with a beautiful woman. A beautiful woman who knew how to accurately read his playbook, he amended, recalling their final conversation. No pleading with him to spend the night. The perfect evening. No muss. No fuss. No strings.

Jeff continued breathing, ignoring his increasing agitation. His nose burned with the exotic, heady, sensual scent of jasmine— the smell conjuring memories that quickly overwhelmed his senses. His peripheral vision took in her quiet, slumbering neighborhood. Lights off, cars parked in neatly laid out driveways. A lone truck parked on the street outside Marisol's house. Suburbia at its finest. All the things Jeff wasn't missing in his life. Would *never* miss. Would never, ever want for himself. He watched the light wink on in a room upstairs. Her bedroom.

Still jacked-up, he took another step toward his car, but Jeff's gaze remained glued to the light. A shadow moved fleetingly across the curtains. He wasn't sure if he'd actually seen Marisol or simply imagined it . . . taking her clothes off . . . slipping on the faded baseball shirt she'd pulled on earlier. He could easily visualize her sleeping in it. Mari wasn't the type to wear sexy lingerie. She wouldn't feel the need to impress. She was comfortable with who she was— in every way. With the decisions she'd made in her life. With the decisions she continued to make, adjusting her path according to what was best for Hector.

It was her words. Jeff froze on the path as he recalled them. That she'd only been a challenge for him. The finality in her expression as she'd said them. As though she *knew*. As though she knew— him. And she'd already accepted that he would likely move on.

Or— was she telling him *she* was moving on? Because that wasn't necessarily how the playbook worked. Was this about Hector? Or had he merely been the answer to a need? What had she said? Something about sex— about not having it for a while. About needing to feel wanted. . . Jeff had never pried over her previous relationships. He'd sensed from Mari's extreme caution there had been someone before him. Someone important. Someone who'd hurt her. But she'd built such a wall around herself he hadn't tried to learn more. Her past had seemed off limits.

Frankly, with the women in his past Jeff had been cool with that. He hadn't particularly cared about their baggage because the likelihood was he wouldn't be sticking around. But tonight, it had grown in importance. He wanted to know what was going on in Mari's head. And get it right with her. Get back on track. Just because there couldn't be anything deeper between them. . . it didn't mean they couldn't continue what they'd shared tonight. It didn't mean they couldn't be friends.

Jeff winced over that lie. They already *were* friends. But now, that would be thrown off. Sex always changed things— and sometimes not for the better. Clearly, tonight proved that. Maybe she was worried about Hector— in case they stopped seeing each other. Hell— maybe Marisol just didn't want him in the little boy's life— or hers.

Okay . . . so maybe he'd panicked. Maybe Mari had sensed it. Something about *her* had knocked him on his ass tonight. But Jeff assumed he'd covered his tracks pretty well. He'd remained his usual charming, level-headed self. He hadn't shown fear. He sure as hell hadn't fallen all over himself looking desperate for more. But Marisol was observant. If she'd picked up on his vibe of uncertainty . . . maybe she'd resented it.

But how the hell was he supposed to act? Like everything was fine? When every molecule in his body had been screaming for him to get out. *Now. Fast*. Before something dangerous happened. Something huge and overwhelming.

The whole night with her had been like . . . standing on the edge of a cliff. All he'd wanted was to dive over the side with her. But— what the hell? He *barely* knew her. He'd slept with her once. Okay— more than once. But for God's sake . . . it was too soon. A *year* from now would be too soon. The vice around his chest tightened as the battle inside him grew more heated. He could never risk it . . . could never accept that sort of drastic change in his life. Not this quick. Hell— probably not ever.

But what he was *really* unprepared for . . . what he couldn't allow— was letting it end this way. To see Mari at the park tomorrow . . . and know he couldn't touch her. To see those beautiful eyes and remember how she'd gazed at him tonight. With sensual heat and drowsy satisfaction. With fondness. And vulnerability.

Tomorrow, Marisol would stare at him with coolness. With distance. Spinning on his heel, Jeff jogged back, taking the porch steps two at a time. Before any sense of composure could return, he pressed her buzzer. His free hand rapped on the door. Though he acted with instinctive purpose, Jeff had no clue what he would say. But damn it, whatever it was— she would listen to him.

He was still knocking when Mari jerked the door open. He read the flash of annoyance in her eyes before it was replaced with concern. Her expression suggested he probably wasn't exuding anything resembling confidence or charm. "Jeff— what is it?"

Her voice. The husky, melodic, sexy accent exploded across his nerve endings. As his gaze finally refocused, Jeff noticed the blessed heat that had risen in her cheeks. At least he had a clue to go by. He was releasing a sigh of relief when he noticed her red-rimmed eyes. And everything inside him stilled. His heartbeat began to slow from its current gallop. His racing, jumbled thoughts synthesized down to one immediate fact. Marisol had been crying. "I need— I want . . . to say something."

She stood, not quite patiently as the silence lengthened between them. As he'd imagined, Mari's tee shirt was covered haphazardly with a robe. Hair hanging past her shoulders, the wild disarray cried out for his touch. Instead, he fisted his hand at his side.

"It's getting late, Jeff. What did you want?"

His anger dissipated, replaced with a new, more unnerving anxiety. "Mari— I'm sorry about tonight." There. He'd said it. Feeling lightheaded, Jeff sucked in much needed oxygen.

Her eyes revealed nothing. "You're sorry. About what?"

Hell— wasn't 'sorry' good enough? Why did women always push for specifics? "I know that— I mean . . . you probably thought I was acting a little strange . . . after-" He acknowledged the flash of pain in her eyes before the shields rose.

"Then perhaps I should apologize, too."

Communication. Relief surged through him. This was good. Everything would be fine-

"I expect your usual evening is dinner first, *followed by* sex. Then you get to bolt. I'm sorry I messed up the plan. All that awkward . . . conversation. It's probably more work than you're used to." Mari wrapped her arms around her waist, the subconscious tell revealing less about anger than a need to protect herself. "We don't have to do this again."

His step toward her was involuntary as a chill strafed down his spine. "Marisol— no. That's not what I meant-"

She smiled, revealing more misery than warmth. "I know how you operate. You wanted me. You pursued me. I *allowed* you to have me."

"Mari-" Jeff heard the gravelly hoarseness and wondered whether he'd ever sounded as desperate as he felt just then.

"It's okay." Her tone sounded of pity as she patted his hand. "There's nothing to feel guilty over— if that's what you're feeling. I wasn't led on. I'm not hurt."

Her lie was betrayed by the redness of her eyes, by the husky catch to her voice. She leaned in to kiss his cheek, her smile brave. "You're free."

Capturing her in his arms, Jeff held her, drinking her in— the startled confusion in captivating eyes, her haunting scent, the way she'd begun trembling as she held herself rigid against him.

"Mari. . . you weren't a challenge." The tortured confession broke free on a whisper. "I mean— the day we met . . . that's how I saw you. I'll admit it. I took one look at you in that parking lot and I was a total jerk. But since then— I've gotten to know you . . . we've become-"

"Friends?" Her expression remained unmoved.

He dragged in a rasping breath. "You can't honestly believe that's all I wanted. . ." God— where the hell was he going with this? "Look . . . I don't know what happened tonight— but it's never happened before. And whatever it was. . . I'm not exactly sure I like it."

Her head popped up over his admission. Encouraged by the relief coursing through him, Jeff took another half step toward honesty. "I'm sort of . . . afraid of it."

"Then why are you here?"

Great question. One requiring honesty. It was *go* time. Or he'd be forced to walk. The way his gut was churning, honest was gonna suck. But revisiting the icy despair he'd just experienced— would suck worse. "Because I don't want this to end."

Yet.

Jeff left the door open for escape, if only in his own head. It was the only way he'd be able to regain control of the ground shifting under his feet. "I like you. Tonight was amazing. I've never-" He stopped himself before he made the mistake of revealing something he might regret— something she might misconstrue. Mari didn't need to know everything. Just enough to keep her-

"I want . . . to keep seeing you."

He felt the shiver course through her, felt his own body absorb it. "I like you, too. But don't you think it would be better to end this now? While we can still remain friends? We have to work together for the next few months. I don't want-"

To hate him when it ended?

"I don't want to fall for you." Mari stared up at him, her eyes worried. "I don't want Hector relying on you. He already does." Her admission slipped out in a voice thickening with tears. "He's been through too much. *I've* been through too much to risk-"

Her startled gaze shifted from him as she left the sentence unfinished. Jeff wanted to pursue it— to discover exactly what had her running scared. To pry it out of her. No matter that he was feeling the same way. But instinct told him their reasons were very different. And hers was an important clue into the secrets she kept from him.

"I can't promise-" Anything. Hell— he'd never come this far with any woman. To the point of speaking about feelings? To the point of negotiating something that might resemble a relationship? "I'm sort of in uncharted territory here. But— I'm willing-"

Jeff knew he had to say it right. Knew Mari would reject a careless effort. He had to reveal what he wanted. "I'd like to see where this goes . . . if you— would like that, too."

Marisol released a gusting breath. He waited, unwilling to acknowledge how everything would come down to this single moment. How important this instant had suddenly become to his plans— whatever the hell they were.

When she smiled, his pulse surged with relief. With victory. His heartbeat roared in his ears, nearly drowning out her response. But when she slid her fingers through his, he knew. As she led him up the stairs, Jeff was nearly drunk with both relief and anticipation. When they stripped off their clothes, they met eagerly, with a new familiarity he welcomed. And when he held her in his arms after they made love, no unruly thoughts disrupted the peace— that he didn't want to be there— that he shouldn't stay— that he was breaking one of his own rules. There was only Mari. His mouth grazed a warm, satin shoulder as he pulled her tighter against him. And when he slept, he dreamed of her.

Fingers fluttering against the curtain, Marisol noticed the truck parked out front. "Dios!" She remembered to lower her voice as she scowled at the sight beyond the window. Glancing over her shoulder, she acknowledged the incredibly handsome man sprawled in her bed, dead asleep. Had last night been a dream? She still wasn't completely certain Jefferson was real. He'd returned. He'd spoken. Voluntarily. Of feelings.

Her scowl dissolved in a smile. *Don't get crazy, Mariboo.* It wasn't as though he'd talked of picking out china patterns. Slipping on her tee shirt, she unearthed the pair of running shorts she wore more for the expandable waistband than for actual athletic pursuits. Allowing herself one last admiring glance at Jeff's seriously chiseled body, she crept down the stairs, finger-combing her hair into a less wild version of the bedhead she'd spied in the mirror.

She tiptoed to the hall closet and removed Hector's bat, remembering to step over the creaking spot on the hardwood floor. Silently, she unlocked the front door and slid out to the porch. Mari took a moment to breathe in the heady, early morning scent of flowers and dew before she half-walked, half-ran to the end of the driveway. Pausing to catch her breath, she peeked around the hedge to assess the vehicle parked there. The pickup truck was nearly new, red and shiny. The windshield fogged from the early morning humidity and the heavy breathing of the man she knew she would find snoring in the front seat.

Her brother Manny. Here, in Arlington. *Spying* on her. Suddenly, her mother's stammered responses made sense. Papi was behind this. Thumping the end of the bat against her palm, Marisol enjoyed the pleasant thwacking sound. What she wouldn't give to see Manny's expression when she bashed in the windshield and woke him up. She enjoyed the vision in her head for several moments before reluctantly setting it aside. If she hurt his truck, Manny would kill her.

It took two more precious minutes to retrace her steps to the side yard where she gathered up a handful of crab apples. Two more minutes before she was lobbing the first pitch at his windshield. Three apples and forty-five seconds later, Manny flew up in the seat, his head— or some other body part hitting the steering wheel as he jolted out of sleep. She winced at the ear-splitting blast of his horn, belatedly remembering it was before seven on a Saturday.

Her brother lumbered from the truck, still half comatose as his feet hit the pavement. "Jeez, Mari— que demonios estas haciendo?"

"What the hell am *I* doing?" She approached him slowly, bat in hand. "Since I'm armed, I think I'll be the one asking questions. How long have you been tailing me?"

Manny rubbed sleep from his eyes, his overnight growth of whiskers making him appear remarkably similar to a bear awakening too early from hibernation. "Papi's orders," he growled, again, not unlike an angry grizzly. "If you dented my truck-"

"You're lucky I threw apples. You want to see dented? Keep trying to change the subject." She took a step closer, annoyance and amusement fueling her movement. If this was what her sister Caridad had endured over the past two years, Mari had a newfound understanding— and perhaps fear— of the torture her parents could inflict on them. "Maldita sea! How long?"

Manny raised thick fingers to his neck and grimaced as he began massaging an aching spot. "Two days," he admitted. "How the hell do you think I feel? I'm wasting vacation days on this."

"For the love of God, Manuel! What is *wrong* with them? Will they ever let this rest?" Mari continued to sputter at her brother . . . in fact was only getting warmed up when she saw his expression change. "What now? Don't think you can avoid my wrath-"

"Mierda."

With an eye still on her brother, she pivoted and discovered Jefferson striding toward them, jeans slung low on the most amazing hips she'd ever had her hands on. His hair looked as though he'd bolted from bed and slid down the banister before he was fully awake. Jeff's expression was one of mild curiosity— until he spied the bat in her hand. In a heartbeat, his demeanor changed to one of fierce intent. *Mierda* was right.

She'd taken only one step toward him before Jefferson had closed the distance between them. His eyes had iced over, a frigid, angry green she'd never seen before. A shiver coursed through her when Mari realized what he was thinking. A large, burly man accosting her at dawn. Not pausing in his forward motion, Jeff brushed past her, jerking her arm to shove her behind him in one liquid movement. The Louisville Slugger clattered to the street. "Who the hell are you?"

Manny's glare matched his. "I could ask you the same, gringo."

Jeff's gaze remained locked on the enemy, his stance battle ready. "Mari— what's going on? Do you know him? Is he bothering you?"

Part of her wanted to see Manny get punched. Marisol read her brother's expression from behind Jeff's shoulder— saw from Manuel's smile he knew exactly what she was thinking. But she also knew her brother could dish it out as well as he took it and she would hate to see one of Jeff's beautiful eyes blackened. With a sigh of exasperation, she relented. "Jeff, this is my overbearing, interfering brother, Manuel." She squeezed his arm to assure him everything was okay. "Manny, this is my . . . friend— Jeff."

The two men sized each other up for several seconds before reluctantly shaking hands. Jeff finally broke the silence. "What brings you here so early?'

Mari snorted. "He's spying on me for our parents."

Manny ignored her outburst. "I've been in town a day or so. I'm leaving shortly," he shot back.

Jeff's gaze drifted to the spot beyond her brother. "That your truck? I saw it here last night . . . *late* last night."

There was no missing the emphasis in his words. To Mari's surprise, her brother's face reddened. "Yeah, it's mine. Like I said, I'm leaving."

From a well of thoughtfulness she didn't realize she possessed, Marisol relented. "You want coffee before you go? We were just about to make some. I have to pick Hector up at nine."

Manny ran a hand through his already scruffy looking hair. "I don't suppose I could steal a shower, too?"

"That depends. Did you plan to rifle through my bathroom cabinets for contraband?" He winced as her remark hit home. "Because I should probably tidy up first."

Her brother rolled his eyes. "Jeez, Mariboo— just a shower."

Though clearly still confused over exactly what was taking place, Jeff watched the exchange with barely concealed humor. Mari turned to him. "What do you think? He's been spying on me for days. Should I let him in my house or just give him a thermos and kick his ass to the curb?"

"Okay, Mari— get it all out of your system. I deserve it. In my defense, you know how Papi gets when he's worried."

Jeff finally spoke as they made their way back up the driveway. "Since he's your brother, I'd give him a break. Speaking from experience, we do stupid things sometimes— especially when it involves sisters."

Manny nodded. "See— he knows what it's like."

As her two gentlemen visitors settled around the table, Marisol tried not to be nervous in the kitchen. She heard Jeff answering questions about the construction going on at New Beginnings and asking a few of his own. This was too soon— this meeting of family and boyfriend. And in such a ridiculous way. Caught spying. She couldn't imagine what Jefferson was probably thinking. That the Ortega family were a bunch of crazies? That there was something seriously wrong with her? That she couldn't be trusted by her own family?

It was simply too weird. Marisol retrieved cups and plates and started the coffee pot, scowling when the faucet drowned out the discussion. Then the pot started rumbling and she knew she'd have to get back in there ASAP or miss out on the entire conversation. Knowing Manny, he might just blurt out her entire life history— including the awful Nick part. And it was way too soon for the Nick part. A lifetime would probably be too soon for that.

Once the cinnamon rolls were finally in the oven, she carried the coffee pot in, setting it on the table. Suddenly anxious, she wasn't sure who to make eye contact with— Manny to glare him into silence, or Jefferson— to apologize for the disruption to their morning. She didn't have to wait long to decide.

"So, your brother tells me he was down here checking up on you. Does this have anything to do with the Phil incident?"

Mari froze. "Phil? That happened nearly a week ago."

"What incident?" Manuel scowled. "Who's Phil?"

"Big Pete filled me on several details you neglected to mention." Accepting a mug, Jeff poured coffee before offering it to Manny who nodded his thanks.

"Why were you talking to Pete?"

"He said it was more serious than you made out." Jeff glanced at her. "And I'd have to agree."

"Pete thinks everything is serious." She couldn't believe what she was hearing— and from Jeff, no less. "He's paranoid, remember?"

"He was logical when we discussed the problem." Jeff kept his gaze on her while explaining the 'problem' to Manuel. "I found him to be highly observant and detail-oriented." His eyes widened. "In fact— in the same conversation, he said he'd been keeping an eye on a mysterious, red truck." His gaze slid to her brother as he sugared his coffee. "That was probably you— spying on your sister."

"Doing a favor for my parents," Manuel corrected, his sigh one of exasperation.

"Exactly when did shelter customer service issues become your business?" Marisol held her temper. "Your job is building the addition— that's it."

"Customer service is complaints about the meatloaf." Jeff's eyes heated. "Lunatic ex-husbands threatening you *are* my business."

"And mine," her brother added, his tone belligerent. "How desperate is he?"

"Now *you're* going to meddle at my work, too?" Had everyone gone crazy? She turned on her brother. "Are you taking a leave of absence from your job?" When the oven timer went off mid-lecture, she glared at him, switching to Spanish for a rapid-fire string of insults. Any hope of Jeff believing her to be normal had passed.

"You're burning breakfast, Mariboo."

When she threw up her hands and stalked into the kitchen, she overheard Jeff . . . trying to speak while cracking up with laughter.

"I can figure out 'estupido'. . . but what was the rest of it?"

Peeking around the corner, she saw her brother grin, erasing the sullen, sleep-deprived expression he'd carried since she'd tried to take out his windshield with crabapples.

"Some things, amigo . . . you're better off not knowing."

"So— what would you do? Why do you think Annie won't go out with me?"

Jeff glanced up from the set of blueprints. "Seriously? You're asking *me* for advice on your love life? It took me over a month to convince Marisol to go out with me."

"Yeah, but it's already been another month and you seem to be doing great with her." Hank shrugged, his expression befuddled. "Frankly, we all figured you'd have blown it by now."

He stared hard at his foreman. "You bastards have a pool going, don't you?"

"Damn straight. That should've been the easiest money I ever made."

Hell, Jeff would have wagered against himself, too. Curiosity won out over irritation. "How much?"

Hank averted his eyes. "I had twenty bucks on her dumpin' you after the first date."

Jeff grinned, unable to take offense. He'd earned his reputation. Why it was still working with Mari was a mystery to him, too. The whole concept of a relationship was completely foreign to him. But the longer it lasted, the more right it felt.

"I'm sure Annie likes me. But I can't seem to get her to leave this building." Hank's face wrinkled into a question mark. "She always wants to eat here."

He raised an eyebrow. "You're complaining about a woman who doesn't spend your money frivolously?"

"You know what I mean. How many hours can she volunteer here?" His friend's voice heated. "And her boys are stuck here for all the hours she stays to work. I wanted to take them out to the farm . . . you know— see the horses, throw a ball around. Have a barbecue."

"And?"

He shrugged. "She got all panicky lookin'— like I was asking her to take her clothes off or somethin'. Even her boys were ticked. They really wanted to go."

Jeff slid back his chair. "Why don't you just ask her?"

"Then she'll think I'm being nosy."

Obviously, Hank just wanted to argue. "No offense, but you're starting to sound like a woman."

Hank scratched his head. "I think her ex-husband is a jerk. Tommy and Jason don't say much, but it sounds like he doesn't spend any time with them. Maybe she just isn't into taking another chance."

"You mean— sorta like you were after Gayle?"

Hank did a doubletake. "I never thought of it that way."

Jeff took pity on him, if only to end the awkward conversation. "You want me to ask Mari for you?"

His friend sighed with relief. "Yes— I really like her. And unlike you, Super Stud, I clearly need help."

Jeff was hard-pressed to figure out why everything was going so well with Mari. They were great together. Early on, when he'd been trying to score with her, he'd been thinking only of the physical side. And he'd always known that would be fantastic. What he hadn't counted on was how good— how relaxed everything else was with her. And Hector. Being with them was . . . easy. And that made it different from anything he'd experienced before.

When they made plans, Jeff didn't panic. He didn't waste time wondering whether she would eventually try to corner him. Since meeting Mari, it hadn't crossed his mind that he might be missing something better.

Free time was spent with them. Quiet dinners. Baseball practice. Playing in the park. Every night after Hector was tucked in, he'd spent hours getting to know Marisol. Warm. Intelligent. Funny. Sometimes brutally honest with him. He never had the sense she wouldn't tell him exactly what was on her mind. When she kicked him out of her bed so Hec wouldn't discover him in the morning, Jeff regretted it. Though he respected Mari for insisting, he'd increasingly hated leaving.

She was still curiously protective of Hector— and herself. Jeff was with them all the time, yet . . . not. Though she didn't come out and say it, he sensed Mari didn't want him growing too attached. She didn't want Hec viewing him as . . . permanent. For the most part, he'd been cool with that. Chances were— he *wouldn't* become a permanent fixture. But lately, the idea that maybe she didn't see them working out— bothered him.

There'd been a time when that notion would've sent Jeff fleeing in the opposite direction. Yet with Marisol, he wanted to know more. Her moods, her interactions with Hector, her thoughts on the shelter . . . her descriptions of her family. Jeff sometimes felt as though he already knew them, though he still didn't know why her brother had been spying on her.

When he'd asked, Mari's expression had taken on the guarded quality he witnessed periodically. She'd been quiet for several moments, as though struggling with an inner turmoil that ran counter to everything he knew about her disposition— before finally confessing she wasn't ready to discuss it.

Her unwillingness to trust him roused his curiosity. And concern. He frowned over the plans he was reviewing, fully aware he wasn't seeing a damn thing. Why would her family send Manny to check up on her? Mari wasn't a teenager. She was twenty-seven. A homeowner. A mother. What were they so afraid of?

Tossing his pencil on the table, Jeff checked his watch. Since she'd been complaining about his 'disappearing act', he'd agreed to meet his mother for lunch. The memory brought a smile to his face. If Mona knew he'd blown off their standing Wednesday night dinner to spend every available minute with a female— the *same* female— one he'd pursued for a record-breaking five weeks before she'd relented . . . his mom would probably have palpitations.

On the drive to the restaurant, Jeff's thoughts drifted to his parents. Their relationship. He winced over the word. *Relationship.* If he started thinking of Mari that way, he might panic and do something stupid. Instead, they existed in an easygoing bubble— one that didn't include promises or plans beyond the next few days. No expectations. They didn't speak of the future. Even Marisol seemed more relaxed taking things a day at a time. It was the perfect non-relationship. Why that was starting to make him uneasy, he wasn't sure.

He spied his mother's Mercedes when he pulled into the lot. A few minutes later, Mona waved from a table in the corner. She stood to hug him. "Jeffie, what on earth have you been doing lately? I haven't seen you since dinner at Jake's house."

He waited until their drink orders were taken. "Now that you're seated, I'll give you the news."

His mom's eyes widened. "What news?"

"I'm seeing someone."

She raised an eyebrow. "Sweetie, how is that news?"

"The *same* someone," he emphasized. "You know— like I'm dating only one woman." He sighed over her gasp of surprise. His mother's shocked expression conveyed her thoughts of him as the millennial version of Hugh Hefner. "Aren't you overdoing it? I've dated women before-"

"Not *one* woman," she interrupted, her eyes sparkling. "Not for an extended period. Jeffie, I'm so proud of you. How long?"

He grinned, suddenly feeling as lighthearted as she appeared to be. "It took me a month to convince her to go out. Now, we've been dating a month."

She peppered him with questions throughout lunch before finally asking the most important one. "Who is she? Anyone we know?"

He sipped his iced tea. "It's Marisol Ortega— from the shelter? I think you've met her. Dad worked with her on the drawings."

His mom's eyes lit with excitement. "I can't believe it actually worked. Your father will be so pleased-"

His glass halfway to the table, Jeff froze. "What do you mean?" When she flushed guiltily, a chill swept over him. *What worked*? His mind raced over the possibilities. What the hell had Linc done?"

"He hoped working with Mari might lead somewhere. She's such a sweet, beautiful girl. Your father just loves her."

His pulse throttled back from overdrive. For a brief, terrible moment Jeff experienced a sick premonition that he'd been the butt of a joke. That Marisol had somehow been party to it— humoring his parents while having a laugh at his expense. "*That's* why Dad pulled the disappearing act? So I'd step in and handle the project?"

She nodded. "Linc felt if he stayed away long enough, you'd jump in at the shelter and see what amazing people they are."

"Well, that certainly happened." He released an unsteady breath. "So— Mari didn't know what he was up to, right?"

Relief flooded him, her expression reassuringly mortified. "Good Lord, no. I didn't know myself until a few weeks ago."

Jeff didn't want to analyze the crazy, desperate reaction he'd just experienced. When— for the briefest, painful moment he'd imagined it not being real. Picturing Marisol— only dating him because his father had meddled. Or worse— donated money. *But that hadn't happened,* his brain reminded. Their relationship was real. No one could mess it up—except him.

He forced the disturbing thought aside. It was probably time to shift their conversation to higher ground. "Jake and I noticed you seem to be spending a lot of time with Dad. What's that about?"

Suddenly very interested in her salad, his mom shifted her gaze. "We've always stayed on good terms-"

Jeff choked on his tea. " You two didn't seem all that tight during his granola chick phase. Zoe. . . Chloe . . . Moonbeam. . ."

"That's enough," she scolded. "Despite our differences. . . we've always been respectful." Her smile didn't match her eyes as she fidgeted with her fork. "A part of me will always love your dad. It's not as thought we broke up over another woman . . . or some huge character flaw."

"Why *did* you break up?" He sensed them drifting again . . . into dangerous conversational waters. Yet, Jeff realized he wanted answers— to questions he'd always been too hesitant to ask. After their divorce, he'd been too young to ask adult questions— the whys and how-did-this-happen sort of questions. Immediately, he'd needed reassurance— that his world wasn't snapping off its axis. Jake had been in college, but Jeff was still living with his parents when they'd called it quits.

"I— was lonely." She shrugged. "Over the years, your dad had become a workaholic. I waited . . . and waited. First, he said he needed to work eighty hours a week to get the business going. Bucky wasn't much help back in those days— with Sarah's drinking problem. Your father had to pick up the slack."

Her eyes looked so stricken, Jeff almost wished he could withdraw his question. "Mom— I'm sorry. I shouldn't have asked."

She offered a brave smile. "It's okay, Jeffie. Nothing new here, just a long time buried." She picked up her teaspoon, twisting the stem in suddenly restless fingers. "Anyway— that was the first fifteen years. After the business was successful . . . I assumed Linc would finally be a husband again. He'd made plenty of money. You boys and your sister were set— you know . . . college and money for your future." Her pensive sigh lanced him with guilt.

"Then Linc's excuse became one of maintaining productivity. I finally had to admit the man I married wasn't ever coming back." Her gaze drifted to the window. "Seven years into that decade, Bucky passed away. Jake and Harrison were still in college-"

The silence lengthened. "You know the rest. I'd spent nearly twenty-five years of our marriage alone."

Like a part of your life that had always been there— like a painting on the wall you stopped noticing long ago, Jeff had stopped noticing how alone his mother was. How alone *they* were. As a teen, his dad had never been around.

"I thought every dad was like that— you know? Working fourteen hour days?" Like a visiting phantom, he saw Linc only occasionally. Most nights Jeff never caught a glimpse. Two strangers sharing the same space, breathing the same air, yet never seeming to occupy it at the same time. He tried to imagine being married to someone like that. How lonely his mother must have been.

"You know he did it for you— for us." Mona's defense of him was automatic, despite the fact that she'd lost him to Specialty.

"I'm not criticizing, Mom. When you're a kid, you don't really understand what's happening. You pick up on the vibes and you wonder what's happening . . . and how it'll affect *you*." He shrugged. "Sounds pretty selfish, right?"

Her hand found his across the table. "No, Jeffie. It sounds exactly like what a kid would think. Surprisingly, you seemed to absorb it better than your brother."

"Not really." Jeff hesitated, not wanting to hurt her feelings after all this time. "I think I just *hid* it better than Jake."

"What do you mean?"

God— did he really want to go there? "I was scared. It knocked me on my ass. The whole thing just seemed to come out of nowhere."

She turned, but not before he saw the flash of pain in her eyes. The one solid, sure thing Jeff had always known was that his mother would never have inflicted harm to her kids, intentional or otherwise. "I . . . I'm sorry, Jeff— I guess I always wondered . . . how you'd handled it so well."

What choice had there been? To a seventeen year old, an absentee father was still better than *no* father. But Jeff had never voiced his opinion. He couldn't be the one who made things worse for his mother. He'd had to be cheerful— or at least not make her cry. He'd done the same for his dad. Not making waves. Keeping their conversations light— the rare times he saw him. Burying his own anxiety about the breakup. Along with the guilt and relief he'd experienced the following year when he escaped— leaving for college. Running from the quiet, empty house that no longer felt like home.

"It was a long time ago, Mom. I'm fine."

Her expression thoughtful, she stared at him for several moments. "I never wanted to blame your father. He's a *good* man. I never wanted our breakup to be about choosing sides— although that's what it became for your brother."

At least Jake had been able to get angry— cruelly so, perhaps, because he'd blamed their mother over the divorce, instead of Linc's work. But at least Jake had burned it out of his system. Even though their dad had been AWOL for most of their childhood,

Mona had been the family rock. Always there. In the morning before school and waiting every night. Dinner warming in the oven . . . sometimes for hours depending on which sport season they were in. The table usually set for just the two of them. Their father forever working while she'd attended his soccer games in the fall, basketball in the winter and they'd road-tripped to Jake's college games in between.

At least, that's how it had been *before* she'd announced the divorce. After that, Jake hadn't wanted to see her. Hadn't wanted to see *anyone*. He'd even turned his anger on *him* when Jeff refused to take sides. The months of isolation when Jake cut him off had left him feeling anchorless.

Thankfully, the snub had only lasted a few months. To his gut-shredding relief, once Jake worked through his anger, he'd reconnected. Jeff finally regained his brother. But that period of his life had been a nightmare— a reversal of everything he'd believed to be firmly planted . . . to be solid and true. Instead, he'd been completely uprooted. As though a tornado had touched down in his life and he'd been the only person left standing. He'd walked out of the wreckage, seemingly unscathed, with everyone shaking their heads over the miracle. When all the while, on the inside— he'd been absolutely flattened.

Ultimately, his parents' divorce had taught him valuable lessons. The first was that nothing lasted— even those things you wanted more than anything. The second was no matter how he really felt, it was always safer to maintain a good front. That way, no one got hurt.

CHAPTER 8

"Mari, what's wrong?"

Sharon's voice filtered through the clamor in her head. Too shaken to speak the terrifying words tangled in her throat, Marisol handed her the note she clutched.

The older woman's forehead creased with concern as she scanned the telephone message. "Damn that woman. When is she going to leave him alone?"

Her heart pounding, Marisol stared at her friend, desperate not to cry. She should be furious— with the woman who used her son as a bargaining chip. Instead, her heart drilled with fear. "D-did you see? It says 'several calls'. Apparently she's been calling for two weeks."

A shudder tore through her. *Two weeks.* Wasted. Two weeks she could've been strategizing . . . contacting social services . . . maybe hiring a lawyer to see if she could petition to move up the custody hearing.

"Sugar— *how* could we not know? She has to be lying. There's no way we've been getting calls for two weeks and not hearin' about it. Everyone knows to be on the lookout for any contact from Luz. Someone would've told you."

She'd thought that too. But now, Mari wasn't so sure. "Look at this place, Sharon. It's crazy loud . . . there are people everywhere. We have new interns. I know we haven't mentioned Hector's circumstances at the last four staff meetings." Or was it five? Or six?

Construction of the new wing had taken precedent over everything else. There were constantly decisions to make and they were always urgent. For two months, the less pressing agenda items had slid to the back burner. They'd been operating in a vacuum ever since. Noise. Confusion. Dust. Strangers everywhere. Keeping the feeding areas clean had become a top priority. And security.

After another threat from a drunken Phil, they'd taken as much precaution as possible. But even that effort was cobbled together based on the construction schedule. One day they were a stronghold. A fortress. The next day— another wall would come down, a new footprint through the building would be required and a new set of faces would arrive. And their security would slip again.

"We need to get a better handle on the stuff we've let slip," Sharon agreed. "I had no idea the construction process would occupy so much of our time. It's like there's always something that has to be relocated or cleaned and put back together."

"The phone system was out for three days last week," she reminded. One of the subcontractors had sliced wires that, according to the blueprints shouldn't have been there. The receptionist had been relocated twice in the past month so construction could take place around her. Next week she would move back to her original location.

Sharon released a gusty sigh. "It's worse because we didn't want to close while the wing got built. Linc recommended we shut down operations for several weeks . . . but where the hell do all the hungry people go?"

Mari wanted to commiserate but couldn't seem to focus on anything beyond the immediate, terrifying problem of Hector's mother, Luz Covas. The drug addict who was now demanding visitation— when she hadn't bothered to contact her son in nearly a year.

"She probably *has* been calling to see him." Mari hadn't been as vigilant as usual. With Jeff in their lives, she'd allowed her fears to subside. Guilt swamping her, she admitted she'd relaxed her guard. *Too busy being happy.* She hadn't wanted any ugliness to intrude. Eager to shelve her worries and watch time elapse until the custody hearing in September.

Now, she faced the possibility she could be forced to allow Luz access to Hector again. And who would protect him this time? Luz held the power to damage him. Her visits were sporadic and selfish. Weepy and demanding— she wanted from Hector things he was far too young to give her. Then— thankfully, she would disappear again. But in her wake she would leave a shadow of sadness and misery that affected Hector for weeks. Now that he was older, he remembered more. Weeks after a visit, when Mari would be certain he was finally back to his normal, cheerful self, Hector would repeat something Luz said, her cruel, manipulative words meant to chip away at his happiness. And it worked.

There was also the fear Luz would try to kidnap him again. He'd been only two the last time she'd slipped him out of the shelter. A tremor of foreboding slid down her spine. Thankfully, the police had found him before. . .

Shaking off her terror, she released a cleansing breath. If she kept thinking *that* way, she would lose it.

"Just because she *claims* to want to see Hector doesn't mean she gets her way." Sharon gave her hand a reassuring squeeze. "I'll get DSS on the phone to see what our options are this time."

Drumming nervous fingers on the desk, Mari nodded. "You're right." She knew the rules. She knew the system. Luz couldn't possibly win, but she could keep showing up just often enough to delay her own chances to finally gain full custody. She wanted Hector free and clear. She wanted to *never* see Luz again. Logically, she knew Luz couldn't win. But it was impossible to think rationally when it impacted her son.

Once Sharon left her office, Marisol stole a few minutes to calm herself. She'd learned the deep breathing exercises during her counseling sessions after Nick. They offered a method of coping with feelings that were too big. Fear. Anxiety. In a way, the situation she faced now was similar to the anger and guilt she'd experienced after Nick. Weighed down by feelings of betrayal and shame— mostly at herself for allowing it to happen. A few minutes earlier she'd been overwhelmed by fear of a person who shouldn't have the power to hurt her. Luz would not win. The stakes were too high. No matter the cost, she would protect Hector.

When a hand grazed her shoulder, Mari flinched, instinct rocketing her away from the source. *Out of reach of his fists.* Her chair careened back, thudding against the wall before she recognized it was Jeff.

"Easy, hon. I didn't mean to scare you."

Hand at her throat, Marisol forced an uneven laugh, heart pounding violently. "S-sorry. I didn't hear you coming."

One look at her face and Jeff's eyes flared with concern. "What's wrong?"

Releasing a shaky breath, she schooled her features, struggling to regain control. *Snap out of it.* She hadn't experienced a flashback in nearly a year. "Nothing— H-how can you tell?"

He helped to right her chair before tugging her against him. "Well, for one thing you nearly launched yourself through the wall into Katie's office." He nuzzled her throat, pressing his lips to her erratic pulse. "I'm happy to fix the drywall. But-" His mouth drifted higher, making her shudder. "I'd have to charge you for a change order."

"Perhaps we could arrange . . . a barter." Mustering a lighthearted tone her body didn't yet feel, Marisol prayed he wouldn't notice.

"With you, that can *always* be arranged. Are you cold?" Large, warm hands stroked the goosebumps on her arms. "Do I look *that* bad?" She felt his grin against her cheek. "I forgot to shave this morning, but I didn't think it would actually scare you."

Warmth seeping into her where his body touched hers, her smile was half-hearted. "Y-you caught me off guard."

When his scrutiny began to feel as though she were being examined under a microscope, she dropped her gaze. What was wrong with her? For a terrifying second, she'd imagined Nick had returned. Worse than the flashback was the helpless anger it churned up— an angry, frothing wake she'd believed had been set adrift. How could a man she hadn't seen in *two years* . . . still hold the power to frighten her? To make her question herself. Cause her to distrust *every* other man— including Jeff.

"I'm fine." As Jeff held her, too many questions in his eyes, Mari forced a levity she didn't feel. "It's nothing."

"Babe, it's not nothing."

He still didn't know. About Nick. He didn't know anything of that terrible time . . . her history . . . her issues. He knew *nothing* about her. Nothing that actually mattered. Because somewhere along the way, they'd decided it was easier not to learn about each other. More fun not to delve into each other's problems. Or hopes. Or dreams. They didn't confide in one another. Because nothing between them was permanent. She'd known instinctively it was how Jeff would prefer their relationship. But she was equally to blame. Because . . . keeping it light . . . having fun— *was* easier. And in the long run— keeping Jefferson at a distance was less risky to her heart. "Your eyes are red." Jeff stroked a finger down her nose. "And you're too pale." Leaning against her desk blotter, he tugged her between his legs. "Come on. What gives?" His hold on her suddenly tightened. "Is it Phil again?"

Raising her gaze, his expression had turned grim. "It's not Phil. But if it was . . . we would handle-"

"Marisol— this isn't up for debate." Exasperated, he cut her off. "He will *not* get anywhere near you again. Is that clear? I won't allow it."

"Won't *allow*?" Irritation flared in her chest. Despite Mari's worry over the more immediate issue with Hector's mother, Jeff's ultimatum set her off. She opened her mouth to remind him exactly who was in charge at the shelter. But before she could find the right words, Jeff raised his fingers, pressing them gently against her lips.

"I know you're upset . . . but I don't think it's with me." His voice gentled to a husky whisper. "At least not this time," he amended. "But if you'd feel better yelling at me— then go ahead." He paused a beat. "Or you could tell me what's wrong so maybe I can help."

His dead-on assessment left her deflated, yet her anger dissolved in a heartbeat. With his fingers massaging the tension from her shoulders, Marisol realized she would love nothing more than to confide in Jeff. She wanted desperately to lean on him . . . to dump her problems on the table and allow him to help her sort through them. Because he would fix everything. It's what Jeff did. He solved problems. He kept his clients happy.

And since he was sleeping with her, Jefferson was apparently willing to bend his rules and become involved. At least for now. Before he grew bored with her, she should probably take advantage of his offer. "I just found out Hector's mom is back," she confessed. "Apparently . . . she's been calling. She wants . . . to see him."

Worry flared in his eyes. "But— she abandoned him." His grip tightened on her shoulders. "She can't take him, right?"

She released a shuddering sigh in an increasingly futile attempt to calm herself. "No— but if she k-keeps showing up, she could delay my adoption."

"How can that happen? Damn it, Mari— Hector needs you."

Appreciating the hot anger behind Jeff's words, she still felt dangerously vulnerable to the possibility that Luz could cause trouble— and probably planned to do just that. "She has to be declared unfit— which happened once a few years ago."

"Then why-"

"No one was interested in adopting Hector back then." Her voice quavering, she continued. "When it happened the first time, I hadn't started fostering yet because I wasn't old enough." And she'd been busy falling in love with Nick. Even without the distraction of her demanding boyfriend, Marisol wouldn't have been mature enough to handle the commitment. "You have to be twenty-five. That's when I started fostering Hector."

"So— after two years of loving him . . . taking care of him. . . of being the only *real* mother he's ever known— she can *still* show up and wreak havoc in his life?" Jeff's eyes burned vividly green with his fury.

"Luz-" She glanced up. "Hector's mother— spent a few months in jail the first time-"

"Jail-" His expression was completely dumbfounded. "What the hell?"

Gulping in a breath, she acknowledged that while Jeff's anger wasn't changing the situation, it was certainly making her feel less alone. "Luz is a drug addict. When she visited . . . s-she kidnapped Hector-" Swallowing around the lump in her throat, she swiped the tears gathering in her eyes. "We found her— them . . . at a crack house-"

His fingers tightened reflexively. "Why was Hector at a crack house?"

"She was . . . attempting to sell him for-"

"Sell him?" Jeff staggered back a step. "Sell him!"

"Luz was going to trade him . . . for drugs."

"Hector was at a crack house." His voice hoarse, Jeff released her, only to pace the tiny footprint of her office. When he reached the doorway, he spun around. "How do you— how do you not lose it, Mari?" His expression was agonized when he met her gaze. "I want-" He jammed a hand through his hair. "I want to hurt her, Marisol."

"I have to work *within* the system," she whispered. "If I become paralyzed with anger. . . I stop being effective. If I give in to my desire to h-hurt her . . . she could win."

"This is wrong on so many levels." His hands clenched, he lowered them as though unsure what he was supposed to do with them. "H-how did you find him?"

"We lucked out. There was a note in her social services file . . . referencing a location commonly frequented by addicts. Luz had been picked up there several times." For her reckless behavior, she'd spent only months behind bars . . . before she'd been released due to overcrowding. Worse for Marisol was the judge's ruling that Luz's problems be deemed mental health related. Instead of child abuse or abandonment. Or the criminal sale of a precious baby boy for drugs. That meant Luz hadn't lost her parental rights. She'd merely lost custody.

"So— it was a miracle." Jeff's eyes had grown bleak. She recognized he held on to his temper by a thread.

Released from jail, Luz had disappeared. Which had thrown a wrench into Marisol's desire to adopt him. The courts didn't seem to know how to react when the mother flitted in and out of her child's life. Each time she resurfaced, Luz reset the clock. Hector's future was perpetually in limbo. Since then, her visits had been sporadic and always supervised. But Mari had never made the mistake of thinking Luz wasn't dangerous. Over the past eighteen months, she'd prepared. After registering with DSS, she'd completed her home study with the social worker assigned to Hector and she'd petitioned the court for permanency. She'd waited. And prayed.

"What has to happen before Hector never has to see her again?" Jeff's eyes sparked with determination.

"One of two things. Either DSS finally terminates her parental rights . . . which should have happened when Luz tried to sell Hector-"

Wincing, Jeff cursed under his breath, making her smile, despite her simmering frustration. "That's what my court date in September is about. The court finally heard DSS' petition a few months back. That's when they gave it six more months."

"What's taking so long?"

She shrugged, helpless. "Backlog. Juvenile court typically runs six months behind."

"Damn it— what's the other way?"

"Luz has to voluntarily release Hector for adoption. It's called a Release and Entrustment Consent."

"What sort of hell do we live in that she gets a choice?"

"The law says-"

"The law sucks, Mari."

As sick as she felt over the situation, Jeff's words eased the ache in her heart. Marisol almost felt like smiling. She loved how Jeff loved Hector— how he protected him. She loved how he was so not afraid to show it. He'd embraced her son, taken him into his world without hesitation. She thought of all the hours he'd spent with him . . . coaching him about baseball . . . teaching him about construction. Showing Hector how to be a man— a kind, considerate, thoughtful man. All the hours they'd spent together— as a family. Laughing and talking about everything . . . and nothing.

She loved him. She loved Jeff.

Unaware of her epiphany, Jeff's eyes burned with frustration. "There has to be a way to end this."

"Eventually, when enough time elapses with no word from the mother, the court makes a decision." Clearly, there were still flaws. While deciding for the parent had positive attributes, the reality was it often left defenseless children in dangerous situations. "I believe in second chances . . ." She hesitated. "But those chances should involve rules and training and supervision."

"No shit."

His disgruntled comment made her lips twitch. How could he make her smile when everything was falling apart? The system *could* work, but when the law was decimated by budget cuts and understaffing— it left gaping cracks that exposed children to abuse from parents who had already proven themselves seriously lacking in judgment.

"We've filed the papers, but if she sporadically shows up. . ." She sniffed in an effort to force back an onslaught of tears. "The adoption could be delayed."

"Let me guess— she doesn't want him . . . but she doesn't want you to have him either."

Suddenly, it was all too much. The uncertainty over Hector. The fear that Luz could find a loophole. The uncomfortable discovery that she was seriously, hopelessly in love with the man standing before her. Tears spilling down her cheeks, she nodded.

Jeff gathered her in his arms. As Marisol wept against his shoulder, he tried to sort his jumbled thoughts. For about five minutes, everything in his life had started making sense. After lunch with his mother, he'd experienced a new sense of clarity. With a fresh understanding of his parents' marriage— he'd begun examining it through the adult eyes. And the view through twenty-nine year old eyes was suddenly far different from the view he'd had at seventeen. He'd just never allowed himself to think about it.

He'd been uncomfortably aware that his actions— some of them, anyway— may have been colored by a perspective that was no longer accurate. While part of him loved being able to do any damn thing he wanted, whenever he wanted— there was another part he'd only recently become attuned to. A part of him that maybe . . . wanted something more. Something substantial. *Someone* who mattered.

As far as freedom went, he'd never been completely free in the truest sense. In the get-on-his-Harley-and-ride-off-into-the-sunset way. He had obligations. Tons of them. He had a large family he loved. He shared ownership of Specialty. He had friends. A job that rarely allowed him the freedom he'd experienced after college. And Jeff wouldn't change *any* of it.

So, the question now was why. With all the important commitments in his life— why couldn't he also have *someone* who mattered?

His parents' marriage had ended after years of inattention from his father. His seventeen year old self hadn't recognized that. He'd been too self-absorbed and far too immature to read the subtle vibes of a marriage slowly dying from neglect. Jeff's takeaway from the divorce had been simply that marriages failed. Randomly. That loving someone was dangerous— and could only end in disaster. Pain. Agony.

After talking with his mother, Jeff left the lunch date with a new awareness. A *hyper* awareness. That he wasn't bound by limitations, even those he'd self-imposed. Maybe— he would discover he wasn't cut out for a relationship with anyone. It was entirely possible he didn't have what it took. It didn't take a rocket scientist to see he liked doing things his way. But— what the hell? Everyone was like that. It didn't mean he wasn't *capable* of sharing his life with someone. Since he'd never allowed himself to think that way— how could he know for sure?

He'd driven back to the shelter with something he could only define as impatience. To see Marisol. For the first time, Jeff embraced the eagerness without questioning the hell out of it. Without wondering if they'd still be together a month from now. He wanted to see her— with fresh eyes.

Instead, he'd found her— pale and terrified. And all his hypothetical what-ifs had flown out the window. In that moment, all Jeff wanted was to make it better. No matter what problem she faced. Imagining Hector losing Mari made his chest hurt. Seeing her break down offered another gut punch of powerlessness when he would have given anything to be able to fix it.

But witnessing fear in Mari's eyes . . . and being unable to shield her— made him feel violent. His need to protect her— to protect Hector— was stronger than any emotion Jeff had ever experienced. Tightening his hold on the beautiful, strong, fragile woman in his arms, he acknowledged he would do anything to help her— to keep her safe. And for the first time . . . maybe ever— that awareness didn't terrify him.

Perhaps he was capable of change after all.

"She's really thin."

Sharon frowned at the television screen. "And jittery. I'd say it's been three days. Maybe four. She's probably hurtin' for a fix."

"Why does she keep showing up?" Marisol sighed, her gaze never leaving the screen. "We need to double down on security. Has DSS authorized a visit? I don't want her slipping out of here with him."

"Supervised visit. Probably sometime this week." Sharon nodded to the screen. "But I don't think she can last that long without makin' a score. If we're lucky, she'll show up high and we can deny the visit."

"What can we do about security?" Trying to control her worry, she sought Sharon's reassuring eyes.

"Already takin' care of it, Sugar. I met with Hank this morning."

Sharon's bracelets jangled against her arm, the familiar sound comforting. Mari wanted everything to be normal. She wanted certainty— that Hector was safe . . . that the adoption she'd planned for the past year would finally happen. She wanted to relax and enjoy him without the fear he could be taken away.

In spite of her worries, she wanted to explore her relationship with Jefferson— see where it would lead. She'd grown tired of questioning herself— of comparing him to Nick. She'd kept Jeff at arm's length lately— sending mixed signals she knew were confusing. If she could sort out her fears— she might be able to resolve them. There was guilt— that she hadn't actually told him about her past. The more time passed, the more awkward that conversation would become.

What was she afraid of? Perhaps loving him was making her skittish. Because now wasn't a great time to appear vulnerable. Yet, she knew Jeff cared about her. In a dozen little ways, he'd shown he was as capable of change as anyone.

Remembering the flowers sitting on her desk, she smiled. And the perfect, summer peach he'd delivered the day before. Jeff presented his gifts shyly— almost as though he'd surprised himself. Definitely unlike his usual, charming self. Mari could tell he wasn't accustomed to offering thoughtful gestures, yet he was so very good at them.

Jeff was thoughtful. And kind. And so damn good with Hector it made her ache watching them together. Whatever was meant to happen between them would finish playing out. Ultimately, that meant her heart might end up broken. But before that happened, it might just be incredible. Because everything with Jeff felt good. Natural.

"How are the flashbacks, Mari? You need to talk with someone?" Sharon's gaze was laser sharp.

Why had she mentioned it? When she *knew* it was stress. Until the shaky, scrawny, disturbed drug addict in the DSS video decided to move on, Marisol's existence had become a nerve-wracking, sleepless, fearful holding pattern.

Still concentrating on Luz— the taped interview she'd had only days earlier with social services, Marisol shook her head. "Getting better. With Luz showing up, I was caught off guard. It's only been a few times . . . Jeff— when he surprised me."

"Does he know?" Sharon's kind eyes expressed concern. "About Luz? Did you ever explain about Nick?'

Ignoring the guilt sliding through her, Mari nodded. "Yes to Luz; no to Nick."

"Marisol-"

Reluctantly, her gaze shifted to her friend. "It's never seemed the right time. First— it was too new. I didn't think Jeff would be sticking around, so I didn't discuss it with him. It's too personal to just dump on every man I meet."

"And now? Jeff isn't 'every' man, right? Stud Muffin's got stayin' power. If you can't see that, Sugar— you're blind."

"Now— it's hard to bring up. I still don't know where we're going, Sharon." Chewing her lip, Mari's gaze drifted back to the screen. "It's not wrong to keep something so . . . personal to myself when Jeff could leave as soon as the new wing is done."

Sharon chuckled. "Now you're a fortune-teller? You're painting yourself into a corner, Mari. He could walk outta here tomorrow or you could still be with him twenty years from now."

She found a smile. "Sometime between now and then . . . I promise I'll tell him."

"There's way too much drama in here today. I can't get anything done." Disgusted, Hank hung up the phone, throwing his pencil on the new set of changes they reviewed. "Everyone is runnin' around like crazy. I can't get answers to simple questions. What the hell will it take to get a little production around here?"

Jeff eyed him curiously. Distracted by the seemingly insurmountable problems facing Mari and Hector, he wondered what he'd missed. Production was going fine. The concrete was poured; the building shell was taking shape. With Linc finally back in the picture, he'd finessed the last of the color decisions out of the women so Jeff could place orders for all the finishes. The building was about the *only* thing in his life that was going smoothly.

"What's the problem?" Relieved to shelve his own worries, if only temporarily, Jeff was eager to latch onto a construction problem— any problem he could actually fix. "Is it Big Pete again? Has he ticked off the concrete guys, too? I know he's eccentric but-"

"Quit your babbling. I ain't talking about Pete." Hank scowled in his general direction. "I'm worried about Annie and her boys."

Understanding dawned. Evidently, Hank had made progress. "So, you've finally progressed to actual dates with her? And what'd it take you? Nine . . . ten weeks?" He lifted his hand in support. "High five."

Raising his gaze to the ceiling, Hank snorted. "You are the most unobservant person on the planet."

"What'd I miss this time?" Jeff would be the first to admit the last several days had been crazy. First— his epiphany about his parents— and how, over the last decade, he'd been conducting his life under basically false assumptions. Then the scare with Hector's mother— who thus far, hadn't materialized. And now there was Marisol— acting nervous and distracted and definitely not herself. She'd become skittish around him. And that probably bothered him most of all.

"Annie finally told me last night— *she's* the one Phil is after. She and her boys-" Hank hesitated, his face flushed with anger. "Damn it, Jeff— they *live* here. Annie volunteers because she's a *client* at New Beginnings."

Shock jolted through him as he remembered Hector's words. Two friends . . . and their dad who hit them. In no way had he ever suspected it could be Annie. Sure, he'd wondered why she was always there— seeming to volunteer twelve hours a day. Yet, it absolutely made sense. Her troubled demeanor, her suspicion of him at the beginning.

But— she hadn't looked like a victim. The arrogance of his thoughts slapped him upside the head. *What does a victim look like, Jeff?* He didn't know jack about abused women. And thinking about it now made him uncomfortable. All this time, they could have been helping her— helping the staff protect her.

"Mari never said anything."

Hank's eyes were troubled. "That's why I have such a hard time gettin' her to leave. She's afraid he'll grab the kids. He's threatened to grab her— and force her to go back to him."

"But they're divorced, right?"

"Yeah— but he's one of those control freaks-" He ran a large hand over his military crewcut. "Claims she's his property and he'll never let go. The poor girl spends her time runnin' from one shelter to the next— never able to live a normal life. Tommy and Jason— they keep changing schools . . . changing friends. It's not right." His sigh was one of frustration. "Did ya know she's a nurse?"

"No kidding? So— he even prevents her from earning a living?" Anger smoldered through him. Between Hector's mother and the news about Annie— it was all getting to be too much. The unfairness of it all. And the tangled mess of a legal system that was overloaded and ineffective. Annie could have a life— a good life. Her kids could be enrolled in a permanent school— living in a real home. Playing baseball and making friends. If that bastard would just leave them alone.

Hank stared at him for several seconds, his eyes speaking volumes. Jeff waited him out— knowing when he finally spoke, it would be something important. "I'm thinkin' I might do something about it."

Jeff stilled. He'd been thinking along the same lines— about cutting through the red tape strangling Hector. He'd contacted Specialty's attorneys to see what Mari's options were, but had learned the process was slow. It was so damned frustrating. And it was destroying Marisol. She was edgy and tense. She jumped when he entered the room— almost fearful of him. He hated seeing her so defenseless. "What do you have in mind?"

Hank's gaze was somber. "I'm thinkin' of tracking him down. Should be a piece 'a cake. Tail him a day or two— get a bead on his routine."

Jeff's pulse ticked up. "Hank— you can't kill him."

His expression hardened. "I won't need to kill him. Just scare the bejeezus out of him— like he's doin' to her." Hank settled into his chair, warming to the subject. "Big man— beatin' up on a woman. He's hit the boys too— when they tried to protect her." His face flushed with anger. "Frankly— I think I'd enjoy scarin' the shit out of him."

Hesitating only a moment, Jeff's sense of control slowly shifted back into place— for the first time in days. "Why don't I give Charlie a call? He could probably give us a few off-the-record pointers. You know . . . so you don't do anything that gets you arrested."

"If it gets Phil out of her life, I don't much give a damn." Hank stroked the salt and pepper whiskers on his chin. "The way I figure— Annie won't relax until he's out of the picture. I don't like seeing her scared all the time. And I really like her, Jeff. I like her boys. And they like me."

Jeff smiled. "I'm really happy for you."

"Every time we're together— those boys just drink it up. They want to live at the farm. Hell— they wanna go to school in one place for a whole year." Retrieving his pencil, Hank drummed it on the table. "They want me to marry their mom. And I'm thinkin' I do, too."

"Whoa— Freeman . . . slow down. You've been seeing her for what? Eight weeks?" Jeff didn't know whether he should be happy for his friend or perform an intervention on him.

"You're a whole lot younger than me, Jeffie. Me and Annie are in a different place. I've been alone a long time— too long. And Annie hasn't had much of a life these past few years. First an abusive husband— then being on the run. She has kids to raise. And I can help raise them. I want to help," he emphasized. He paused. "You've never been in it for the long haul with anyone— but I have. And it's a great feeling. I never thought I'd find it again after Gayle passed. But I really miss it. And I finally want it back."

His friend's truthful comment found its mark. But the twinge of jealousy he experienced left him baffled. At least Hank knew what he wanted. Jeff had never had *anyone* in his life he'd wanted around permanently. Anyone he could envision being around a few *months*— never mind a lifetime.

Mari was the first woman he'd ever actually chased. And once he'd caught her— Jeff had surprised himself. By continuing to pursue her. Hell— he'd been as surprised as everyone else. Yet, he'd stayed in the game. Even when Marisol would have ended it— he'd pushed back. He'd actually fought to stay in. The old Jeff would have turned and run.

All the stuff he'd viewed as strings tying him down didn't feel like it anymore— at least not with Marisol. For the first time, his instinct had been to jump in. To take on more. To become . . . necessary to her. Like she and Hector were becoming necessary to him?

His brain had skirted the issue for days. Because thinking about her made him nervous. And Jeff wasn't sure why. Could he commit to one woman? Could he be a good father to Hector? Was he even ready? How the hell did anyone ever know for sure?

What made him more uptight— what made his stomach four-chili-dog queasy was imagining them with someone else. If he messed up with Mari— she'd dump him and move on. She was beautiful. Giving. An open heart. She was open to a relationship. To . . . marriage. The thought constricted his chest. Because she had Hector to look out for. And she wanted a family. Marisol would give all that love to someone . . . who wasn't him.

What sent panic crashing through him was the sneaking realization that he might finally have someone in his life he couldn't bear to lose.

"Okay, gentlemen . . . just so we're *all* clear." Sharon paused, waiting for the conversations to stop. Jeff poked Big Pete to get his attention. "What we're doing here is slightly unorthodox. We do *not* make a habit of deputizing outsiders into service."

"We're happy to help," Hank interrupted.

Sharon eyed him with humor. "I know, honey. But you boys have to understand we're deviating from protocol here. So, let's make sure we're all on the same page."

"We understand you're in an awkward position. We won't do anything that could get New Beginnings in trouble." Jeff was relieved Sharon was willing to cooperate. How much help could the construction crew be when they didn't know who to look for? "Pete's the only one who's seen Phil. And none of us know what Luz Covas looks like."

Understanding dawned in her eyes. "Let's just make sure Miss Sharon doesn't lose her job in the process." Herding them into her office, she checked the hallway and shut the door before snapping on the television. "This first one is an interview with Luz Covas. It was taken late last week by DSS. You don't need to hear what she's saying—just see what she looks like."

She waited while the men focused on the set, memorizing her features. "Okay— this next one is taken from our security cameras the last time Phil was here trying to reach our client."

Jeff sensed Hank stiffen next to him. Tension crackled in the room as he stared at the set with the intensity of a welding torch.

Pete took a step closer, muttering as he stared at the screen. "That's funny."

Sharon paused the footage. "What?"

"That's when he entered through the side door." Pete pointed to the screen, placing Phil in the shot. "I was right there. And Miss Marisol . . . she was over here."

"That's how I remember it too," Sharon agreed. "This is right before you cut him off."

"I can't believe I missed it." Big Pete's expression changed from the ever present scowl to one of agitation. That alone was enough to send warning jags down Jeff's spine. But seeing Mari and Hector enter the frame . . . before Mari pushed Hector away had blood pounding in his ears. Terrifying was probably a better word for that.

"What is it, big guy?"

"I shoulda been flash-blasted for that." Pete took another step closer to the screen, his scowl fierce. "Look at his hand. When I blocked Miss Ortega— I was lookin' at his face."

All eyes swiveled to Phil's hand . . . to the knife he clutched, before slipping it into his trench coat as Pete's hulking frame stepped in front of the camera.

"Babe— what's going on?" Jeff hoped he sounded neutral, though he sure as hell wasn't feeling that way.

"What do you mean?"

"You jump every time I walk in the room." After seeing that knife in Phil's hand, he wasn't sure he could ever feel neutral again when it came to Mari's safety.

She'd done it again— jerking back from him as though he were a stranger. And it stung. Sure— he'd surprised her, but Mari reacted as though he might hurt her. And Jeff didn't like it. He fucking hated it.

"I— you just startled me . . . that's all." Distracted, she focused on the document in her hands.

"Are you sure that's all it is?"

"Jeff— I'm preoccupied. I'm worried about Luz. I have donors who are late." Her eyes flashed with something close to guilt— which sent unease tracing through him. Was there something she wasn't telling him?

"The construction is making *everyone* crazy with the noise and dust," he reassured. Three days into his new perspective on life, Jeff had reached the conclusion that the whole becoming-self-aware-thing was exhausting. Before Marisol, he'd never paid much attention to what a woman wanted. Because— selfishly, he now admitted, he was pretty much going to do whatever the hell he felt like doing. And women accepted it— or they were out of the picture.

But now, Jeff couldn't imagine acting that way. It embarrassed him to remember the way he'd treated some women— perfectly nice women who'd deserved more consideration than he'd given. Not that he'd ever meant to hurt any of them . . . he just hadn't cared enough to try.

Closing the distance, Jeff pulled her against him, relieved when she promptly wrapped her arms around his neck. *This* was the Marisol he knew. Her kiss heated and at the same time, soothed. Everything about her felt so right— so worth any effort. His fleeting stab of insecurity was laid to rest when she clung to him.

"Why didn't you tell me Annie lives here?"

Marisol pulled back to frown at him and he loosened his clasp on her waist. "We keep that information classified. To protect our clients. How did you find out?"

"She told Hank." Unable to resist her scent, he nuzzled her hair, dropping a kiss near her ear. Again, he experienced relief when her breath hitched in her throat. Whatever else was going on, Marisol was still attracted to him. And while it annoyed him to admit it, Jeff wasn't above using their explosive chemistry to remind her.

Her eyes registered surprise. "Wow— she must really like Hank to confide in him. That's a huge step for her." She smiled. "It's nice Annie trusts him so much."

Did Marisol trust *him* like that? Jeff frowned. Were there things she wanted to tell him . . . but kept to herself? The problem with all this new self-awareness was that it made him— aware. And doubtful. Of things he'd never doubted.

"Mari— our crew could protect Annie if we knew she was the one Phil was after."

Unaware of his gloomy thoughts, she squeezed his hand. "You aren't here to protect the clients. You're here to build them a wonderful new facility."

"You know what I mean." Frustration flared. "If that bastard shows up while I'm here, I'll take a two by four to his face."

She raised a brow. "*That's* why we keep our clients confidential. By the time women arrive here— they've lost everything. Their homes. Jobs. Even clothing. They have nothing left. Here— they keep their dignity. They volunteer to feel better about themselves and to learn skills they can possibly use in the job market. These women are *guests* . . . not people to be viewed as victims."

"While I get all that . . . you need to understand how we feel-"

Marisol frowned. "We?"

"Hank," he hastily substituted. Damn it— him, too, if he ever decided to man up and be honest with her. Jeff wanted the Hector issue settled. He wanted Mari back. He wanted-

"That's what I thought."

Disappointment slid through him when she confirmed his suspicion. Did she still view them as temporary? "Hank thinks he's in love with Annie. If something happens that he could have prevented-"

"Jefferson-" She took his hands in hers. "We have to operate within the law. I *must* deal with Luz in a legal manner. I protect Hector from her— within the DSS guidelines this shelter operates under." She hesitated. "It doesn't mean I agree with it. I'd love to smuggle him away." She tightened her grip. "I'd *love* to hire a lawyer who could keep slamming Luz with orders she doesn't have the money to respond to."

Her eyes tearing, she regained control, reminding him again how incredibly strong she was. "But that would be selfish. I'm here to help mothers reunite with their children— *if* it's in the child's best interest. In Luz' case, she's dangerous and unstable. But there are mothers out there who are just too young— or too poor. Or who just don't know any better. But they love their kids."

"And you think this system works for them?" Jeff was humbled by her. By her ethics— that she would work through a fractured and broken system because it was all that was available. No matter that she risked losing the little boy she loved more than life. Marisol saw the big picture— what helped the most people.

She nodded. "I have to believe that . . . or I couldn't do this."

"Mari, love— you're the most amazing person I know."

"I don't feel amazing," she admitted. "I'm terrified of losing Hector. I take him h-home every night . . . and we— we have a life. It's a small, wonderful life. I don't want to lose it. But there's always the possibility. . . I could."

There was nothing small about her wonderful life. And Jeff was never more grateful to be part of it. "Babe . . . while you may not have the money to make Luz respond to legal demand letters— you realize I do, right?"

"Jeff— you can't-"

"How can you stop me, Mariboo?" He smiled when she stiffened against him.

"I usually punch Manny when he uses that name."

"Duly noted." Relieved to see a spark of the old Marisol, he smiled. Skimming his hands down her arms, he loved the softness of her skin.

"I was only polite that day because you were meeting my brother for the first time."

Her grumpy admission widened his grin. "*That* was polite?" A telling blush heated her cheeks. "You looked pretty comfortable with that bat in your hand," he admitted. "For a minute . . . I thought you were gonna use it on him."

"On his truck, actually."

Jeff cracked up. "Remind me never to piss you off."

"I was worried you'd think I was strange for having an overprotective brother stalking us."

"You still haven't explained what that was about," he reminded. "I'm dying to know why Manny was cruising our jobsite for two days— and sitting outside your place overnight. That's some serious family closeness."

"There is— something I need to tell you-" Mari hesitated. "It's not important now."

"Whenever you want." He stroked the sudden tension from her back. This was right. Being with Marisol. Despite the fact that he'd never felt more— exposed. Realizing that he . . . *cared* for her left Jeff distinctly vulnerable. But as unfamiliar as that felt, this . . . caring— also made him feel so damn good.

Whether Mari liked it, he was going full court press with Specialty's attorney. Deborah was already researching how to shut down Luz Covas and speed up the adoption. And he would have that chat with his brother-in-law, Charlie. Until the Phil situation was resolved, they needed to beef up security around New Beginnings. Any measures they put in place seemed to get shredded by the construction schedule.

Jeff realized he wanted Pete more involved. If he hadn't been holding Marisol in his arms, he would have laughed. Despite the giant's numerous idiosyncrasies, Pete was damned talented when it came to noticing— everything. Between Pete and Hank, they had two highly trained, former military, kick-ass stars in their presence— united in the protection of women and children. They should be able to develop *plenty* of creative ideas— though probably leaning more toward physical resolution over diplomatic.

Maybe the best thing for New Beginnings would be Phil disappearing— or damn well wishing he had.

CHAPTER 9

It had been an eventful week, Marisol realized a few days later.
"Mama, hurry up. I needs to go potty."

Inserting her key in the lock, she hastened her pace on Hector's command. "Remember to wash your hands."

As he raced down the hallway, she tossed her keys in the bowl, her mind splintering in ten directions. Jefferson would arrive soon for baseball practice. Smiling, she took a moment to bask in the glow of how well things were going. Jeff had been true to his word. He'd promised Hector he would try to attend his games . . . and he'd made every game. Every practice. Hector was lapping it up. He loved being with Jeff— loved talking baseball. Loved being tucked in every night. Jeff was a presence in their home nearly every evening now. Increasingly, she couldn't help thinking about their future— that they might actually have one together.

Her experience with Nick made her more conscious of the stages of her relationship with Jeff. Though she tried not to compare them, Marisol was vibrantly aware of time. At the three month point she'd been head over heels with Nick. Now, at the three month point with Jefferson, when she analyzed her feelings, it was so much deeper and stronger. There could be no comparison to her younger self. Despite knowing that, she increasingly suspected she was holding back . . . reining herself in against the giddy elation she experienced with Jeff. She hated being so cautious. It wasn't fair to Jeff *or her* to remain so guarded when what she really wanted was to have everything with him. Sharon was right. Soon, she would have to sit Jeff down and discuss her past.

The tap on her door came at the same moment Hector burst from the bathroom. "Mama— what's for dinner? I'm starvin'"

She opened the door to Jefferson, smile on his face and a pizza in his hands. "You have perfect timing."

Leaning over the box separating them, Jeff kissed her, lingering over the task. "You know— I've heard that before."

"C'mon, Jeff. You can kiss mommy later. We need to eat before practice. I don't want to be late."

"Okay, Hec. Let's get the plates out." Winking at her, he headed for the kitchen. "Remember, I'm kissing you later."

"It's a date." Obviously, the Nick discussion would not take place this evening. But Marisol made a mental promise that she would get to it soon.

"So— Luz has made contact?" Jefferson frowned. "How do you feel about that?"

Marisol rested her head against the couch. They'd finally gotten Hector to bed twenty minutes earlier. "Sharon took the call." Probably a good thing, she admitted, unsure how she would have handled it. "So, I haven't actually spoken with her. But Sharon says Luz claims she doesn't want to make any trouble this time."

Jeff set his drink on the coffee table. "From what you've told me, that would be a first, right?"

"She claims to have Hector's best interests at heart, but I can't imagine Luz having some sort of epiphany about him. Supposedly, she's moving on and she wants the best for him." Shifting to face him, she sighed. "It can't be true, though. We watched the video DSS sent over. Luz was clearly strung out— so she's not off drugs . . . or if she is, it's only been days. Not weeks or months of sobriety."

His expression darkened. "I don't like this, Mari. Can't we stop her from seeing him?"

She loved how Jeff said 'we' when he spoke of Hector. Jeff was clearly crazy about her little boy. "I want to be thrilled by this development— that she might *finally* be ready to sign over custody voluntarily, but I can't bring myself to trust her. She's never, ever kept her word— to him . . . or us."

Lowering her voice, Marisol was conscious of how sound carried. "She's hurt him so many times— with her promises." She would never want Hector to overhear them discussing his mother. No matter how awful Luz was, Marisol would never turn him against her. When Hector was older, he could draw his own conclusions.

Jeff pulled her closer, until she rested against his shoulder. "We'll get through it. If this is her last visit, then we're lucky. If not, we make the best of it. We're not going to let her get anywhere near him where she could hurt him. I promise you that."

"Jeff-" It was there . . . hovering in the air between them. Marisol wanted so badly to just blurt it out. That she loved him. That she needed him. So much— she needed him. She'd never felt this way before. That another person had become so essential, she'd question whether she could do it alone. Of course, the sensible, practical Mari *knew* she could do it on her own. She'd proved she could. But increasingly, she just didn't want to do it alone anymore.

"I'm so glad you're on my side." Brushing a kiss along his jaw, Mari recognized how much faith she had in him. It was comforting and worrying at the same time. "Just talking with you makes me feel— stronger. More confident."

Gentle fingers stroked along her arm. "If I'm completely honest, what I really want is to stop Luz cold . . . to go over her head and get a court to side with us and make her go away permanently."

Increasingly, Jeff held power. If she'd learned anything from her previous relationship, it was that power could be abused. With Nick it had always been about him. *His* needs. *His* wants. His moods. Nothing and no one else was important to him. In a lifetime, she couldn't imagine Nick embracing Hector into his world.

Sighing, Jeff kissed the top of her head. "But I know talking strategy won't set your heart at ease. And I want you to feel better. So— for tonight only, I'm settling for reassurance instead of action."

Contentment washing over her, Marisol shifted in his arms. In her soul, she knew Jeff would never abuse his power. Gorgeous green eyes were lit with a combination of amusement and impatience. "Since you like fixing everything, I can only imagine what this restraint is costing you."

"Well, I need to take charge of something," he admitted, his expression disgruntled. "I think maybe now is a good time for the kissing to start."

It was much later when Marisol woke in their bed. "Jefferson— wake up."

"Huh? What's . . . wrong?"

"It's after midnight. You need to go home," she whispered, guilt poking her over his sleep-roughened voice. "Hector can't find you here in the morning.'

Groaning, Jeff sat up, his tousled bedhead looking dangerously sexy. She resisted the impulse to finger-comb it.

"Mari— I'm coming back in the morning anyway. Hector's game is at nine."

"But. . . I shouldn't let him see a man-"

"I'm not just *some* man, Marisol. Hector has seen me here for months." His expression shifted from sleepy to disgruntled. "If I promise I'll be up by six-thirty and dressed before he wakes up?"

Marisol bit her lip to keep from laughing. Jeff's negotiating voice was equal parts surly and persuasive. "What if we oversleep?"

"I *never* oversleep." Sensing her weakening resolve, Jeff turned to face her, his beautiful eyes more alert now. "I like staying here with you. I don't sleep well in my bed anymore."

"Why not? I thought you needed space. You certainly hog the bed here," she teased.

"What can I say? This ripped physique requires extra room." His sleepy grin revealed a dimple. "Besides, I'm hardly ever at my place anymore."

Hiding her smile, she decided to make him work for it. "Didn't you tell me you loved sleeping in your bed?"

"I've sort of— gotten used to this one," he admitted, his voice hesitant. "When I'm home, I wake up all the time."

"Why?"

"It's like I'm . . . looking for you." Yawning, his shoulders rippled with a shrug. "I like knowing you're there."

Though her heart soared over the admission, Mari wasn't through teasing him. "What about— my bathroom? You hate showering here. You always complain about my girly stuff."

Unwilling to concede defeat, Jeff stayed in the game. "If we busted out a wall, I could give you an awesome bathroom."

"With more shelves for my girly things?" She coughed to cover her laughter.

"With cabinets," he corrected, warming to his idea. "Maybe cherry. We could hide all that shit-" Recovering quickly, he grinned. "I mean . . . there'd be plenty of space for everyone's stuff." Sliding back under the covers, he pulled her down on top of him. "I could build you a big, roomy shower— we could do just about anything in there."

Her pulse stuttering, Marisol realized somewhere along the line, she'd lost control of their conversation. "While I'm rather enticed by-" She paused, throat suddenly dry as the heat of strong thighs nudged hers apart. "By . . . the idea of a new bathroom— we still have the original issue-"

"What issue is that?" Jeff's voice was distracted as he shifted amazing hips under hers. Rising up to accommodate him, Mari experienced the familiar, urgent pull of his body. Rational thought would disintegrate rapidly. "H-hector . . . waking up and . . . waking up-" His strong, capable hands were busy guiding her hips over him. ". . . finding you h-here-" Those amazing hands. The strength of them— anchoring her to his body. Arching into him, she bit back a groan. "Jefferson— hurry . . . *prisa*."

When he surged into her, they moaned in unison. "I have . . . an internal clock." Jeff's rusty voice scraped over her as she tried to focus on his words. But the sensation of his body moving within her was taking up all the room in her brain.

On a shiver of exquisite pleasure, she gasped. "Yes . . . like that." His eyes intent with concentration, Jeff smiled up at her, happy to accommodate her demand for more.

"Baby, trust me . . . I'll wake us up on time."

"Jeff— hey Jeff."

It was the second time that night someone was shaking him awake. Jeez— he just couldn't catch a break. Opening one eye, Jeff met Hector's steady brown gaze.

Hector. Standing at the side of the bed.

Hector. Code red.

"Hey, buddy." Shooting for the appearance of cool, calm and collected, Jeff shook off the sleep clouding his brain. Was he naked? Was Mari? Should he look? Would that be obvious? Holy cow.

"Jeff — if you was sleepin' over . . . why didn't you stay in my room? We coulda built a tent and played flashlights and everything."

"Next time, Hec," he croaked. "I promise." *Next* time he'd remember to lock the door. His brain rallying, Jeff took stock. Okay— he felt the sheet over them. He also felt Marisol's shoulders shaking with laughter behind him. Damn, she'd been right.

"I'm hungry. I need Mommy to make breakfast."

"Okay, little dude— here's what we're gonna do." Propping up on one elbow, Jeff ran a hand through his hair. "Go put on your sweatpants-" *Excellent* idea. That would give him a minute to jump up and find some clothes. He spied his shirt on the chair . . . but where the hell were his pants?

"Are you naked?" Hector's voice rose in curiosity. "Aren't you cold? I'd be cold."

Marisol was outright, no-holds-barred cracking up now— as she slithered further under the blankets. "I— uh . . . get really hot during the night." He ignored the jab to his ribs. Damn it, she wasn't helping any. "That's why I. . . You know what? I have a great idea, Hec. Let's make breakfast together. That way Mommy gets to sleep a little longer and she can come down when it's all ready."

"I get to help?" His eyes widened. "Just you and me? Awesome!" Running for the door, Hector shouted over his shoulder. "I'll be right back." About to tear the sheet off and leap from the bed, Jeff froze when Hector stopped at the door.

"Don't start anything without me."

His heart pounding as though he'd been caught holding up a bank, Jeff nodded. "Not a chance, bud." The moment Hector disappeared, he bolted up in search of his briefs.

"Hey, sailor— nice butt."

Tempted to flash her, he remembered the meter running. *Eyes on the prize, Traynor*. He could hear Hector trashing his room in search of the elusive sweatpants. Only when Jeff had secured the lower half of his body, did he turn to respond. "Okay— lay it on me. You were right. I can admit it."

Covers drawn up to her chest, Mari's sexy hair tumbled over her shoulders. "You *do* get really hot during the night."

Grinning, he met her gaze. "You could've helped me out there."

"You know, carino, I agree your ripped physique is capable of . . . so many amazing things." Her gaze ran over him suggestively— making Jeff wish he wasn't on pancake duty just yet. "But your internal clock is definitely on the fritz."

"Where's Hank?"

Annie's worried expression broke through the hazy daydream Mari was indulging in when she should've been working. This is what love did, she realized. It made you goofy and happy and light-hearted in the middle of an average day at work. She was in love with Jefferson. Hands down, full on, smacked-in-the-head love.

Seated across from her, Sharon set aside the budget she'd been reviewing, bracelets jangling. "Don't worry, Sugar. He's just takin' a day or two off. That's what Stud Muffin told me this morning."

"Are you sure? Because— I thought maybe-" Her voice trailing off, Annie blushed pink.

"Maybe what?" Sharon was on the scent now— a hound to poor Annie's fox— or more appropriate— defenseless kitten. Sharon would be unstoppable. Mari nodded encouragingly. May as well give it up.

Checking the hallway, Annie took another step inside. "Well— he and I . . . I don't exactly know how to say this-" Her gaze on the far wall, she took a deep breath. "We— uh— were out at the farm . . . and Hank— well-"

Unable to resist a smile, Mari took pity on her. "You slept with him?"

Releasing an embarrassed sigh, Annie nodded. "I mean— I'm thirty-eight years old, right? I'm divorced. . . I can do this. I . . . I'm supposed to get back out there."

"So, what's the problem, Sugar?" Sharon's voice was no-nonsense. "He's a fine lookin' man and you're an available, pretty woman."

"I was— sort of-" When the fragile blonde's eyes filled with tears, Mari quickly rose, shutting the door and gently pushing Annie into her chair. "I sorta . . . freaked out."

"Hank was good to you, right?" Sharon's gaze caught hers over Annie's head.

"Of course he was." She sniffed. "He was amazing and kind."

"Then what's the problem, sweetie?"

"Being with Phil— he . . . made me ashamed when we— you know." Wiping her eyes, Annie hesitated. "Early on, things were okay, but the last eight years . . . he made the whole experience so . . . awful. When I finally worked up the nerve to let Hank— see me . . . I guess he sort of— could tell I was afraid. And he was *wonderful* to me." Annie's eyes filled again. "But . . . afterward . . . I think he seemed— angry. And now— he's not here today."

Jeff's words replayed in her head. Biting her lip, Marisol caught Sharon's attention. Was Hank out there— looking for Phil? The older woman shook her head in warning.

"Sugar— Hank has been working six days a week for three months, now. Jeff told me he just needed a day or two off. Said somethin' about him having a few appointments he'd been putting off because of the construction schedule."

Releasing a gusty sigh, Annie blew her nose. Her eyes relieved, she nodded. "You're probably right. I just— this is so . . . new." She smiled. "I just panicked, that's all."

"Of course you did." Sharon nodded, her friendly, brown eyes steeped with understanding. "Everything is gonna be just fine. You'll see."

Rising from the chair, she gave Sharon a hug. "I'll— get back to work. Thank you both."

Waiting until they were certain Annie was out of earshot, Sharon frowned.

Marisol lowered her voice to a whisper. "Jeff said Hank was really angry about Phil showing up here."

"If that damn, stubborn fool has got it in his head to go after Phil— I'm gonna personally take a shovel to his thick skull."

Marisol agreed. Engaging with him would only serve to enrage Phil— making it even more dangerous for Annie— and everyone else at the shelter. Unless Hank could make Phil disappear permanently, he would guarantee only more violence. "We'd better warn everyone to be on the lookout."

"Lord have mercy— please spare me any more jealous men." Sighing, Sharon picked up the phone, her eyes weary. "If Hank challenges him— then Hurricane Phil is sure to make landfall shortly after."

The next afternoon, Marisol peppered Jeff for details as they walked the perimeter of the building, reviewing the exterior. The tilt up walls in place, the roofers had begun framing to close it in. She was excited by the progress, yet still concerned about day two of Hank Freeman's disappearance. "Is Hank really running errands— or has he gone after Phil?"

Taking her arm as they walked the rutted site, Jeff was firm. "Hank is taking care of some personal business— which is none of ours," he reminded. "The guy hasn't taken a weekend off in months. He needs a few days."

"But Annie said-" Marisol hesitated, uncertain whether to share what she'd relayed in confidence. "She thinks Hank is mad at her."

Hands on his hips, Jeff released an exasperated sigh. "What is this? High school?" Checking his watch, his vivid, green eyes lasered in on her. "Maybe I could pass him a note in gym class."

"Okay— I get it. We're overreacting." Marisol couldn't help smiling. In his hardhat and jeans, Jefferson looked both annoyed and edible— at the same time.

"I'm late for a meeting with the roofers." He raised his head to the guys three stories up. "Can we please talk about this tonight?"

When she nodded, Jeff leaned in, giving her a swift kiss. Smiling, she released his hand, then turned to head back around the building to the side entrance. Mari hadn't taken two steps before she felt a tug at her elbow. Turning, she discovered he'd followed her. "I thought you-"

Pulling her against him, he sealed her mouth with his, not coming up for air until she sagged against him. Setting her back on her feet, Jeff smiled at her dazed expression, ignoring the cheers raining down from the roof. "See you later, carina."

It was her new pumps that tripped her up. Returning the next day from a successful meeting with a willing and influential donor, Marisol was humming as she juggled her briefcase and the temperamental side door. Construction had shifted the main entrance again. "Where is Pete," she wondered, realizing as she said it that they'd all grown terribly spoiled. Big Pete was always there— opening doors, carrying heavy boxes and just— taking care of them.

Finally jockeying the heavy door open, Marisol tripped, the heel of her pump catching on the rubber mat they'd laid to catch all the construction dirt at the door. Before she could right herself, she was jerked by a pair of hands. Crashing into an unyielding chest, she instantly smelled alcohol.

Hurricane Phil had made landfall. Shoving back against him, Mari cried out when he twisted her arm behind her back. "Shut up, bitch. Or you'll get it, too. You've been protecting that whore-"

Heart pounding in her ears, Marisol stopped fighting him. Hours of security training kicking in, she went limp in his arms. As expected, Phil floundered with the added weight as he was forced to hold her up.

"Stand up."

As he jerked her upright, pain radiated through her arm. Not losing focus, Marisol utilized the momentary distraction. With her free arm, she eased her hand into her pocket, activating the panic button they'd all begun carrying two days earlier. All she had to do now was keep him there— in the vestibule outside the dining area. Unsure of the time, Mari didn't want Phil gaining entrance to the dining room, where Annie was possibly setting up a service.

The gleam of his knife flashed in her peripheral vision. Fighting the terror welling in her throat, she dragged in deep breaths. The panic buttons carried GPS. About now, she envisioned the team in action. Her panic button had grabbed a shelter phone line— sending a signal to the police substation— notifying them of a hostile intruder. The switchboard had also sounded an emergency code for shelter staff. Already, someone would have seized Annie— hustling her to a safe room, where she was now locked in with a guard protecting her. That thought reassured, in spite of the desperate man trying to break her arm. At least the kids were still in school. Tommy and Jason wouldn't witness yet another violent incident with their unstable father. And Hector- Despite her resolve, a shudder of fear tore through her. Hector was safe— at school.

"That's right, you better be scared of me."

"Phil— if you let me go, the police might not press charges," she lied easily. "If they storm in here and you're still holding me— you'll have no choice."

"I want my wife. Where is she?"

He was sweating profusely— alcohol seeping from his pores. Trying not to gag at the smell, Marisol's job was to stall and distract. Phil hadn't noticed the sudden stillness— the ceasing of activity as groups of employees and volunteers made their way to her location. They would come from all directions— not to attempt disarming him— but to witness. The more people around, the less likely Marisol would be injured. Angry ex-husbands were bullies at heart. They enjoyed terrorizing their victim- But it was only the person he was emotionally invested in that would give Phil the sense of power he needed to feel like a man. There was little satisfaction in hurting strangers. And a large group of witnesses would only add to his embarrassment.

Sensing movement to her left, Marisol shifted subtly to the right. If she could distract him long enough-

A split second later, Mari crashed to the floor when Big Pete body-slammed Phil into the wall. *It was over*. Rising unsteadily to her feet, she was surrounded by shelter staff. With Phil still in a chokehold against the wall, Pete glanced at her over the crowd, his eyes worried.

Again, Marisol was reminded how fortunate they were that Pete had taken such an interest in the shelter. A thrashing drunk still struggling under his grip, Pete's first concern was that she'd been injured. Though her nerves were still arcing like a live wire, Mari forced a smile, giving him a thumbs up.

Her arm aching, she allowed herself to be led into the cramped kitchen for an icepack. Nothing was broken, but she'd probably have a sizable bruise from the episode.

"Mari— you're sure you're okay?" Poor Sharon's eyes were wide as saucers. "I know we've practiced that a hundred times— but damn, girl. When it comes down to it, it's still awful scary."

"I'm . . . good." Her nerves stretched taut, Marisol smiled reassuringly. She'd be alright in a little while. But she needed quiet. In her office with a cup of tea— she could decompress before it was time to pick Hector up at the bus stop. "We aren't out of the woods yet. If Phil makes bail— he'll be back," she reminded.

"We'll get on that right away." Distracted, Sharon hesitated. "Sugar— I hate to hit you with this now— after you've just dealt with Phil but-"

In an instant, Marisol went cold with dread. "Oh God— not Luz. She's here, isn't she?" Her friend blurred in her eyes as she staggered with the knowledge. Not this— not now— so soon after one shock.

"Not yet, but she's comin' this afternoon. To see Hector. I made the appointment for four o'clock. I didn't want her here for any of his afternoon routine. I don't want her knowin' anything about his schedule."

On autopilot, Marisol nodded, not really hearing anything over the insistent drumbeat of fear in her head.

"Deep breaths, Mari. Deep breaths," Sharon coached. "It's just a visit. She said she's not makin' waves. I got the impression maybe she's leavin' town." The older woman squeezed her hand in encouragement. "Maybe she's gonna offer to sign the consent. It will be over. Hector will be yours— and you won't have to wait 'til September. We can petition for permanency next week."

"Okay," she whispered, wanting desperately to be alone. So she could just— lose it. Releasing a deep breath, Mari forced a calm she did not feel. "Okay, Sharon. Okay. I need to sit here. . . for a little while. I need to— think."

"Whatever you want, honey. I'll take care of the police out there. You can give them your statement later." Sharon checked her watch. "I'll check your calendar. If there's anything— I'll just reschedule. And we'll keep everyone away."

As the door finally clicked shut, Marisol felt herself crumbling, the barriers she'd erected around the seething cauldron of bitter fear collapsing in on her. She felt small. Alone. And powerless. As tears splashed down on the blotter, she buried her face in her hands.

Grimacing, Jeff jerked into a parking space, the metallic taste of terror acrid in his mouth. Resisting the urge to jump out and leave the car running, he remembered to lock up and take his keys. "She's alright," he muttered in a futile attempt to keep the raw panic at bay. Pete had explained to him— in clinically detached, highly specific detail that Marisol was safe.

"Mari's okay," he repeated. But— he didn't want to hear the words. Jeff wanted to see her. Hold her— proving for himself it was actually true.

Crossing the parking lot at a run, he jerked open the side door. Police were milling through the vestibule taking statements. As he entered the dining room, his eyes snapped pictures of the normal activities taking place. The volunteers were readying the room for lunch service. *Mari.* Where the hell was Marisol?

As several volunteers approached him, Jeff waved them off, heading for the office corridor. He needed to see her. Before anything could ever be right again, he needed to see her. *Now.*

"Jefferson- wait."

Drawing a ragged breath, Jeff was forced to stop, but only because Sharon was blocking the damned hallway like a linebacker. "Sharon— where is she?"

"She's here but I need to talk with you before you go back there."

"Please, Sharon. I can't-" Raking agitated fingers through his hair, Jeff fought for the patience to be polite. "I have to see her— to make sure she's okay. I'll come back, I promise."

"Hold up there, Sugar." Sharon shifted again, blocking his access. "This is about Mari. And we both care about her. So, you're gonna have to listen to me."

"For God's sake, Sharon— what is it?" Reigning in his impatience, Jeff allowed himself to be pulled into the conference room. "Just tell me she's alright."

"Mari is *not* injured. He twisted her arm behind her back, so she's gonna have a bruise but-"

When he would have risen from the chair, Sharon gently eased him back. "But we have another problem."

Jeff stilled, finally hearing the urgency in her voice. "W-what is it?"

"Luz is coming this afternoon. I had to hit Marisol with the news right after the Phil episode."

He swore violently, then remembered the older woman's presence. "Jeez— I'm sorry Sharon."

"It's okay, Stud. Those are my sentiments exactly." She rested against the edge of the conference room table. "So— here's the deal. If you go in there all fired up about the Phil thing-"

"Hell, Sharon. I'm sick about it. I wasn't here. She could've-" Jeff shuddered at the possibilities.

"I know, Jeff. But right now, Marisol is terrified. If you go in there yelling about Phil— you're not going to be able to help her get through this afternoon. She's this close to losing it." Sharon held her fingers an inch apart. "I need you to talk her down. Reassure her she's not going to lose Hector."

Dispelling a ragged breath, Jeff wrestled for control. Sharon was right. He was jacked up. With fear. With anger. And guilt— for not being there when it happened. But none of those emotions would help Mari. From the fear roiling his gut, he needed to somehow summon calm.

"You're . . . you're right." Meeting her gaze, he nodded. "I can't show her how scared I was. I need to focus on her."

"Luz is coming here at four. That means Mari can get Hector from the bus and walk him back here to the daycare before she arrives." Her voice was a low, reassuring buzz in his brain. Soothing, yet focused. "We'd rather Luz not know any of the particulars about Hector's routine-"

"Because she could still pull something, right?"

Sharon scowled. "I assume Mari explained what happened once before?"

Not trusting himself to speak, Jeff nodded. "How do you do this job, Sharon?"

"Not every situation is this bad. Lots of mothers leave here successful . . . they land jobs, they take care of their kids and they move on with their lives." Her eyes reflected a weary history. "Those stories help us get through days like today— with Phil trying to hurt Annie. And Luz— unwilling to let her son be placed with a capable person who clearly loves him."

"I need to see Mari." Rising slowly, he squeezed her hand. "Thanks, Sharon. I promise I'll do my best to be helpful."

"I know you will, Stud."

Worried how he would find her, Jeff entered her office cautiously. After Sharon's description, he assumed he'd find Marisol weeping hysterically. Instead, she was quiet . . . gazing out the window. Almost deceptively calm. Unsure what he should do, he crossed the room and pulled up a chair.

"Mari, honey? Are you alright?"

Barely acknowledging him, Marisol continued to stare out the window. "I don't have any tears left. I guess that's a good sign."

Why wouldn't she look at him? "Sharon wanted to remind you about Hector getting off the bus." Checking his watch, he paused. "That's in thirty minutes. Why don't I go with you?"

"I don't know."

The defeat in her voice sliced through him. "Honey— can you look at me?" When she didn't respond, Jeff sighed. He was about to enter uncharted waters. Comforting someone he cared about— and not knowing what the hell to say. "I know . . . you're scared. I know it all seems hopeless. And I— know I can't . . . change any of that," he admitted. What was he doing? Hell— he was supposed to be making it better. But how could *anyone* make this better? "The truth is . . . I'm scared, too. I don't want to imagine your life without Hector in it. But, Marisol— we're not going to let that happen."

Still nothing. It was as though she had built an impenetrable wall around herself. As though it somehow might stop her from feeling pain or fear. "Let me help you, Mari. Please? Let me in, love. Can you look at me?"

Her gaze finally dropping from the window, she turned slowly toward him. "I can't keep doing this, Jeff." Her voice was a painful whisper. "I can't bear it. She does such a number on Hector when she shows up. She works him over-"

"We can help Hector get through this," he reminded. "No matter what she says . . . we'll be there to counteract her words. We love him. That means we can protect him." Cautiously, Jeff slid closer. "Let's do this together," he suggested. "If you just lean on me, Mari— I swear I won't let you fall. I'll be there with you . . every step of the way."

Relief coursed through him when she finally nodded. Helping her stand, Jeff took her carefully in his arms. For the first time since meeting her, Marisol seemed vulnerable. Isolated. As though the world was crushing in on her.

For a long time, Jeff just held her, not saying a word. There was nothing he could say to make the ordeal better. There was only hope that by doing it together, he would help her get through it. When it was finally time to meet the bus, Jeff led the way, Mari's fingers locked tight in his.

Hector was thrilled to see Jeff waiting for him at the bus stop. Trusting him completely, he launched himself into Jeff's arms, completely skipping the last two steps off the bus.

"Carino— you shouldn't leap off the bus like that. What if Jeff wasn't looking?" Offering a wave to the smiling bus driver, Marisol knew her scolding was pointless. But she'd learned that focusing on normal, everyday activities helped her cope with the dread of dealing with Luz. It also helped mute her worried vibe so her mood wouldn't affect Hector.

"Jeff was lookin' right at me. How could he miss?"

Forcing a lightheartedness she didn't feel, Marisol smiled. "What if he dropped you?"

Hoisting Hector in one arm, Jeff smiled. "With these biceps? Honey— get serious."

Giggling, Hector flexed his arms. "When I get old, I'm gonna have big guns just like Jeff."

"Old?" Jeff shot him an exaggerated grimace. "Dude— you're killin' me."

Hector leaned against him. "I meant big," he corrected. "When I'm *big* like you."

"Guns?" Giving Jefferson the once over, Mari relaxed a notch, his playful mood proving infectious. "Already, you've taught him that terminology?"

His expression sheepish, Jeff captured her nervous fingers with his free hand. "Gotta have strong arms to power the ball into the outfield, right Hec?"

"Jeff says if I eat a bunch 'a spinach, I'll be able to swing the bat so hard— it'll bust open the baseball."

She smiled over his boast. "I see you're employing the Popeye method of strength training?"

"Hey— it worked for me," Jeff admitted. "I ate tons of vegetables because of that cartoon." Mari couldn't help noticing how wonderful it felt— his sturdy hand holding hers, Hector snuggled safely against his chest, giggling as Jeff told silly jokes. His magic worked on her as well. Instead of locked in worry over what the next few hours would bring, Mari was smiling, soothed by Jeff's easygoing confidence. Making her laugh. Making her happy.

Any passerby watching them would smile over the idyllic scene, the perfect little family. Because they were perfect together. Jefferson was so at ease with Hector. Marisol had no trouble envisioning him behind a stroller— or with a sweet, tiny infant cradled in his arms. At one of the most stressful moments of her life— not knowing yet what game Luz played, it occurred to her that Jeff was the man she wanted by her side as she endured it. This was the man she wanted to spend her life with.

The discovery made her even more appreciative of his reassuring presence. Raising their entwined fingers to her lips, she pressed a kiss to his hand, letting him feel her smile. "Strong arms can be useful," she admitted, "for many things in life."

CHAPTER 10

"What happens next?" Jeff waited while Mari closed the door to the daycare before he spoke.

Pausing to watch Hector chat with Miss Robin, Marisol smiled. His earnest brown eyes were wide and animated as Hector relayed a story to his teacher. "We wait."

"When do you tell Hector that Luz wants to see him?"

Marisol sighed, drifting from the door. "When she actually appears at the door. Half the time, Luz never shows." Nodding toward her office, they walked together. "About a year ago, we stopped telling Hector when she might be visiting."

Jeff hesitated beside her. "What was he— four?"

"It did more damage than good. He was old enough to understand. He'd get excited— thinking she would be . . . better. Normal. That she finally wanted to be his mom." Mari sensed his body tensing next to her. "All it did was get Hector's hopes up. Then, he'd be devastated when she didn't come. Or worse— Luz *would* show up. Filling his head with lies before she disappeared again." Resting her back against the corridor wall, she acknowledged Jeff's sober expression. "Weeks after a visit, Hector would still be asking when Luz was coming back for him. . . because she'd promised— that next time she'd take him home."

"How is he so happy? Still smiling. Still laughing. He's the most amazing kid, Mari."

She knew exactly how Jeff felt. "I think it actually helps that he was so young when this all started. Hector was only two when DSS got him the first time. He was three when I started fostering him." Mari's smile was troubled. "I guess we're lucky he doesn't know any different."

"So— we just wait? We can't just— tell her to go to hell? I want . . . a judge who will finally listen." Pulling her against him, Jeff held her close, dropping a kiss on her forehead. "I'm sorry. I'm not exactly helping by talking this way."

Loving the reassuring sound of his heartbeat under her ear, Mari lifted her head. "You've helped a great deal. This afternoon— I was . . . lost. You got me back on track." Resting against him, she sighed. "On a terrible day— you had me laughing . . . feeling joy." Her gaze met his as her voice dropped. "I'd say that was pretty amazing."

"I don't know how you've done this for so long. It needs to end."

Absently, she rubbed her aching forearm, wincing when she brushed over the tender spot. Probably, she should have iced it longer— but there hadn't been time.

"Is that where he-"

Forgetting that Jeff was watching so closely, Mari startled, lowering her arm. "It's just sore. Maybe a little bruise."

The flash of anger in Jeff's vivid, green eyes did not match the softness of his voice when he finally spoke. "Mari— for your sake— and *only* your sake," he clarified, "I'm filing this away until later."

Weariness seeping through her very bones, Marisol couldn't summon the energy to placate him. "Good, because I need to pretend to get back to work while we wait for Luz to show up." Just thinking about it made her pulse tick up. "And I may need you to talk me down again later."

In a heartbeat, Jeff's expression softened. "I'll be right here," he promised. "And— under the circumstances, I think we need to do something *seriously* fun tonight."

"Seriously fun sounds great." Delivered to her office door, Mari was once again amazed by his ability to soothe her. Together, they would get through this.

Hector was quiet that evening. While Marisol seemed to take his mood in stride, it bothered Jeff. Mari had been through this before— probably a dozen times. But *he* hadn't. The meeting with Luz had been disturbing. Unsettling. Clutching Marisol's hand as they watched Luz on a closed circuit television, Jeff had experienced a degree of helplessness he'd never known was possible.

A strung out woman, shaking with nerves, or more likely the need for a fix— as Mari had corrected him, was in a room down the hall from where they sat. Making demands of the DSS staff person sitting with Hector. Sweet, vulnerable Hector. Sitting across from a weepy, defiant, belligerent shell of a woman. Who was *supposed* to be his mother.

Jeff was surprised to realize he knew how to read the little boy. Hec's eyes had held the shimmer of confusion— of *wanting* to like his mother, yet also fearing her because she was acting so strange. His body language had been guarded— as though he half expected her to leap over the table at him. It would go down in memory as one of the hardest things he'd ever endured— sitting there with Mari . . . helpless . . . while Hector was subjected to the ranting of a crazy woman.

"Hey bud, wanna go out and throw the ball around? We still have time before it gets dark." He needed to move— walk— *anything* to shake off the remnants of that dreary image. More than anything, Jeff wanted to help the little boy feel better. Feel safe and secure. But that was probably the last thing he could provide at the moment.

Hector set aside his toy soldiers. "Could we take a walk? Like . . . just you and me?"

Glancing toward the kitchen, where Mari was putting away the brownies they'd just devoured, he called out to her. Her head appeared around the doorway, as though she'd heard their conversation. "Go ahead. But Hector needs his bath in twenty minutes."

Pretending not to see the worry etched on her features, Jeff forced a smile. "Come on, Hec. Let's take a spin around the block. But I'm warning you— after that gigantic brownie sundae, you might have to carry me part of the way home."

The little guy rewarded him with an impish smile. "Don't worry. I had three broccolis for dinner, so my muscles are already growin'. I'll carry you."

"Make sure to take Jeff's hand when you're in the street, carino." Mari turned hastily back toward the kitchen, but not before Jeff spied the glimmer of tears in her eyes. And maybe for the first time, he finally understood *exactly* how she felt.

Dusk was settling as they left the house, the sweet scent of jasmine blanketing the humid air with its perfume. As Hector's fingers slipped into his hand, Jeff felt a corresponding ache settle in his chest. "You okay tonight, Hec?"

Hector's gaze was focused on the street, his eyes seeking out anything unusual in their path. Jeff followed his lead as they drifted first to a pebble he wanted to kick, then a stick. His expression excited, he picked it up. "We should keep this, Jeff. When we go to the park, we could drop it in the stream and watch it float."

"Why don't I put it in my pocket for you?"

Handing it to him, Hector hesitated, his mind clearly on bigger issues. "Sometimes— seein' her makes me sad."

Five minutes in— and Jeff was already out of his depth. Pausing as he searched for the right words, he finally gave up. There were no *good* words for this situation. "I think whatever you feel is okay to feel."

"What if I feel . . . mad?" Little fingers fluttered anxiously in his hand.

Squeezing his hand, Jeff turned Hector to face him. Then dropped to his haunches. It was suddenly very important that he be able to look him in the eye. "Hec— I think you're the bravest, coolest, smartest boy I've ever met." His gaze was unwavering as he stared into unhappy brown eyes that had seen far too much in five years. "If you feel mad— I think you've gotta go with it. But— being mad without knowing *why* doesn't help get rid of it."

"What do you mean?"

Spying a bench as they neared the playground, Jeff nodded to it. "Let's sit for a minute, okay?"

Settling on the park bench, Jeff scooped the little boy into his lap. "When I was a little older than you, I got really mad at my dad because he took my older brother to a baseball game— and he didn't take me."

Hector's eyes widened. "Didn't he like you?"

Jeff smiled. "He liked me a lot. But he thought I was too young to go to the game so he only took Jake. He told my mom he would take me the next year. But I didn't know that part." He paused as

Hector settled back against his chest. "So— I got mad . . . and I stayed mad for a whole week after the game. And it made me quiet and sad-"

"Did you cry?"

"I did— almost every night in my room," he confessed. "But here's what I learned from that. When my dad finally figured out I was mad at him— he asked what was bugging me. And when I told him how angry I was about the ballgame, my dad was floored."

"What do you mean?"

"It means— my dad never *knew* how angry I was. He said if I'd only told him what was bothering me— he would have fixed it sooner." He tipped Hector's chin up to look at him. "So— I was mad for a week, but I held it all inside. So— no one could help me fix it. And no one could make me feel better."

"What did your dad do after that?"

Jeff released a steadying breath, praying he was getting his point across. Was he doing the right thing? "He sat me down and told me he was sorry that he'd hurt my feelings."

"So— telling your dad made you feel better?"

"Telling my dad made me feel way, way better." He gave Hector's hand a squeeze. "And once he knew how I felt, he took me to a game the following week— just me and my dad."

"What if— the thing you're mad about is really, really big?"

Swallowing around the lump in this throat, Jeff winced. "Then you should tell someone you trust. Because, maybe that person could help you feel better."

"Can I tell you?"

His whispered request had Jeff's heart plummeting to the pit of his stomach. "You can tell me anything, Hec. Always."

"I . . . don't like that lady— and I know . . . I'm supposed to." Hector's confession came out on an anguished whisper. "An'. . . I don't wanna see her again. She's scary and mean."

Throwing his shuddering frame into his chest, Jeff caught him in a tight hug. "It's alright, buddy. It's *okay* to be mad at her. And it's okay to not like her."

"It is? Are you sure?"

"Sometimes people want to be good— but they're not strong enough to be nice. Being mean is easy."

"Is being nice hard?"

"It's more work," Jeff explained. "Because you're thinking about the other person instead of just yourself. Like remembering to say please and thank you, right?"

"But people like when you do that. Mari says I have to be polite."

"Mari is absolutely right. But some people don't like being nice. And when they realize they're mean— they take it out on other people so they don't feel bad about themselves." Jeff paused, searching for an example he would understand. "Like a bully. They act mean because they're afraid you won't like them the way they really are. So they'd rather have you be afraid of them."

Hector's head popped up from his shoulder. "You mean like Tommy and Jason's daddy? He was mean to them."

"Exactly. Tommy's dad doesn't want to make the effort to be nice'"

"Or polite," Hector interrupted.

"So, what I'm telling you Hec, is that it's okay to not like that woman. But you shouldn't waste time being afraid of her."

"But she's scary-"

"Bud— you're gonna have to trust me on this one, okay?" With everything he had, Jeff didn't want Hector to be afraid. "We won't let her hurt you. I promise."

"But— if she ever did . . ."

Jeff realized that simply telling him not to worry wouldn't stop Hector from being afraid. He needed to feel in control. "Okay— here's what you're gonna do," he directed. "If she ever scares you— *ever*, then you have my permission to be mean."

His eyes widened. "Mari would get mad at me."

Jeff shook his head. What the hell? Let him feel empowered. "Mari would want you to fight back. If that woman ever scares you— then you can do *anything* you want to fight her. You can yell *really* loud. You can punch. You can kick."

Hector's shoulders began shaking with his laughter. "Can I . . . bite?"

"Yup."

"Scream?"

"The louder the better."

"Spit in her eye?"

Chuckling, Jeff gave him a squeeze. "If your aim is good- go for it." When Hector finally stopped laughing, Jeff settled him against him. "But you won't need to do any of those things because there are lots of people watching out for you."

"She wiggles too much an' she talks funny— like she's goin' too fast." Stifling a yawn, he paused. "We get in trouble at school if we don't sit still." Hector slung his arms around his neck. "I want Mari to be my mommy."

Rising to his feet, Jeff planted a kiss on his forehead. "Mari loves being your mom."

"She's nice to me. An' she never yells at me. And she cooks good. And I like my room— and all my stuff."

"Pretty soon, she'll be your mom forever."

Hector went slack in his arms. "Can you carry me back, Jeff?"

"I thought you ate three broccolis?" Hector's sticky smile brushed against his neck, filling Jeff with a sense of contentment he'd never experienced before.

"I fibbed. It was only two."

"Mama— can I take a bath later?"

Hector's ear-splitting yawn made Marisol smile. As did the sight of her son splayed across Jeff's chest. "You must have walked a long way to come back so tired."

"Jeff can put me to bed. I don't need a story."

Meeting his gaze over Hector's head, Jeff's smile gave her encouragement. "Okay— we'll scrub you up tomorrow morning before school."

"I'm not even dirty," he protested.

"Dude— you don't want to be the smelly guy at school," Jeff reminded. "It's not cool."

"Okay. I can wash up tomorrow."

Raising her gaze to the ceiling, Mari smiled. It was so unfair that Jeff could get Hector to agree to anything. Jeff's grin told her he knew exactly what she was thinking.

Lifting his head, Hector's sleepy eyes sought hers. "Mommy— Jeff said he wants to take us to his farm this weekend. Can we go? We get to sleep over for the weekend— an' his nephew will be there. And— he's my age . . . almost."

His eyes had their sparkle back. Hector seemed so much better. So much more like her excited, happy little boy. Jeff had spent fifteen minutes with Hector— and worked his special brand of magic. After she'd put away the brownies, Marisol had allowed herself a mini meltdown in the kitchen. Then she'd splashed cold water on her face and waited anxiously by the window for her boys to return.

"It sounds like the best place in the whole world," he embellished.

"In the whole world?" She ruffled his tangled curls. "Okay, mi pequeno. If it's that great, we definitely have to see it."

"I'm not your little one," he grumbled. "I'm getting big."

"If you're big, that means you can walk upstairs by yourself." Amusement in his eyes, Jeff faked lowering Hector to the floor.

"No— Jeff. You have to carry me. I'll be her pequeno," he promised under duress. Fighting to stay in his arms, Hector squealed when he tickled him.

"I'm sorry— I didn't hear you. What did you say?"

"I said I'm her-" He shrieked with laughter. "Stop ticklin', Jeff."

Any trace of sleepiness left him as Hector wrestled with Jeff. After the day they'd endured, Marisol didn't mind throwing the rules out the window. "If Jeff's putting you to bed, then you need to give me a kiss, pequeno."

Jeff swung Hector around to accommodate her request before stealing a kiss for himself. "I'll be your big pequeno."

Mari chuckled. "You'll be my big 'little one'?"

His eyes glinting with promise, he kissed her again as Hector made gagging noises from his arms. "I'll be your *only* one."

"Are you *sure* you should be bringing us? It's a family cookout— your whole, entire . . . *huge* family." For two days, Marisol had been excited and nervous about the Traynor family's Memorial Day barbecue. At a farm owned by Linc and Mona. Hector had been over the moon.

The invitation couldn't have come at a better time. More than ever, Marisol was grateful for the long weekend. The further they drove from the city, the more unburdened she became. For the next two days, she would not give another thought to New Beginnings . . . to Hector's mother . . . to her faltering donations . . . to the haze of construction. For once, she would leave every worry behind and just enjoy her time with Jeff and Hector. And Jefferson's gigantic family.

Smiling, Jeff's gaze remained on the road. But he'd shifted just enough for her to confirm his adorable dimple. The one that made him pretty much irresistible. "That's the point. You get to meet everyone all at once. It'll be perfect."

"Stop bouncing back there, carino." The feet thumping her seat paused. Marisol smiled, knowing it would only be a temporary reprieve. Hector was having all he could do just to contain himself. Jefferson had filled his head with talk of horses and baseball and a nephew close to his age.

"How much longer, Jeff? Are we close?"

"Pretty soon. Did you bring your bathing suit, Hec? The pond will be cold, but all the guys have to jump in."

"Only the boys? Awesome." The thumping started again.

Mari turned to stare at him. "How cold?"

Jeff lowered his voice. "Just enough to make you question your sanity. But it's tradition. Every Traynor male has to jump in the pond on Memorial Day weekend."

"Freezing to death in a pond is your tradition?"

"It's— a guy thing. You wouldn't understand." Knowing that statement would annoy her, he couldn't help grinning. "Let's just say that for the entire rest of the year— your manhood is seriously questioned if you don't do it."

"Ah. That makes perfect sense, then." She shot him a look. "Do the Traynors have any other unusual customs I should know about?"

Hector piped up from the back. "I brought two suits . . . just in case. And I gots my glove and a bat . . . and three balls. And my Lego set."

Jeff's grin widened. "Sounds like you're all set. You're gonna like my nephew, Alex. My brother Jake says Alex can't wait to meet you."

Checking the rearview mirror, Jeff confirmed Hector was occupied looking out the window. "There are one or two . . . *sacred* traditions I need to discuss with you privately." His dimple winked at her again. "Later tonight," he promised.

Surprised when Jeff reached over to take her hand in his, he brought it to his lips, his mouth warm against her skin. And her insides liquefied with pleasure. Each day that passed, Jeff grew more comfortable with her. And she was getting spoiled by his affectionate gestures.

"Well, now I'm dying of curiosity." Heat crawling through her, Mari squeezed his fingers. "I'm very glad you invited us."

"Be prepared for an onslaught from the female members of the family. You're the first woman I've ever brought home, so they'll be ready to pounce on you."

Rather than nerves, a burst of pleasure made her lightheaded. She probably shouldn't read too much into Jeff's confession, but damn, it still felt amazing to hear.

True to his word, there was a crowd awaiting them thirty minutes later when they pulled up to the farmhouse. Marisol eyed the sprawling front porch. "This place is huge. And no one lives here?"

Jeff pulled up next to the barn. "Believe me, it still gets a workout. In the summer, we all take turns using it. Then, we're all here together for the major holidays. You should see it at Christmas. We have a big sled for the horses to pull. And the snow is beautiful."

"It sounds wonderful."

"Personally, my favorite time to visit is in the fall. The hiking is incredible and the trees are beautiful." Staring at her over the roof of his truck, his eyes heated, sending shivers down her spine as she read his thoughts. "There's a great fireplace for when the nights get cold. Lots of quilts to stay warm."

"Can we come back, Mari? I wanna hike with Jeff." Hector wrapped his arms around Jeff's neck as he climbed out of his car seat.

"Of course I'll take you hiking, Hec. You're my best bud."

"I love you, Jeff." When Hector kissed his cheek, Jeff's stunned expression was completely unguarded. Marisol could feel the weight of his pause before his beautiful eyes lit with pleasure, a huge grin suffusing his face.

"I love you, too, buddy."

Marisol pulled her lawn chair closer to the bonfire. Moments later, Kendall Traynor joined her. Smiling, she watched Kendall's husband Harrison make a fuss over his tiny wife.

"Do you need a pillow, Kenny? Are you tired? How's your back?"

"Harrison— I'm *fine*. The baby is fine. Marisol is fine . . ." Turning to her, Kendall's distinctive, smoky voice was amused. "Mari— you're fine, right?"

Marisol held her smile. "I'm great."

"So we hear." Kendall rolled her eyes. "Harry, why don't you go have a beer with Jeff and listen to him tell you how wonderful Marisol is, okay?" Leaning back in her chair, she sighed. "When Jeff gets boring and repetitive, you can bring me a brownie."

Harry's serious face transformed with his smile. "Okay. Nothing against your perfection, Marisol . . . but my pregnant wife needing chocolate will be the perfect excuse when Jeff starts gushing."

"I'm not perfect," Mari protested, heat staining her cheeks. "Jeff is merely being nice."

Kendall leaned over to pat her knee. "We're just joshin' you, Mari." As Harry left them, she called over her shoulder, instructing him to make it a big brownie. "Personally, I think it's hysterical that a woman has finally brought that man to his knees. I've only been in the family a little over a year now, but even I'm enjoying the change in Jeffie."

Mari could only agree. "He's been wonderful with Hector."

"I always suspected he had it in him." Tipping her head back, Kendall gazed at the stars. "What do you think of the Traynors? I know when I first came on board, they were a pretty overwhelming bunch."

"Actually, they remind me of my own family," Mari admitted. The day had been amazing. Boisterous, laughing, loud. Hector had experienced probably the best day of his life. At Jeff's urging, he'd leaped into the pond like a pro. Tonight, after fireworks and the bonfire, Hector would be bunking in with his new best friend Alex and his older sister Megan. Today had been a spectacular day.

"There are four kids in my family. I have only one brother, thank goodness. And two sisters— which is sometimes problematic, but mostly wonderful." Mari took a deep breath of the sultry, summer night, the scent of charred wood drifting toward them. "None of us are married, so the gatherings aren't quite as big as this one."

"That probably helps." Kendall stifled a yawn. "Sorry— I'm having trouble staying awake these days."

"Mari— can you put the marshmallow on my stick?" Hector threw himself across her lap, interrupting their conversation. "Mine keeps fallin' off."

"Excuse me, Hector," she reminded as she finessed the marshmallow on his whittled stick.

"'Scuse me, Miss Ken," Hector parroted back, shifting impatiently while he waited. "Miss Ken?"

"Yeah, sweetie?"

"Why does Lurch only have three legs?"

Kendall smiled. "He was like that when I adopted him from the shelter. He'd been hit by a car."

Hector's eyes widened. "You *adopted* Lurch? Didn't you want a dog with all his legs?"

Leaning forward in her chair, Kendall squeezed his hand. "I knew the moment I saw him that we were meant to be together."

"Mama? Can we adopt a three-legged dog?"

Mari smiled as she slid the marshmallow on his stick. "Shouldn't you be asking whether we can get *any* dog?"

"Please?" His velvety, chocolate eyes pleaded. "Lurch likes graham crackers, too."

Returning his stick, she smiled. "We'll see how well you do your chores this summer." When he scampered away, she winked at Kendall. "Don't run with that," Mari called the reminder after him, knowing there was virtually no chance he was listening.

"Good luck with that." Kendall grinned. "He's a great kid, Mari. I've been watching him all day. So happy and easygoing." She shifted in her chair, trying to get comfortable. "I was an only child. And only one parent, so it took me a while to get comfortable holding my own with all these Traynors running around." She patted her stomach contentedly. "But now, I wouldn't have it any other way. I'm so grateful our baby will be born into such a big, rambunctious family."

"Do you know what you're having?"

Kendall leaned over conspiratorially. "We found out last month but we haven't told anyone yet, because then the baby-naming wars will start early."

Marisol smiled. "Who causes trouble? Lincoln?"

"Well— you know the whole presidential thing, right? All Traynor babies are named after a president— even the girls. Jake and Jen swiped Roosevelt and Madison for the twins."

"I guess that narrows down the name list arguments, right?' Marisol chuckled. When Jeff had told her of the tradition, it made her smile. She loved how tight-knit they all were. Even Mona and Lincoln. They certainly didn't act as though they were divorced. She'd noticed them today, heads together, smiling and talking; bantering back and forth as though they were still married. "So, what's your dilemma?"

Kendall's husky voice dropped to a whisper. "Well, I like Truman for a name, but Harry is leaning more towards Carter."

A boy. An image floated in Mari's head— a little boy with startling green eyes and a smile that would excuse him from all sorts of trouble. "I'm surprised you wouldn't go with Adams. Wasn't that your maiden name?"

Ken's eyes widened. "Good Lord, I never even thought of that."

A few minutes later, Harrison returned, large brownie in hand. "Honey, you want something to drink with this?"

Her eyes drooping, Ken smiled. "Darlin' I'm too tired to eat it. You need to take me to bed."

Not missing a beat, Harry winked. "I live only to serve you, Mrs. Traynor. Allow me to   help you up from that chair."

"Not so fast, Traynor. Marisol has just given me a fantastic idea. I'm gonna need to lay it on you before we go to bed."

Mari chuckled, loving how comfortable they were with each other. She wanted that. A loving relationship with your best friend. Heck— she'd found that with Jeff. All day, he'd been attentive to her and Hector . . . making sure she had someone to talk with. Making sure she had a plate of food. She'd watched him with Hector . . . hitting the ball to his niece and nephew.

She'd tried not to stare when the Traynor men stripped down for the annual pond jump. But her gaze had remained glued to Jefferson's incredible body. Soaked to the skin, holding her little boy in his very capable arms— Jeff embodied every fantasy she'd ever had. All she could envision was him holding her like that. Feeling the heat rise in her cheeks, Marisol had been grateful for her sunglasses.

Her relationship with Jefferson was perfect. If only *he* could ever realize it, too.

CHAPTER 11

Marisol was smiling as he approached the bonfire. Jeff had been watching her all night. Her eyes sparkling as she talked with his mom; her amazing smile when his crazy sister-in-law Kendall said something funny— because she *always* said something funny. This was his Mari. No worry in those gorgeous, aqua eyes. Relaxed and happy. And so damn beautiful. She was perfect.

Jeff grinned. Hell— Harry was right. He *was* gushing. When had this happened to him? Somewhere along the way, he'd become so finely tuned to Mari that he didn't know how to shut it off. He was so damn aware of her— of what she said . . . and what she didn't say. What her eyes told him. What her body said when her words said something different.

Not for the first time since he'd met her, Jeff felt unsure of himself—as though he could make a mistake. As though he could blow it. Because he finally had something precious to lose. The fleeting image of that television screen . . . of Phil with a knife sent a tremor of fear through him before he resolutely set it aside. He'd sworn he would not think about any of that here. Their day had been perfect. All worry had been temporarily suspended.

Slipping into the chair next to Marisol, he leaned in for a lingering kiss. "I've missed you with all these people around," he confessed. "Can I get you anything? Are you having fun?" Seeing Hector by the fire, Jeff relived the fun day he'd had with him today. And acknowledged how much he wanted to do it all again.

"Everything I want is right here." Marisol's whispered confession sent pleasure ricocheting through Jeff's chest— as it had when Hector said he loved him. And when he'd said it back. It was all just a little overwhelming. And amazing. And perfect.

"I have a proposition for you." Mari's eyes widened expectantly. "There's something I'd like to show you— a special place I want you to see."

"Tonight?"

"That's one of the best times to see it."

When Marisol smiled a sexy, knowing smile, Jeff's body instantly tightened. Grateful for the darkness, he was glad he was already seated.

"Are you forgetting the little wild man I have to get bathed and ready for bed?"

"That's where my proposition comes in. I've bribed my mother to herd all the kids to bed tonight." Smiling in anticipation, he watched acknowledgement flare in her beautiful eyes.

"Your mom can handle all three of them?"

"She's in the room adjoining my dad's. The kids are actually bunking down in his room, so she'll have help."

"I see you've thought of everything." Marisol's eyes sparkled. "I would love to take you up on your proposition."

Thirty minutes later, they slipped away from the bonfire like guilty teenagers. The million cricket symphony covered their getaway. Now, loping through the fields under a thick blanket of stars, Jeff inhaled a deep breath of the cooling night air and began to relax. Another night he would take Hector to his special place, but tonight . . . he wanted only Mari. To be alone with her. To show her the beauty of a place that had captured him as a child. He wanted to see her reaction. Wanted her to know it as well as he did.

The kids were well on their way to being trooped inside for baths, hot chocolate and bed. Jake and Jenna had bunked down for the night, taking advantage of the twins' early schedule to catch some much needed rest. Andrea and Charlie had left for the evening, since Charlie had pulled a shift for the following morning.

Linking her fingers with his, Jeff smiled when Marisol giggled.

"Why do I feel like I'm in high school again?"

"Like we're slipping away from camp to go make out?" Jeff's heart thumped with anticipation. This moment with Mari— was more exciting than anything he'd done in years.

"So— where are you taking me?"

"To my favorite spot on the farm." Marisol kept pace easily as they climbed the first slope. "I probably should have thought of this earlier, but there's a little bit of a climb at the end." He paused on the trail. "What kind of shoes are you wearing?"

"I'm good. These are flat." He swung the beam of his flashlight toward the ground to confirm.

"My dad bought this place when I was ten. I found this spot the very first summer."

"How big is it?" Mari stopped on the trail to turn back and look around. "And why is it so hilly? I thought farms were flat."

"Give or take . . . a few hundred acres." Jeff tightened his grip on her hand as they circumvented the pond. "And you're right. We call it a farm, but it's built into the hills. We have orchards." He stopped again, turning her to the east. "On that hill, there's a small apple orchard." He turned her again. "Over there, we have peaches. And over there, we have Christmas trees."

Leaning back against him, Marisol's scent washed over him. "You have your own Christmas trees? How cool is that?"

"Mom liked it because she always said Dad couldn't complain about the price of our tree."

"It must be a guy thing." Marisol chuckled, the throaty sound rippling over him. "That's how my dad was. Every year— like clockwork, he'd pitch a fit over the price of our tree. And every year, my mother pretty much ignored him and got the biggest one on the lot."

"We always cut one down for the house in Stafford, and then we'd cut another for our celebration out here." Resuming their climb, Jeff took the lead, not really needing the flashlight. He knew these acres like the neighborhood he'd grown up in. There wasn't an inch of land he hadn't explored with his brother and cousin. "Then— one year, Linc claimed he was too busy at work to drive out here to cut the tree down."

He felt Marisol miss a step and waited for her to regain her footing. "You okay? Need to rest?"

"I'm good." Taking a deep breath, she took another step. "So— what did you do that year?"

"I was fourteen by then. Jake was seventeen so he didn't much care— or at least that's what he claimed. I made my mother drive us out here and I cut one down for her."

"So— there must have been a few years when it was just you and your mom, right? Is Harrison about the same age as Jake?"

Jeff hesitated. As much as he wanted to take this next step— to open up to Mari so she would see that he was serious about her— it was still hard. He felt a little naked. And when she gave his hand a squeeze, it was almost like Marisol knew what he was thinking. "Harry's a year younger."

"They were in college when it happened?" Her voice encouraged him to continue.

"The divorce, you mean?" Their ascent began to steepen. Pulling Mari closer, he placed his hand at her back, the skin above her waistband warm to his touch. "Yeah— I was basically the only one left in the house. Andrea was already grown and married."

"That must have been hard for you— witnessing that. Living through it." She slipped then, her hands reaching down to the ground for balance.

"I won't let you fall, Mari," he whispered the promise, knowing in his heart it was true. "It was hard," he admitted. "I never thought it affected me that much, you know? But now that I'm older— I've started to realize what an impact their divorce had on me. Weird, huh?"

"Not to me." She hesitated. "I think there's lots of stuff in our past that makes an impact. But we don't realize it has . . . or sometimes we don't want to admit it."

Jeff wondered whether she spoke from her work experience or something more personal. "We're nearly there."

When they broke through the clearing, he was eager for her reaction. Her gasp of surprise sent warmth cascading through him.

"Jeff— this is . . . amazing." Turning slowly around on the plateau, Mari couldn't contain her smile. "I can see the farm." She pointed down through the woods. "And the pond. And there's the barn."

"Wait 'til you look up." Dousing the flashlight, Jeff watched as she raised her gaze to the stars overhead. With the sliver of moon visible, he was able to see the wonder in her face. Watching Mari's delight made it new for him again.

"Thank you so much for showing this to me. I— I'm honored you wanted me to see it."

"I've experienced some of my best and worst moments right here." Jeff wasn't sure why he'd confessed that— only knew that Marisol would understand.

Her head tilted back to view the stars, her lips curved in a smile. "Tell me some of the best moments."

"Well— there was that first summer, of course. Discovering this place. And then there was my twelfth birthday, when my parents let me camp out up here with six other kids."

Her gaze rested on him. "You must have been the coolest kid on the planet."

"Yeah, I thought so, too. Until my friend Bobby got sick in the middle of the night and Linc had to carry him all the way down to the farm so Mom could take care of him." He chuckled at the memory. "He threw up in the tent, so it went from extremely cool to disastrous in about five minutes."

"Tell me some more," Mari encouraged, her fingers slipping through his.

"When I made the varsity baseball team. That was a big one. I was a sophomore," he added. "Then again when I found out about college . . . getting into the school I wanted, after pretending it wasn't a big deal."

Jeff wasn't sure exactly when he'd decided to bring Mari here, because he truly didn't believe he'd planned it. But watching her all day— interacting with his family— everything had sort of shifted into place. He'd suddenly just— *known*. That Marisol was the one. Finally realizing he was in love with her had been a colossal moment. And ever since then, the night couldn't get here fast enough.

"And now, tonight . . . sharing this with you." When she shifted closer, Jeff caught her— eager to hold her— eager to share his discovery with her. As though he'd waited his whole life for this very moment.

"I can see why you love this place. Beautiful and a little remote from a distance . . . but up close, it's steady and constant, watching over everyone below." Lowering her gaze from the sky, she smiled. "I would have loved having this place— like my own secret hideout."

When Marisol smiled, his heart lurched. Right now, he needed her. So very much. As a boy, Jeff had envisioned bringing someone up here— someone special— who would appreciate the significance of his hidden treasure. Years passed and he'd grown jaded. He'd convinced himself he didn't need to share this place with anyone— that it had been a childish fantasy better kept to himself. Like he'd kept his life to himself.

"Mari- I know it's only been a few months . . . and— I think you know me well enough by now to believe me when I say . . ." Suddenly overcome with doubt, his fingers tightened convulsively on hers. What if *she* wasn't ready? He'd never been in this position with a woman—of not knowing the outcome. Maybe this wasn't the right time . . . Maybe he should just wait. What if— she didn't want to hear this?

"Jefferson? What's wrong?" Confusion flared in her beautiful eyes.

"I should have planned this better," he confessed. "In my head— I swear I sounded so much better. I'm just going to say something— and I'm not looking for you to answer— yet . . . because this has sort of taken me by surprise-" Summoning his courage, Jeff dragged in a steadying breath. "What I'm trying to say is . . . I'm pretty sure-" Shaking his head, he corrected himself. If he couldn't be honest now, when the hell would he? "Actually, I'm completely sure. Marisol, I'm . . . in love with you."

Staring at him, her beautiful eyes shocked— it seemed as though days passed before Marisol's radiant smile eased some of the tension coiling through him.

"That's a huge relief. Because . . . I'm completely sure I'm in love with you, too."

Slipping her arms around him, Marisol felt a shudder ripple through him. And knew her heart would burst from the sheer wonder of this moment. Jefferson *loved* her. He trusted her. With something he cared deeply about. She knew what this place meant to Jeff. From what he'd said . . . and what he hadn't. As though he'd been afraid to let her know how important it was.

"I should have said it better," he muttered against her forehead. "You deserve beautiful words."

"Your words were perfect." Smiling, Mari reached up, brushing her lips against his. And felt his amazing arms wrap around her, steadying her. Jeff took his time, nibbling at the corner of her mouth, before drifting to her jaw.

"I love you, Mari. I've never said that before," he confessed. "I guess that's why it took me so long— first to realize it . . . and then to finally admit it to myself."

"I was praying I wasn't the only one." When his mouth found her racing pulse, he raised his head, his smile knowing. She shuddered. "This is too beautiful a spot for you to be torturing me."

"You've tortured me for three months now," Jeff admitted. "And I'm starting to realize this feeling will never go away." His breathing unsteady, he grazed her bottom lip with his teeth.

Moaning, Marisol moved against him, equal parts frustration and desire. He was full and hard against her stomach. And she was slowly going up in flames. "Dios— we should have brought a blanket."

Pausing in his effort to drive her slowly out of her mind, Jeff smiled against her lips. "Baby, turn on the flashlight."

Her thoughts scattered, she had trouble concentrating. "Why?" Guiding her hand, he clicked on the light. She followed the direction of the beam . . . to a spot just beyond where they stood. And Mari laughed with delight. On top of a thin foam cushion, a blanket was spread out. Next to it sat a backpack. On a corner of the blanket lay a bottle that looked suspiciously like champagne, along with two glasses.

"This is the most romantic thing anyone has ever done." Grateful for the darkness, she hoped he wouldn't see the tears she blinked back. But she suspected he could hear them in her overwhelmed voice. "I love you, Jeff."

"Te amo. Only you, Marisol." Removing the flashlight from her trembling hand, Jeff took her in his arms. In the moment before he kissed her, she would have sworn her heart stopped beating. The expression in his beautiful eyes was one she'd never seen before. When he kissed her, it was unlike anything she'd ever experienced. It felt . . . sacred.

And then, there was only him. His strong arms holding her, guiding her to the blanket. The whisper of clothes being tossed aside as they met eagerly. The delight of touching him and being touched— by someone who knew how to make her body sing. And when he finally entered her, her sob of wonder joined his groan of fulfillment.

Much later, as they lay side by side on the blanket, Jeff felt Marisol's hand searching for his. An overwhelming sense of rightness settled over him when their fingers entwined. Staring at the stars overhead, he realized this moment was exactly the way he'd imagined it all those years ago. Sharing his favorite place with the perfect person. The one meant for him. Marisol shivered next to him as the breeze cooled their overheated bodies. Shifting toward her, he propped himself up on one elbow, admiring her beautiful body. Unable to stop himself, he lowered his mouth to an irresistible, perfect breast, pausing when it pebbled under his tongue. "So beautiful, Mari."

Her sharply indrawn breath made him smile. For two hours, he'd made love to her— his body relentless in bringing her pleasure. And each time it grew better. Every shiver, every moan. Each time Mari quaked in his arms . . . each time her beautiful eyes widened, then glazed over with passion— his body answered. And now, as Marisol stirred next to him, wanting him as desperately as he wanted her— Jeff acknowledged what he'd finally confessed to her tonight.

He loved her. He loved Marisol. And he would never stop loving her. When it hadn't been in his life, Jeff had never understood how anyone could possibly believe in love— in the theory that there was a single person out there who could complete your life. He'd always assumed Jake had gotten lucky. And then Harry, too. But he'd never believed it would happen to him.

"As much as I would love to do this again, we should probably be heading back." Reluctantly, he draped his shirt over her shivering body.

She sat up, beautiful hair in wild disarray. "No fair. You shouldn't start something you're unable to finish."

Jeff grinned over her disgruntled expression. "Unable?" In a heartbeat he shifted over her. "Is that a challenge?"

Mari's eyes were luminous as she answered his smile. "It's okay. I know you're tired . . ."

"Never for you, Marisol." Tugging the shirt away, he tossed it aside. His fingers traced slowly down her stomach, each muscle contracting at his touch. When he reached her fold, he caressed her, his fingers confirming she was already wet for him. Her body rose against his hand, suddenly making it difficult for him to breathe. Entering her swiftly, he swallowed her gasp of excitement. As she tightened around him, Jeff grew mindless to anything but the pleasure she was giving him. When he came deep inside her, it was an explosion of light and sound that left him reeling. He muttered yet another truth to her. "I will never, ever be tired of you."

The next week passed in a whirlwind for Marisol. In a few short weeks, Hector would be out of school. He was already looking forward to attending summer day camp. The end of school would free Mari up in the afternoons to visit donors instead of being tied to the school bus schedule. She needed to make a final push for donations to finish paying Specialty for the new wing.

"Damn those framer men. They're trackin' sawdust all over the place. We need to talk with Hank about this. He needs to make them clean up their mess every day." Seated across from her, Sharon fumed about the latest inconvenience. Marisol nodded to make her happy.

Construction at New Beginnings had reached a boiling point of progress that involved a frenzy of activity both in and outside the shelter. Though the noise and dust and crowds of work crews were testing Sharon's and the rest of the staff's sanity, Marisol passed through the cacophony in a haze of happiness.

"I know. Jeff leaves his clothes everywhere."

Glancing up, Sharon's eyes narrowed in suspicion. "Sugar? Are you even listenin' to me? Earth callin' Planet Lovestruck. Are you there, Mari?"

"Of course I'm here. I'm sitting right across from you." She was in love with Jefferson Traynor. And Jeff was in love with her. Her days were spent smiling, no matter what issue arose.

Sharon snorted. "You've gone as moony over Stud Muffin as Annie has over Hank. I've lost my foreman and my best volunteer in the space of a week. Are you next?"

"I'm busier than ever," she protested. "If I'm mooning, it's productive mooning." Mari grinned when the older woman rolled her eyes.

"Spare me all this love going 'round. What are we going to do when Annie moves out?"

Aware that Sharon was working up a head of steam, Mari shifted her focus. "Annie was excessive with her hours because she was basically trapped here. Now that's she's safe to move, we won't lose her forever. Until she finds a nursing job, she's going to continue to help us out."

"At least we're freeing up a family space," Sharon agreed. "That waiting list is long. Whoever has the misfortune of being next on the list will have big shoes to fill."

Checking her watch, Mari rose from her desk. "Hector's bus is in fifteen minutes. I need to head out there."

Nodding, Sharon's gaze was fixed on her computer. "When you come back, can you check in with Hank to remind him we need an updated construction schedule? Now that they're working inside, we need to huddle with the staff at least once a week so we can plan how to work around the construction."

Waving to Pete as she left the shelter, Mari's mind sifted through a dozen different issues. Work was getting crazy— her days running together in a blur. To top it off, her parents were visiting this weekend. She still hadn't managed to find the right time to tell Jeff about her former relationship with Nick. Now— she'd be forced to do it tonight. The last thing she wanted was for her parents to mention the incident casually in his presence. It wasn't fair to blindside Jeff with something she should have explained months ago.

This would be the first time her family met Jefferson— with the exception of Manny, who, as far as she knew, hadn't returned since stalking them in April. Though he'd certainly reported back to her father on the details of his surveillance trip, she hadn't heard a peep from her sisters. Surely, if her mom knew the full story, then Serafina and Caridad would have pounced on her for details.

It wasn't as though she was worried about their visit. Her mother and sisters were going to love Jeff. Her overprotective father— perhaps not so much. But that would be the case no matter who she'd eventually brought home. Luis Ortega would spend the entire weekend grilling Jeff like a Cuban chorizo over a low, steady heat. In spite of the quiet strum of dread pooling in her belly, Mari chuckled. Jeff was about to experience a close encounter with a patriarchal cattle prod.

Her thoughts drifted to Luz Covas. Since the visit with Hector ten days earlier and her belligerent demands for a reinstatement of parental rights, she'd gone suspiciously quiet. Relief over Luz' disappearance warred with Mari's desire to just get the adoption over with. Luz's demands fluctuated with her drug use. Before her recent visit, she'd gone eight months without contact. And it had been wonderful. When Luz was using, she didn't care about anyone or anything. But Hector's mother was never really gone for good. Unless the court agreed to move up the date of her adoption hearing, the best Mari could hope for was Luz just staying away.

Ignoring the seductive aroma of baking bread, she studiously avoided the bakery as she turned the corner. She'd be faced with the same dilemma on the return trip— only with Hector, it was always the brightly iced cupcakes he wanted to indulge in. Clearing the corner with her willpower still in check, Mari heard her phone beep and smiled when she heard Jeff's husky voice. "Hey, I'm on my way to pick up Hector at the bus stop. Are you at the shelter?"

Savoring the sound of his confident, sexy rasp, Mari slowed her pace to a stroll. Something about talking with Jeff on the phone felt intimate. It reminded her of talking with him late at night, sharing their thoughts in the dark. "You don't have to meet us. We'll be back in probably— ten minutes." Since he was obviously excited about a small toy he'd picked up for Hector, she let him convince her that he should join them for the walk back. "Okay, I'll be waiting at the bus stop."

Checking her watch, Marisol hastened her pace. Hector's driver was usually prompt. Gladys had been driving the route for nearly twenty years. Only a block away, Mari saw the bus in the distance and hustled the last half block. As Hector's bus approached, Mari could see Gladys at the wheel. Smiling, she raised her hand to wave.

Gladys' expression went quickly from friendly recognition to puzzlement. By the time she pulled to the curb, Marisol sensed an undercurrent of anxiety. Something was wrong.

Jerking the bus to a halt, the elderly woman slammed on the brakes. Concerned, Marisol took a step back. When the door jerked open, Gladys flew down the steps, her skin blanched, her eyes shocked. *What on earth*— was she ill? Lord— was she having a heart attack?

"Gladys? What's wrong?"

"Oh my God— oh my God-"

It took only a moment for Marisol's blood to ice over. It suddenly hurt to breathe around the stabbing panic in her chest. "Where's Hector? Gladys? *Where* is Hector?"

Turning around, Gladys lumbered back up onto the bus, snatching her radio. "Dispatch— dispatch— we have a code ten. I repeat, a code ten."

As the scratchy voice of the dispatcher repeated back the code, Gladys grew hysterical. "Call the police," she shouted. "A child has been kidnapped from stop number twelve."

Kidnapped.

"Hector," she whispered. Over the roaring in her ears, Marisol heard the frantic terror in the elderly woman's voice as she provided their location.

Fumbling with her phone, Marisol couldn't prevent the sobs cascading from her chest as she dialed 911.

Whistling, Jeff rounded the corner, eager to show Hector the balsa wood airplane they would assemble after dinner. He'd seen it at lunchtime and promptly remembered how much he'd loved playing with them as a kid. After baseball practice— and prior to Mari scolding them about bath time, he and Hector would have a brief window of opportunity to launch a few test flights from the deck. Grinning, he was already imagining the feasibility of launching from Hector's upstairs bedroom window— and how they'd get away with it without Marisol finding out.

Life was good. Amazingly good. The addition at New Beginnings was ahead of schedule, Jake had just given him the go ahead to price three new projects— and he was in love with Marisol Ortega. Ever since he'd finally said the words aloud, Jeff had discovered he couldn't stop saying them. He didn't *want* to stop saying them.

If anyone had suggested to him three months, two weeks and four days earlier that he would be off-the-charts in love with someone, Jeff would have laughed in disbelief. He would have bet thousands of dollars against the prediction and been completely confident he'd win such an easy sucker's bet.

The strangest thing about this new life— this new perspective— was how freeing it had been. Through the filtered lens of his parents' divorce, Jeff had completely overlooked so many facts. That his parents' marriage had actually been good for many years. That they had truly loved each other. That they *still* loved and respected each other. He'd never bothered to weigh the other variables— too much focus on work, too much outside stress— that had taken such a heavy toll on his parents' relationship. He'd synthesized all the bad emotions— all the anger and fear, the isolation he'd experienced those last few years of high school, and those images had become the ones embedded in his memory. Like a talisman, Jeff had carried them inside him as an adult. As though the only true way to ever prevent being hurt by a woman was to completely avoid any emotional connection.

The sound of sirens in the distance broke into his thoughts. Lots of sirens, he corrected. Growing closer by the second. His skin prickled to attention as Jeff realized the wailing sound was damn close to where he was heading— Hector's bus stop. Unsure what he would find, he began to run. Each step he took, Jeff grew more certain that something was terribly wrong. Rounding the corner, his eyes snapped pictures. The bus pulled over at an odd angle— as though it had pulled up too fast. Marisol— God . . . had she been hit? Police officers milling through the street. Where was Mari? The knot of fear in his chest loosened only slightly when he saw her. Marisol's back was to him, but it was definitely her. And she was alright. Whole. Standing upright. Not bleeding.

But then she turned in his direction. The terror etched on her face caused him to stumble. Her eyes— wide and vacant— as though she'd seen something unspeakable. Jeff was suddenly overcome by a sense of anguished desperation— as though he'd stepped into a force field of agony. Then Mari's eyes finally focused— locking on him as he closed the distance between them— as he ran to reach her. And Jeff knew. It was something awful. *Hector.*

"What is it? What's happened?" Jeff wrestled through the gathering crowd. Onlookers asking questions. Damn them— couldn't they step back? Just get the hell out of the way? He heard the word 'kidnap' from one of the shopkeepers milling around on the sidewalk.

Mari was in shock when he reached her. Her eyes huge and starkly blue in her deathly pale face. Shaking with fear. "What happened? Mari? Honey— tell me what's happened."

"Hector," she whispered. "He's g-gone. Gladys— she . . . let him off t-two stops back."

"Why the hell would she-"

Her shoulders shaking, Mari began sobbing. "There was s-someone waiting for him— she h-had a wig on. And sunglasses."

Cursing, Jeff pulled her into his arms. He wanted desperately to shout, to swear, to hit something. To rail at the gods for allowing something like this to happen. "Luz. It was Luz."

She nodded against his chest, still quaking violently. "Gladys said Hector s-stopped. On the bottom step. As though— he knew . . . he knew it wasn't r-right. But she was distracted. And she sh— shooed him off the bus so she could stay on schedule."

Tightening his hold on her, he rested his head on top of hers, as though by doing so, he might be able to absorb some of her violent tremors into his own body. "Did she see anything else?"

Inhaling a shuddering breath, Mari released it slowly, the effort to calm herself probably the only thing keeping her from completely breaking down. "As she pulled away, Gladys started thinking it was odd for him to be picked up in the wrong place. She watched them in the rearview mirror."

"Did she see anything helpful— a car? Another person? Where the hell is this other bus stop?" One arm still wrapped around her, Jeff tugged out his phone. He needed his brother-in-law. He needed access to information. Charlie could relay details he wouldn't be able to get from the local cops.

"She saw Luz tug him across the street. Gladys says she realizes now that Hector was fighting her, but in the mirror, it just looked like she was in a hurry. She said Luz got into a car parked at the corner."

"What color? What make? Model? Anything? Does she have *anything* that can help us?" His voice hoarse with anger, the desire to shout was growing stronger. But if there was ever a time for Jeff to not lose it—that time was now. He had to stay focused and calm. He had to keep his brain functioning instead of seizing up in terror.

"Only that it was dark blue. And old. Rusted. A car— not a truck." Her eyes distracted, Marisol tried to remember. "And there was at least one hubcap missing on the driver's side."

A cop was approaching them. Jeff saw him separate from a huddle, heading in their direction. Nodding to him, he released Marisol. "Honey— I think they need to talk to you."

Disoriented, Mari lifted her head from his chest. "Okay— will . . . will you wait for me? W-will you still be here?"

His heart aching for her— for them . . . he slowly nodded. "I'll be right here."

Several phone calls later, a beehive of activity had begun at New Beginnings. Jeff had called everyone he could think of to help them. Though it was clearly a matter for the police— and the feds, as of forty-five minutes earlier— Jeff knew he couldn't just sit around and wait for something to happen. Whether his actions would be helpful or not— he had to *do* something. Anything. Or he'd go crazy.

Two hours had ticked by since Hector disappeared. Two hours. He could be anywhere. Luz could be driving somewhere— far away. Jeff swallowed around the lump that had stuck in his throat, his jaw working to dislodge the terror. She could have holed up somewhere. Somewhere terrible. Disgusting. Dangerous. Or she could have done the unthinkable. Though his brain wanted to tumble there— to the terrible, dark place without any hope— he couldn't allow it. Thinking that way would paralyze him.

Hank and Big Pete were mobilizing a group of volunteers. Sharon had contacted Marisol's family. They'd piled into cars and were on their way from Baltimore. After contacting Charlie, who had already heard about the kidnapping internally, Jeff had called his brother. In turn, Jake had called Harry and they'd shut the office down. Through the field grapevine, several superintendents from other Specialty project sites had shut down their projects and were now gathering in the shelter's parking lot, taking direction from Hank. Big Pete had mobilized a motley crew of concrete, drywall and framing subcontractors who were eager to help if they could.

If he hadn't been numb— with fear and despair, Jeff would have smiled over the unity his family had shown— both his work family and his real one. He watched Jake's wife Jenna as she arrived to join his parents. Together, they were helping Marisol hold it together until her parents could arrive. Harry's wife Kendall had driven to Jake's house to babysit all the kids.

"Jeff— can you come here a sec?" Hank's gravelly voice broke into his thoughts. "We think we might have something promising."

Hope flared through him like an electrical current. Anything. Anything would be better than just sitting here. "What is it?"

Scratching his head as they headed for the parking lot, Hank gave it to him straight. "Could be nothin'. Could be a wild goose chase. But Pete thinks he's found a connection."

"Pete? *Pete* thinks he's found something?" His hope dissolving in frustration, Jeff tried not to be discouraged. "God, Hank— he sees conspiracies in every delivery truck."

Jerking his arm, Hank stopped him as they approached the parking lot. "I *said* it could be a wild goose chase, son." The older man stared at him hard— staring right through him. "Now— get yourself together. You're not helping anyone with that attitude. We've got a lot of people here who are willing to traipse into the nastiest areas of this city to look for your boy. So, you need to snap out of it."

Dragging in a tortured breath, Jeff nodded. He'd needed a headslap to clear it— and Hank had just delivered. Big time. "You're right, man. I'm sorry. I'm— I'm a little crazy right now."

"You're actually not much worse than your usual crazy."

Forcing a smile he didn't feel, Jeff knew he would have to go through the motions until they uncovered more information. It would be the only thing to keep him sane. "What does Pete think he's discovered?"

"Okay— so here it is. Pete has been keeping a diary since the start of construction."

"His notebook? Yeah . . . I know." Distracted, he wondered where this was leading.

"Well, I never knew about it until he managed to track me down last week when I went after Phil."

"He keeps track of . . . everything. Cars. Delivery trucks." He thought of Marisol's brother tailing her. Pete's dire warning months earlier about the red truck . . . that had turned out to be Manny.

"Exactly. Among other things, he keeps lists of every car— within a two block radius of the shelter. And he updates the damn thing hourly. That's how he traced Phil's car— through the plate number."

"He— he tracks plate numbers?" A cold chill swept through him. "So— if Luz has been watching this place . . . watching Hector's schedule . . . then she might be in his notebook."

"Might," Hank emphasized. "If she was driving, or— even if she had someone driving her around," he confirmed.

"God— he keeps plate numbers." Lightheaded over the possibility of a lead— even a slim lead, Jeff quickened his pace. "A blue car— dark blue . . . sounded roughed up from the bus driver's description."

Patting his shoulder as they approached the crowd in the parking lot, Hank pushed him forward to where Big Pete stood. "Pete— tell him what you got."

CHAPTER 12

"Here, Sugar. Drink this."

A cup of something hot was shoved into Marisol's hands. Like an automaton, she raised it to her lips— needing both hands to get the cup to her mouth. She couldn't stop shaking. The violent tremors had taken over her limbs the moment she'd heard that Hector was missing. And now they'd taken up residence.

"Marisol— sweetie, your parents are coming." Sharon's sturdy cocoa hands grabbed hers, rubbing them as she spoke. As though she had the power to transfer her warmth into Mari's icy, lifeless body. "They should be here in the next half hour."

Mari nodded, because she knew it was what she was supposed to do. Acknowledge people. Acknowledge kindness. But the fact was, she wasn't even there anymore. It was as though she were outside her body— watching everyone fluttering around the crushed, broken shell of a woman. The other Marisol was hunched over in a chair— her face aged at least ten years— her eyes wide and vacant as they stared at the blank wall. Was this it, then? Was this her breakdown?

The ghost Marisol wanted to drift away from the crowd. From the noise. From the terror she was experiencing. She wanted to be invisible— so no one would be staring at her, talking about her in hushed tones— about her loss. About her trauma. So no one would bear witness to this unspeakable pain.

Even in this otherworldly state, Mari was capable of bargaining. With God. With anyone who could bring Hector back to her. She would take a beating— worse than anything Nick had inflicted. Was she being punished for being so happy? Had she grown arrogant in her life? She would give up her happiness. Would that be enough? Her wonderful little boy. Her new building. And now— the perfect man. Was it all too much for one person to deserve?

The only thing keeping Mari from splintering away from the broken woman in the chair was Hector. The thought of him. Trapped somewhere. Frightened. Cold. Hungry. Possibly being abused. Possibly worse-

Bolting from her chair, Marisol finally felt her soul surging back into her body. And it hurt. Everything in her body hurt. But breathing was the worst— each breath twisting a knife through her chest. "I can't sit here. I've got to do something."

Eyes wide, Sharon stared at her, finally nodding. "Anything, Mari. Just tell me. Tell me what you want to do."

"I want Luz's file. The one we have here— and the one downtown. Do you know anyone who could get us a copy of that one?"

Pursing her lips, Sharon slowly moved to her desk, snapping on the computer screen. "I think I know someone who can help us out."

"Charlie— just listen to me." His fingers clenched tightly around his phone, Jeff wanted to hurl it against the wall. "I've got eleven solid leads on a license plate. Are you saying you don't want them?"

It was probably better that his brother-in-law was safely out of reach right now, or Jeff would seriously be contemplating choking him. What good was having a cop in the family if he wasn't willing to help? "So— I give them to you, but you won't tell me who they belong to? We need help narrowing them down. Addresses would probably do that for us."

Jeff was seething. It was a friggin' miracle. Big Pete had performed a miracle right here on earth. He'd laboriously documented every vehicle that had passed within a two block radius of New Beginnings.

Hourly.

For the past four months.

And now that they had solid information, his dickhead brother-in-law was going all 'strict procedures' on him. "I know about the feds, Charlie. We're living this hell, remember?"

Dragging his free hand through his hair, Jeff settled back against the building. Big Pete, Hank, his brother, and Harry . . . all stood waiting for Charlie to run the damn plates and give them a corresponding address. It wasn't as though they were planning a vigilante mob. Hell— the addresses alone would help them eliminate half the vehicles on their list. The people who worked and lived in the area and by chance had happened to park near the shelter in the past month. One thing was damned sure— Luz didn't live anywhere nice.

Once they had a narrowed down list, the plan was to break up into groups and drive to each address. If anything looked promising, they could call the cops to raid the house. Instead, his brother-in-law was feeding him a state police line of bullshit about the bureaucratic mess that occurred when the feds became involved.

All Charlie's excuses confirmed for Jeff was that the cops would be moving more glacially than he'd previously assumed. Pushing off the wall, he paced the length of the newly poured sidewalk. Not watching where he was going, he brushed past two men, nearly equal to each other in height and burliness. "Sorry," he said absently as he strode past. Barely six feet past them, he exploded, his fury nearly volcanic. "Dammit, Charlie— I love this girl. I love her son. You've got to help me."

Cursing over his brother-in-law's adamant refusal to fork over the addresses, Jeff hung up, resisting the urge to hurl his phone to the pavement. Slowly turning around, he was surprised to see the two men still standing in the growing shadows. Watching him. Waiting for him. Taking a step closer, Jeff finally recognized one of them. "Manny— is that you?"

Marisol's brother stuck out his hand. "Hey, Jeff. This is my father, Luis." Jeff turned to face the father of the woman he loved. Their introduction couldn't possibly have come at a worse time. Barely able to function, Jeff knew he was not acting remotely civilized. Wordlessly, he extended his hand.

Luis Ortega held it, sizing him up in the rapidly approaching dusk. "You're the guy? With my Marisol?"

"Yes, sir. I'm . . . the guy." The guy who was hopelessly in love with his daughter. With a woman who was inside this very building— falling apart. And there was not a damn thing he could do to help her . . . to ease her distress in any way. Yeah— he was *that* guy.

Luis Ortega's face was nearly expressionless, except for his dark eyes, which seemed capable of burrowing deep within him— missing nothing along the way. Marisol had told him a little about her father— in preparation for this weekend. According to Mari's description, Luis Ortega had been tough, strict, loving and loyal. With the exception of his mysterious job, her father was an open book. What you saw was what you got. Judging by the current expression on his face, it was a prickly, brooding book.

"How's my girl holding up?"

His facade beginning to crumble, Jeff hesitated. "Not well. She's— holding up. But— we're trapped in a nightmare-" When he heard his voice begin to crack, he knew he'd be better off not speaking. As though his brother could sense the terrible vibe emanating from him, Jake appeared at his side. "Mr. Ortega? Nice to meet you. I'm Jeff's brother, Jake."

Grateful for his brother's presence, Jeff felt Luis' eyes still appraising him. "Did I hear right? You said you've got license plate numbers?"

"Yeah-" Jake turned to him. "Did you manage to get anything out of Charlie?"

Joining them, his cousin Harry quickly explained to the Ortegas how they'd come up with the plate numbers and that once filtered, the lead was likely a strong one.

"He won't give us the addresses. With the feds involved, he can't risk releasing that information. Says it's a leak and he'd get fired over it. But he promised to let us know as they make any progress." Jeff felt dull, listless. Unable to help Marisol.

He was surprised a moment later when Luis patted him on the shoulder. "Give 'em to me. I can get the addresses. Then we go check each and every one of them." When Jeff handed him the piece of paper, Luis turned to his son. "Manuel— get my secure phone from the car."

"Mari, love— how can I help you? What are we looking for?" Bridget Ortega sat with her daughter, wanting desperately to help. Yet, Mari knew there was nothing that could ever make her feel better. Not until she had Hector back.

"I don't know, mama. I don't know. I just know I have to look."
Marisol poured over the files on the table, as though possessed by
demons. Like a bereaved person who suddenly feels the violent
urge to scour an entire house to fill the aching void of a loved one's
death, Marisol was processing her grief and desperation over
Hector by maniacally reviewing data. Everything they had on Luz
Covas. Every minute detail. Every absurd, stupid, inconsequential
bit of information. Because it was all she had. It was all she could
do.

Her poor mother sat beside her, helpless to console her rapidly
deteriorating daughter.

"Find anything yet?"

Jenna's soft voice pierced through the cottony thickness of her
despair. Like a too-heavy blanket, smothering her, it threatened to
suffocate her. "Not much. Lots of notes from DSS regarding her
health . . . her fitness— or lack of it." Burying her head in her
hands, Marisol felt tears burning the back of her eyes, clogging her
throat. "Why they delayed the adoption for so long— I'll never
understand."

Mona Traynor joined them at the table. Behind her, her former
husband carried a tray of sandwiches and drinks. While Marisol
appreciated Linc's gesture, the thought of food— of anything in her
stomach— made it roil with nausea. But the others were likely
hungry.

"What about the car?" Mona's question penetrated the
uncomfortable silence. "Would there be anything in a file
somewhere that talked about her visits?"

Her vision clouded, Mari raised her head. "What do you mean?"

"Like in prison-" Pulling out a chair, Jeff's mother sat down
opposite her. "You have to sign in and you have to provide your
vehicle information. Would there be anything like that?" The older
woman made eye contact with Sharon. "We'd be looking for
anything we could cross-reference to a visit."

"How could Luz even have a car?" Linc entered the
conversation. "I seriously doubt she could afford one— given her
lifestyle."

Jenna's indrawn breath was audible. "What if the same person
who drove the car today was also the person who brought Luz to
her DSS appointments?"

Sharon's seat scraped back, breaking the deathly silence. "I think you're on to something, Mrs. Traynor. We might even be able to get photo stills— from the parking lot cameras." Most state buildings have mounted cameras."

Latching on to hope— to the slightest possibility that they could find the needle in a monstrous haystack, Mari released a shaky breath. "How long, Sharon?"

"I got a few favors I can call in, Sugar. Let me make a couple calls."

Pacing the darkened parking lot, Jeff nearly crackled with energy. Four hours had passed. The sun had set. More than anything, he'd wanted to go inside the shelter— to console Marisol. To hold her. Yet, he was also afraid. Of seeing her face. The devastation she must be feeling. And to not be able to help her. It was too much.

So, he'd remained outside in the dark, telling himself she was surrounded by family, both hers and his. Telling himself they were working on leads. All while praying for something promising he could report to her. All while wishing he could just go to her.

"Jefferson?" Luis Ortega's subtle accent was unmistakable in the darkness.

"Sir? Do you have anything yet?"

Luis approached him, again with those damned eagle eyes appraising him. This was not Jeff's finest hour. Hopefully, Mari's father would not hold it against him.

"We've got the addresses, but I don't know this area. I want you to review them— make an educated guess on which ones are our likely targets. Let's rank them according to location."

Jeff accepted the printout, wondering why Luis carried a printer in his vehicle. "Okay— we've only got eleven. These three are out in the county. Not bad neighborhoods. I can't imagine Luz has any friends left who lead normal lives. So, I'd rank these last."

Through process of elimination, Jeff was able to get the total down to six possible addresses. After consulting with the motley crew in the parking lot, they narrowed the list down to four. Four addresses within the city's limits. Two of those were in the most notoriously violent projects in the city. The other two were in neighborhoods with slightly better economic conditions, but not enough so they could be ruled out as possibilities.

"So— what's our next move?" Luis stood next to him as they reviewed a map of the city.

"Each group is going to take an address and go check it out. We'll stay in touch by cell phone. If we can rule one out quickly, that team will provide backup at the next one on the list," Jeff explained. Pointing to an X on the map, he tapped the location. "In my opinion, this one is probably the most dangerous. I don't want any of the volunteers going there. I'll take it myself."

Nodding, Luis pulled him aside. "You, me and Manuel," he corrected. "*We're* gonna take that one."

Jake, Hank and Big Pete stood close enough to hear Mari's father. Pete straightened to his full height. "I don't know about you guys, but I'm goin' to that one, too."

Manny glanced at his father as some unspoken message passed between them. Manuel nodded. "Right. I'll get your toolkit."

"Jeff— where are you?" Marisol could barely contain the excitement in her voice.

Fumbling with the map, Jeff managed to get the phone to his ear. Jacked up about what they were about to undertake, he was having trouble with what were normally easy tasks. At least Big Pete had the foresight to task Manny with the driving. Jeff was relegated to the backseat where he could cause the least amount of damage. Him being a basket case and all. "What's happening? Is Hector— did she bring him back?"

"No." Her excitement deflated in the space of a single syllable. "But— we had an idea about Luz and where she might be holed up. Sharon was able to research visitors to the DSS. The parking lot is protected by cameras. Sharon's contact reviewed the film on the dates we knew Luz had appointments with her social worker. He was able to track a vehicle that was used on two of Luz's visits to DSS headquarters."

"Was it blue?"

"One time, yes. One time, no," Mari confirmed. "Did Charlie help you with the license plate idea? Because we have a few names and addresses."

"Uh-" Sensing Luis' gaze on him as he shifted in the passenger seat, Jeff glanced up. Luis gave a slight shake of his head—translating loosely to 'if you give away my secrets, you're a dead man'. "Yeah— uh, Charlie helped us out. Tell me the names you have so we can compare."

His heart already in overdrive, it nearly stuttered with joy when she relayed the names to him. Carefully exhaling a shuddering breath, Jeff kept his tone neutral. "Okay, Mari. I'll call you the second we know anything more-" He was patient while she reminded him to be careful. Despite knowing that every guy in the truck was listening in, Jeff didn't care. "I love you, too. Remember— don't leave the shelter."

The silence in the truck was deafening as Jeff ended the call. "Mari has a list-"

"Jesus, Jeff. We heard all that." Hank's irritable voice broke the silence. "Did you get anything?"

For the first time in the last five hours, Jeff experienced a powerful sense of hope. "Hell, yeah. We got something. One of the names matches exactly to the address we're heading to."

Resolve seemed to charge the atmosphere inside the vehicle. But it was Luis' determined expression that sent a twist of warning down Jeff's spine. He would not want to be on the receiving end of that expression. "Manuel . . . *vamonos*."

Underbelly. Seamy. Forgotten. Without hope. Any of those words would describe their location perfectly. Perched on the edge of the weedy, abandoned lot behind a structure that some might have called a house, Jeff inhaled another breath of decaying trash as the smell carried on the summer breeze. There was no 'downwind' from this neighborhood. The stench of rotting garbage and a decaying infrastructure permeated the air they were forced to breathe.

"Blue car in the driveway," Jake acknowledged. "Does it match the plate number?"

Big Pete, binoculars to his eyes, strained to confirm the number, the only light a dim glow from the street lamp. "First three digits are right. Damn it, Manny— slow down."

Lights out, Manuel crept slowly past the condemned structure before circling back around the block to view it from the rear.

Sliding from the rear seat, Pete and Hank left the vehicle. As the night slowly came alive with people forced by the stifling heat onto their stoops, Luis wanted them on sentry duty so no one could sneak up behind the truck.

"How we gonna do this?" Big Pete squatted next to the driver's window. "There's people roaming around everywhere."

Using a pen light, Luis was busy digging through his duffel. "You, my giant friend, are going to watch our six when we go in the front. Someone needs to guard my truck or it will be on blocks by the time we come out." Pausing in his search, he pointed a stubby finger at the back door, hanging drunkenly from its frame. "Hank will be stationed by the back door." Glancing at the house again, he pointed to Jake. "You will stand at the corner of the house- I want you to watch the windows on the side. No one in or out."

Hefting his duffel onto the seat between him and Manuel, he withdrew a gadget. "But before we do anything, I want to take a reading on the house." Flicking it on, he waited for the red light to turn green.

Hank was mesmerized. "What is that?"

Big Pete's grin was slow with recognition. "That's a damn homing device." Admiration in his eyes, his gaze locked on Luis. "Infrared?"

Luis nodded. "We're going to see if anyone is actually in this place before we hit it."

Sensing Jake's eyes on him, Jeff returned his stare, shrugging. How the hell did Luis Ortega *coincidentally* have a heat-seeking sensor in his possession?

Springing from the truck, Luis held the device in one hand as he slowly ran it over the exterior of the house. Without a word, everyone gathered around him. On the tiny screen, they witnessed two splotches of heat in the front corner of the house. "Okay- we have two on the left front of the house. None in the back." Raising the tool, he scanned back and forth across the second floor. Frowning, Luis focused again on the meter. "Right there. Upstairs . . . far right corner— in the back, I think. It's smaller than the two downstairs."

Jeff's heart leapt all the way to his throat. "Hector," he whispered, not wanting to jinx the hope charging through him. "Please, let it be him."

Luis took his time, scanning the house again. Jeff was jacked up— to go . . . to bust in— to race up those damn stairs and search for Hector. Yet, he knew they had to be cautious. Controlled. Disciplined. And tonight, he sorely lacked those qualities. The part of him that was forced to remain rational acknowledged real admiration for the degree of patience Luis Ortega was displaying. And the rest of him just wanted to shake the older man.

"Hold up— look at this," Luis' quiet voice commanded. Watching over his shoulder, they observed a blob of heat enter the house. Tracing their movement, one of the two heat sources left the corner, moving to the back of the house, to the spot where a kitchen would likely be located in a normal house. The red dots huddled together in the kitchen for two to three minutes, before the heat source moved again to the front door and the other returned to the front corner. Five minutes later, the same transaction occurred.

Unlike the rest of them huddled around Luis' infrared, Big Pete stared at the back of the house. "This is a hit house. That's where the drugs are. The transactions are taking place right there." He pointed to the darkened window. "But this isn't a big time dealer. This feels more like a user— who's only selling so he can keep using."

Turning to stare at him, Hank's scratchy voice asked the question they were all thinking. "Now— how the hell do you know that?"

"He doesn't have any heat. No guards. If this was a distributor, he'd have protection— and we wouldn't be standing thirty feet from his stash without getting shot." His gaze still locked on the house, Pete deflected the unspoken question. "Trust me. I know a little about this sort of place."

After twenty minutes observing the drug house's activity, Luis turned off the display. As he carefully tucked it back into the cushioned case, Manuel waited to retrieve his duffel. "We're going inside in ten minutes." Pausing, Luis scanned each face. "And not a damn one of you saw that equipment tonight."

"Remember, there might be a gun," Big Pete cautioned. "Jake— as soon as we go in, you call Charlie."

"Why don't I call Charlie now? Before any of us gets shot?" Always the voice of reason, Jake voiced the question they all had.

"And tell them what? That we're breaking into a drug house because we think there might be a kid in there? We have no proof— just suspicion. Do we really want to waste time explaining ourselves to the cops?" Annoyance threading his words, Pete sighed. "Look— one of them is Luz. She's what? Eighty pounds? And she's high. The heat in the corner hasn't moved since we got here. The other one is also high. He's dealin' a little, but he's shooting up with her. He goes back to the corner after each transaction."

Hank nodded. "I'm okay with those odds. And I don't want to get tangled up in a cluster with the cops if this is the wrong house. If this one ain't it, then we need to move on to the next."

"Let's go, already." Adrenaline careening through him, Jeff was at the end of his patience. Acknowledging he was on the losing side of the argument, Jake nodded.

Giving him a quick hug, Jake muttered a 'be careful', before Jeff crept into position at the side of the house. Hank was already in motion toward the back door as Manny ran for the far side of the house.

Nodding to Pete and Luis, Jeff offered up a silent prayer the next ten minutes would prove both fruitful and uneventful. That they'd leave this dreary place without anyone getting hurt and with Hector clutched in his arms. As they moved for the steps, Jeff stopped thinking at all.

Since the door was already open, there was no battering required. The acrid stench that greeted them was nearly overwhelming. Choking over the smell, Luis and Big Pete broke quickly to the right— moving toward the heat sources in the corner. His eyes adjusting to the murky darkness, Jeff launched himself up the stairs. Behind him, he heard Luis shout a confirmation of a female. A moment later, Pete's voice confirmed he'd neutralized the male.

His heart in his throat, Jeff reached the top of the stairs. Disoriented, he moved into the first room he found. The heat source had been in this vicinity. Tiny, cluttered with trash and disposed needles, Jeff repressed a shudder as his flashlight panned over the grungy mattress in the corner. Walking cautiously to the closet, he opened the door slowly. Flicking his light over the empty space, his heart stopped when the light passed over a backpack. A kid's backpack. And a thin cording of twine.

"Hector!" His voice suddenly hoarse, Jeff tried again. Turning on his heel, he moved to the next room. "Hector— buddy— are you here?" Hearing steps on the stairs, he met Luis and Jake as they entered the upstairs hallway.

"Anything?" Jake stuck his head into the trashed space that had once been a small bathroom. "Pete's holding the two downstairs. He recognized the woman from the video. Said it's Luz. But she's too high to tell him anything. She said something about selling a kid-"

Jeff's heart clutched with fear. "His— his backpack is in the closet. But he's not here."

Easing past them, Luis moved into the bedroom. Scooping up the backpack, he checked the contents. "It looks like he may have been tied up." Cursing violently, Luis finally revealed some of the tension he'd been suppressing. Cupping his hands to his mouth, he shouted. "Es Papi. ¿Dónde estás, pequeña?"

"We saw the heat spot," Jeff insisted. "Where the hell is he?"

"No one has come out. Hank would've seen him," Jake reminded, his voice grim. "We keep looking. The cops are on the way."

More afraid now than ever, Jeff nodded. "Is there an attic?"

Aiming his flashlight down the hallway, Jake acknowledged the possibility. "I'll check that."

Where the hell was he? Bolting for the stairs, Jeff headed back down, taking them two at a time. Luz was slouched in a chair in the corner.

"Luz! Where is he?" Not caring that he was shouting at her, Jeff wanted to shake her, but was acutely aware he was hanging by a thread. If he touched her, he might actually hurt her. Her glazed eyes told him she'd barely heard him. One eye blackened, she stared at him, unseeing. Two long scratches covered one malnourished cheek. This was Hector's mother? This starving, pathetic creature was the woman who'd borne the kid who'd taken ownership of his heart?

"Don't waste your time," Pete advised, tugging him away from her. "Just keep looking." He was standing guard over the guy he'd knocked out, in the unlikely event he came to. "She ain't going anywhere."

"Hector?" Shouting as he moved from room to room, Jeff finally approached the kitchen— or what would have been a kitchen if the space had been inhabited by humans instead of animals. Scuffed, discolored linoleum lead to blank spaces where appliances had once sat. Gaping holes in the wall where plumbing had been ripped out. Cabinet doors hanging or missing. The strong musty scent of mildew. Like an automaton, Jeff moved into the small pantry. A single light bulb fixture hung by a forlorn string.

"Hector— where are you, buddy? Please, God— where are you?" Running agitated fingers through his hair, Jeff felt the plunging sense of despair start to overtake him. Where would they search next? Had he left the house? Was he wandering in this god awful neighborhood? In the dark? Hiding somewhere they wouldn't be able to find him? Or worse— where someone else would?

The scratching sound from one of the cabinets made him think of a mouse. But the sudden realization that it was large enough to be a hiding place had Jeff dropping to his knees to throw them open.

"Hector? Are you in here?" Finding nothing in the pantry, he quickly retraced his steps to the kitchen. Jerking open the cupboard under the sink, Jeff froze when he discovered the little boy. A groan of relief was torn from his throat as he pulled Hector into his arms.

"Are you hurt? Did they hurt you, Hec?"

As Jeff's eyes adjusted in the murky room, he groped for his flashlight. With a spurt of fury, he discovered Hector's mouth was bound. As gently as he could, Jeff removed the tape. But his hands shook so badly, he did it with little finesse.

"Ow— that hurts, Jeff."

His eyes blurring, he apologized. "I'm sorry, buddy. I don't want to hurt you."

"It's okay." When his curly head flopped onto his shoulder, Jeff experienced the most powerful sense of relief he'd ever known.

Uncertain whether his legs would support him, he sank to the floor
with Hector locked in his arms.

"Can you untie me? I got's my feet undone and I ran downstairs
to hide. But I couldn't undo the knots."

Startled, he realized Hector's hands were tied together with
more of the twine he'd seen upstairs. The bastards had tied him up.
Tearing at the knots, Jeff freed him.

Hector wasted no time, throwing himself into Jeff's arms. "I'm
glad you're here." A moment later, his head popped up. "Is that
Papi yelling upstairs?"

"It's your Papi and uncle Manny," he confirmed, his chest so
tight with gratitude, Jeff could hardly breathe. "And Hank and Big
Pete and my brother, Jake."

"Why are you cryin', Jeff?"

"It's okay to cry when you're really scared or really happy. And
tonight I've been both."

"Cuz of me?"

"Yeah." Clearing his throat, Jeff yelled for Big Pete to notify the
others. Hearing sirens in the distance, he managed a smile. "There
are lots of people out looking for you, Hec."

"I maybe cried a little, too," Hector admitted solemnly. "But I
did what you told me."

As the rubbery sensation left his legs, Jeff rose to his feet,
Hector's arms still locked around his neck. "What's that?"

"I bit . . . and scratched an' punched."

Remembering Luz' black eye and the scratches on her face, Jeff
found his first smile of the endlessly long, bleak night. "I'm so
proud of you, bud. Good job."

With his free hand, Jeff searched his back pocket for his phone.
Dialing Mari's number, he handed the phone to Hector. "Let's tell
mommy you're okay."

"Mama? It's me, Hector."

Though the phone was nestled at Hector's ear, Jeff heard Mari
shriek, before bursting into tears. He heard the cheering in the
background— from countless friends and family— the shelter staff
and volunteers still gathered at New Beginnings— waiting
anxiously for news.

After several seconds, Hector's eyes flashed concern. "Mama's
still cryin', Jeff."

"I know, bud. Just tell her we're coming home."

"Damn it." Marisol fought to control her breathing as the panic attack hit. *Not again.* The last week should have been the happiest time of her life. Luz was in jail. The court, in its wisdom, had finally granted her greatest wish. The custody hearing had been moved forward. After the embarrassment of having to answer uncomfortable questions from the media— about why Hector had been stuck in the foster care system for the past three years. About why his biological mother had been allowed to retain parental rights after she'd tried to sell him-

Sinking into her chair, Mari dragged in shallow breaths. But the sensation of suffocating was so real. And terrifying. It was hard not to be terrified when she wasn't getting enough air. It was as though she'd regressed— back to the days after Nick. Sharon insisted the flashbacks were common after a scare. But knowing that didn't make the attacks any easier.

Now, instead of one giant secret, Mari was keeping two from Jefferson. First— about being beaten up by her boyfriend, and now— despite Hector being almost completely back to normal, she was dissolving into a basket case. How the heck was she supposed to tell Jeff that?

"He already suspects," she whispered. Jeff already sensed something was wrong. Thinking back to the previous night, Mari wanted to weep. Knowing she was troubled, Jeff had asked what he could do to help. He'd rehashed all the good that had come of the incident. When he'd confessed how grateful he was— to have her and Hector, she'd dissolved in tears. And for the hundredth time this week, he'd held her, comforting her.

"That's when you should have told him," she muttered miserably. A few shallow breaths later, Mari felt her heart rate begin to slow. The worst of it was over. *This time.*

How was she supposed to confess her pathetic fears to a man like Jeff? When he was so capable? So confident. Nothing scared him. He'd saved her child. He'd marched into a known drug house, and he'd found her son. Jeff claimed to love her. But— that was because he viewed her as strong— competent. *Normal.*

With all her issues starting to resurface— why would he want her now? Remembering her bargain with God, Mari questioned the fairness of unloading her baggage on Jefferson. When he could have someone completely normal. Someone who wasn't full of doubt. Who was strong enough to be his equal.

Letting him go would be the right thing to do. The sharp stab of agony caught Marisol by surprise. It would hurt. But— it would be worse to see his eyes. When he finally realized what she'd become. The admiration in Jeff's eyes would turn to pity. Would he stay then? Would she want him to? Out of some sense of duty instead of love?

She would always remember him. As the one who seemed to get her— who was completely in sync with her. Who knew what she was thinking without having to ask. She'd found The One. Jeff was it. And it had been amazing . . . while it lasted.

As tears streamed down her face, Mari knew what she had to do. She would tell him. Today. Maybe, if she'd met him sooner . . . there never would have been a Nick. She wouldn't be so damaged. And they would have been so unbelievably happy. But the past had a way of catching up when you least expected.

CHAPTER 13

"Mari, honey . . . what's going on?" Jeff tried to ignore the strum of unease lurking in his chest. She'd been so . . . distant the last few days. At first, he'd attributed it to stress— the overwhelming terror she'd experienced over losing Hector.

She shrugged, her eyes betraying utter confusion. "Jefferson— I've been thinking a lot— and I don't. . . I'm not certain-" Dragging in a shuddering breath, she released it slowly. "I think maybe we should . . . slow things down a little. Maybe take a break."

"Take a-" Though a chill swept over him, he immediately began rationalizing his worry. They'd been through an ordeal. A hellish nightmare that had taken a huge toll on *all* of them. Perhaps Mari most of all. She'd been jumpy and skittish all week— crying when she thought she was alone.

Hector, on the other hand, seemed almost back to normal. Aside from a few night terrors, and a new desire to sleep with a nightlight, Hector was, for the most part, back to himself. "Mari, I know this has been hard, but— I don't think we need a break."

"With everything that's happened . . . I think it will be safer to stay focused . . . on Hector. I can't risk losing him again."

"Luz can never touch him again. Hector is safe, love," Jeff reminded. "We've made sure of it."

"I want this adoption to happen and I'm afraid-"

Something was clearly terrifying her. But hell if he knew what it was. He gentled his tone. "What are you afraid of, Marisol?"

"I'm afraid of getting sidetracked. Jeff— I really care about you . . ."

"You love me," he corrected. Her too pale face was dangerously resolute. *What the hell was going on?*

"But I haven't been paying attention. Donations are slipping-"

It was as though Mari couldn't hear him—as though she'd left him and he couldn't figure out where she'd gone. Sickened, Jeff flashed back to his parents. To the overwhelming sensation he was about to be blindsided. "Am I to blame for that?"

"Of course not," she protested. "But I'm not as focused on my work. We've been in this amazing little bubble— you and I. And it's been wonderful. But this place has been my dream for years and it's finally happening. When you leave— these people still need me to be focused— to continue to help them."

Leave? His head jerked back. "Who said I was leaving?"

"It's what you do, Jeff. Why would I be any different?"

"Because I love you?" Frustration flashed through him. What the hell was this about? Gentling his tone when he wanted to push her to see sense, he tried again. "You know I love you, Marisol." Staring at her— through her . . . Jeff tried to read the dialogue in her head— because this sure as hell wasn't about him.

"Since I met you, I haven't looked at another woman. I— I haven't *noticed* another woman. Because you're it for me, Mari. And — I'm not leaving. But it sounds like . . . maybe you're leaving me. And you don't even have the courage to tell me why."

Pacing the room, he dragged agitated fingers through his hair. "What's the real reason, Marisol? And stop with the bullshit about work, because I'm not buying it. What are you so afraid of? Is this about the adoption? Is this about— a guy?" Dread coiled through him.

"No— yes . . . I mean, there was another guy . . . before you." Distracted, she shook her head, as though even she didn't quite know what was happening. "It ended . . . very badly. It took me a long time to get over it and I don't want that to happen with us."

"You're breaking up with me now so— we don't break up later?" Jeff tried to rein in his mounting desperation. She wasn't making any sense. This wasn't Mari talking.

"I love you Jeff, but I have to think about Hector."

"You don't think I'm good for Hector?"

"No— you're wonderful with him. I just think it would be better if we take a break-"

"You're . . . dumping me?" Jeff's heart stopped— then began thrashing painfully against his ribcage. "Because some other guy treated you badly— you're dumping *me*? Have I at least got that part right?"

The irony of his words was not lost on him. He'd broken up with dozens of women and never known the slightest bit of guilt. He'd deluded himself into believing they'd always known the score. They'd known he would never get serious. With anyone.

He'd never been the person being dumped. And while he'd never, ever made false promises to women, Jeff had known by the expression in their eyes— for some of them . . . they'd been way more attached to him than he'd ever been to them. He knew *exactly* what his own expression looked like. Because he'd seen it before— on the faces of women he'd left behind.

Hurt. Confusion. Bitterness. Wondering what they could have done wrong and whether there still might be a way to fix it. He was living it— right now. Marisol had dealt him a body blow.

Now, she would walk away. And Jeff didn't know why. He may *never* know why. And the pain of that just might prove to be unbearable. "What did he do to you, Mari? What could he possibly have done to make you so-"

Jeff swallowed around the lump in his throat. He was furious. And terrified. Raw, bitter . . . exposed. How could he have done this? He'd finally risked everything. He loved her. In a million different ways.

Marisol was the woman he'd hoped never to find. The one he'd been too afraid to search for. Jeff had known all along— that if he ever found her . . . he would be ruined. He would fall in love and he would never, ever be able to climb out again. Because when she left him— there would be nothing left.

But he'd pursued Mari anyway. He'd risked the pain because he couldn't stay away from her. She had destroyed him for any other woman. And now— she stood before him, ready to toss him aside— like some friggin' afterthought. How could she-

"What did he do?" he shouted, watching her flinch. "At the very least, I— deserve an explanation." His chest felt as though a building had just collapsed on top of him. And everything hurt— breathing, thinking, feeling. "Dammit, Mari— how can you do this to us? To me?"

Marisol winced as his acid words spattered over her. Jeff should have cared— that he was hurting her. That she was in pain. But—

damn it, she was *killing* him. Her face pale and drawn, her expression one of torture. The mesmerizing aqua eyes he adored held a sheen of misery. He would never see that color again without experiencing a gut punch of pain.

"What could he possibly have done to make you so . . . paralyzed with fear that you won't take a chance with me?"

"He . . . beat me."

Her whispered words convulsed into the chasm between them. And Jeff was too shaken by them, too electrified to speak. As they sunk in . . . as they reverberated through his stuttering brain, he staggered back against the wall.

An icy wash of shame drenched him as the blood drained from his head. "No, Marisol," he whispered. "Please . . . God, not you, too." Stumbling to the table, Jeff collapsed into a chair. And then dropped his head in his hands, as everything in his life crashed down around him.

Her brother keeping tabs.

Her family's caution. Her fierce protectiveness of Annie. Of all the women living in the shelter. Because . . . she was one of them. An agonized sound escaped his throat. God— how would he live with himself?

"It's okay," she whispered. "I s-should have— told you . . . a l-long t-time ago."

Mari's teeth were chattering, he realized, as though she'd caught a chill. She was in shock. He'd done this to her. Jeff heard her edge closer to the table, but was too ashamed to speak. He'd deliberately hurt her. So immersed in his own pain, he'd bullied her into explaining something he had no business demanding. Afraid of what he would see in her eyes, he was grateful for the tears blurring his. "Mari— I'm so sorry. God, can you ever forgive me?"

Warm fingers cupping his chin, she forced him to look at her. "There's nothing to forgive." Her eyes were puzzled. "Jefferson— *you* haven't done anything wrong. You've *never* done anything wrong. It's me— I'm not . . . right. I'm not ready-" Swallowing a sob, her voice cracked. "I might never be. I've been h-having flashbacks."

Her skittish behavior. The new wariness around him. He'd known something was wrong. "How can I help you?"

"I didn't want you to know," she admitted. "But I knew . . . you sensed it."

Why would she hide from him? "Marisol—there's nothing you could ever tell me that would make me love you less. When you hurt . . . I hurt."

"You deserve someone stronger. Normal-"

"Screw normal." At her startled chuckle, Jeff pushed back his chair, wanting desperately to hold her, but so afraid he might frighten her. When she slid into his arms, he crushed her against him, holding her as though his life depended on it. And damn it— he was pretty certain it did. When her arms crept around his neck, he drew in rasping breaths of relief.

"Mari— there's no one else for me. There never will be. I love you so much. I should have- I could have been more understanding-"

Her tremulous smile tickled against his neck. "How could you know w-when I wouldn't tell you?"

"Damn it, I should have been kind. I could have tried to discuss it with you. But all I heard was . . . you— didn't want me."

"I was afraid." Her voice was thick with unshed tears. "I'm still afraid."

His heart stopped. "Of me?"

She shook her head. "Never you, Jeff. I'm afraid of me."

Releasing a shuddering sigh, he felt the smallest amount of tension escape his chest. "Why?" Tears continued to slide from her beautiful ocean eyes and he patiently wiped them with his thumbs.

"I'm s-still angry with myself for what h-happened. And it sometimes makes me question my judgment."

Jeff digested her comment, acknowledging the swell of anger it caused. The bastard had injured her in more ways than just physically. But now wasn't the time for anger. It wasn't time for anything other than loving her. Reassuring her. Accepting that it would take her a while to feel comfortable with loving him. "You think . . . because he slipped under the radar— that you might misjudge me, too?"

She startled, her beautiful eyes widening in recognition. "I love you, Jeff. I know I love you. I just. . . I'm a little afraid of it." She sniffed back the tears that wanted to fall in earnest. "I want more than anything for us to be together. Yet— sometimes I feel terrified that if I let you in— you could hurt me. If you were to . . . change your mind."

"I can relate to that." Jeff smiled. "Loving you means I'm handing you the power to hurt me. And— while I really don't want you to hurt me. . . I can't stop loving you." He shrugged. "So— I'm just going with it. I love you. I love Hector. I want us to be together. And I want it as soon as you're sure about it, too."

Mari leaned in and kissed him. Lingered over it, enjoying the spark that ignited between them. Without qualm, Jeff took it deeper, reminding her of the crazy strong connection they shared. If there was even the slightest possibility he could utilize their house-on-fire chemistry to nudge aside any lingering doubt, he was prepared to burn the whole thing down.

Mari was the first to return to her senses, upon hearing one of the chefs in the hallway near the kitchen. Jeff pulled her closer, smiling when she sighed.

He hesitated several moments, uncertain whether he had the right to pose the question he wanted desperately to ask. Jeff knew he would have to accept her answer . . . knew he didn't have the right to push if she wasn't ready. But he wanted to know— everything. He wanted to be able to offer comfort. He wanted to understand what she'd been through.

God help him. He wasn't completely sure he could handle it. Hearing about someone hurting her- His body jerked in reaction.

She felt it, too. "Jeff? What is it?"

Sliding her fingers through his, Jeff needed to feel her warmth. "Could you please . . . when you're ready-" He swallowed around the concrete block in his throat. "Will you tell me what happened? I-I want to know . . . everything— but only if you want to tell me."

"I love you so much, Jeff." Clutching his hand, Mari's eyes were bright with tears. "Yes. I want you to know."

"Well, Jeffie . . . you should be proud." Linc Traynor sidled up to his son, a champagne glass in hand. The dedication of New Beginnings' new wing had been an enormous success. Donors, residents, volunteers, community members and a swarm of Ortegas and Traynors filled the new dining room. Big Pete stood guard, resplendent in the tuxedo Sharon had acquired for him. "This place has turned out amazing."

"Thanks, Dad— but I should be thanking you for pushing this project on me. Without you, I never would have met Marisol." Interrupted by a photographer, they paused to smile for his camera. "I've taken the new beginnings thing literally. And I think it's catchy." Jeff nodded to the spot in the corner where Hank Freeman wooed a radiant Annie.

They were joined by his mother, looking stunning and happy in her sparkling cocktail dress. She nodded approvingly. "I think happy and in love will do that to a person, Jeffie."

Jeff stared at his parents, acknowledging how comfortable they were together, arm in arm. Marisol's comments about their 'friendliness' flashed through his brain. She'd sensed something was up with them. "When are you going to tell everyone?"

Mona flashed a guilty look at his dad. "I knew it," he confirmed. "Mari was right. You two are back together, aren't you?"

"We didn't want to say anything— with you and Marisol announcing your engagement—and Harry and Kendall due any day— we didn't want to draw attention-"

"That's crazy. There's always room for more good news." Jeff pulled them in for a hug. "I'm so happy for you both."

"Well— we'd like to be the first to congratulate you on your engagement." Linc beamed. "You'll never find a finer woman. Where is she, by the way?"

Jeff searched the sea of people, his gaze not lingering to admire the new carpeting, tile, and artwork. He skipped over the double doors leading to the shiny stainless kitchen the chefs would now work in. Finally, they settled on Marisol. And his breath caught. She was especially beautiful tonight . . . her wild mane swept up, her shimmering gown revealing an expanse of honeyed skin he'd grown addicted to over the last seven months.

"She's heading this way." Surrounded by her sisters and the overprotective Manuel, Marisol was radiant. This was her night. Her dream. She'd worked so hard to achieve it. Pride swelled his chest. She was so important here— to so many people. Jeff's gaze locked on her hand, on the sparkling band gleaming there. Smiling, he remembered the climb to the plateau. At his favorite spot in the world, he'd asked her to marry him, slipping the ring on her finger as the sun rose. With the light warm on their faces, he'd kissed her, sealing their promise.

Though he'd never stop chasing her— he'd finally caught her hand. The adoption completed, Hector was Mari's son. Soon, Jeff would officially become his dad. He'd already completed the background check and all the paperwork. All that remained to make it official was their rapidly approaching wedding.

Hector poked him. "I wanna be in here, too." Slipping under Jeff's arm, he entered the circle he'd created with his parents.

"I hear you'll be a Traynor one day soon." Linc lowered his gaze to Hector.

Hec's earnest expression made Jeff smile. "Well, for now, I'm still an Ortega. But when Jeff marries us, I'm gonna be Ortega *and* Traynor. I want both names so I can remember."

"Remember what, Hec?" Hoisting the little boy to his shoulder, Jeff loved the feel of his sturdy little body cushioned against him.

"When Mari picked me."

"Picked you for what, sweet?" Mona gave his hand a squeeze.

"To be her kid." His grin was exuberant. "What if she'd wanted a girl instead?"

His mother's smile faltered. For a moment, Jeff thought she might cry. Hell— for a second, he thought he might, too.

"Are you sad, Miss Mona?" Hector's chocolate eyes were puzzled. "I think it's good she picked me cuz I'm really good at baseball and I 'member to make my bed every day. Almost."

His mother's smile was radiant. "I think she picked the best boy ever. With you and Alex, I'm going to have the two best grandsons ever."

"*Three* best grandsons," Hector corrected. "Remember? Aunt Kenny's baby is a boy, too."

Joining them, Marisol's dazzling smile was directed at him. Still slightly awed by how amazing his life had become over the last seven months, Jeff wondered whether the sense of belonging he experienced every time he looked at Mari would fade with time. Gazing at his parents, he had his answer.

"Where have you been?"

"I was just in the kitchen with our chefs— admiring my extravagant engagement present from Jefferson."

"What did Jake say when you told him you were donating all the kitchen equipment to the shelter?" His father's smirk suggested Linc already knew the answer to that question.

"He understood— eventually." Jeff smiled. "After reminding me again about the four mouths to feed . . . four cars . . . four college educations . . ."

"Mama— you already have a stove at home."

"I know, carino. Jeff gave me this one for our new building."

"We need a toast," Linc announced as he signaled a passing waiter. The cluster of Traynors wiped out an entire tray of champagne glasses. Hector in one arm, Jeff sought Mari's fingers. When she linked them with his, a sense of peace settled over him. Of exquisite rightness.

Linc raised his glass. "To New Beginnings. To all the souls who pass through these doors . . . may they find the help they seek. To all the hard-working volunteers who devote themselves to helping others."

Squeezing Mari's fingers as they shared a glass, Jeff leaned in to brush his mouth against her ear, loving the delicate shiver that coursed through her. "To my beautiful, talented, dedicated fiancée."

Her eyes lit with happiness, she smiled. "Thank you for my beautiful kitchen."

"Thank *you* for finally agreeing to go out with me." Chasing Marisol had been the smartest thing he'd ever done. He gazed at the circle that was his family. A circle that would continue to grow over time. The one constant in his life he'd always known he needed. And for him, Marisol was at the center of it. Everything he would ever want was right there in his arms.

Look for Book 4 of the Blueprint to Love series, Hank Freeman's story, **SHELTERING ANNIE.**
Coming Summer, 2016.

Love Under Construction . . .

Solitary widower Henry Hank Freeman has relearned how to be alone. In a world gone colorless with grief, he views life in varying shades of gray. Until bumping into Annie McKenna, a mysterious woman walking her own lonely path. But when their paths cross, he can see only light. And a rainbow of opportunity.

Annie McKenna doesn't need any distractions. Perpetually on the run from her abusive ex- husband, she has two kids to hide and protect. No job. No money. No hope. Until she meets Hank Freeman at the shelter she's living in. For the first time in years, she's awakened to a sharp sense of longing. For a normal life. With a man she can trust. But Hank seems too good to be true.

Falling for Annie and her boys was the easy part. But convincing her to build a new dream with him might take longer than the addition he's constructing for the shelter. And protecting them from her ex is a full-time job. Believing Henry's beautiful blueprint will take all the faith Ann can summon. She can't afford another mistake. Because where she's escaped from . . . mistakes can kill.

SHELTERING ANNIE
Available Summer, 2016

I hope you will enjoy an excerpt from
OUT OF THE MIST,
the first book in my new series, Can't Help Falling.
Coming April, 2016.

Out of Time . . .

Beaten and left for dead, Juliet awakens in the rain with no memory of how she ended up alone on an isolated road. After another attempt on her life, she'll have to pour her faith into the one man who's made it clear he doesn't trust her.

Injured drug agent Matt Barnes has seen just about everything in a decade battling the worst humanity has to offer. But he's never seen anything like Julie. The beautiful blonde reminds him more of sorority Barbie than a ruthless drug kingpin. But looks can be deceiving. He's got the bullet hole to prove it.

Juliet— and her memory are all he has in a case going nowhere. To erase the worst mistake of his career, his team will utilize her to lure the most dangerous drug lord he's ever battled. But will the woman he's fallen in love with ever forgive him for making her the bait?

OUT OF THE MIST

Available April, 2016.

Julie jolted awake to a cold raindrop sliding down her neck. Followed by another. Thunder vibrated, shaking the ground beneath her. Head swimming, she sat up, the earthy bloom of decaying leaves clinging to her sweater. She was alone in a ditch. With no memory of how she'd arrived there.

Wrestling a freight train of panic threatening to knock her flat, she released a calming breath. Great news— her lungs were working. "Even better." Her spine seemed intact. She wiggled her toes. Super duper. Her face however, held the drunken sensation of an injury she might be afraid to acknowledge in a mirror.

In the smothering darkness, pain slithered over her like crawling insects. "Oh, God-" Terror rose in her throat. *Was it really bugs?* Bolting to her feet, her wobbly stilettos sank in wet moss. If she'd known she was going to be kidnapped, she never would've worn new pumps.

"Ow. Ow. Ow." A sharp torque in her ankle toppled her back to the ground. Shoes should've been the last thing on her mind, but contemplating her shiny, never worn, sort-of-pinched-her-toes-but-she'd-bought-them-on-clearance Jimmy Choos was easier than wondering why someone wanted her dead.

"Try not to panic." Except fear had already taken over, tremoring her hands as she grasped handfuls of weeds to claw her way up the embankment— where she prayed she'd discover a road. "Piece a' cake." Yeah— dropped on the floor, frosting side down. Her desperate chuckle hinted at approaching tears. Who was she kidding? It was the *perfect* time to panic. She wanted to run—to the nearest source of light . . . safety . . . warmth. Cower under a blanket with her eyes scrunched shut.

When tires crunched on the gravel above, instinct had her shrinking back against the slope as she prayed. *Please, please don't see me.* Unable to rationalize her fear, the throbbing sense of dread hovered like the storm clouds overhead. Twin headlights loomed closer, casting exaggerated shadows on her hiding place.

A warehouse. A body. A lion's paw? Images flashed before her as she flattened into the shadows, remaining motionless for what seemed an eternity. *Was he back?* The thought did little to steady her catapulting heart. Once the vehicle passed, she lurched to her feet, a wave of dizziness threatening to drop her again. Finally reaching pavement, she released a sob of frustration at the glimpse of fading taillights. Wanting the car to return. Wanting it to disappear. Wanting to run in the opposite direction. With a renewed sense of urgency, she stumbled down the road.

"Pete. . . I just saw somethin'."

"Half the county's searchin' for that girl. You really think *we're* gonna find her?"

"Dammit, turn around. I saw a flash a color in my mirror."

"We ain't seen the car, Billy. Don't you think we'd find the car first? Or did she let *herself* outta that trunk?"

"People were blowin' their horns like crazy. Maybe the perp catches on— so he changes plans and dumps her."

The old cop pondered. In the span of seven minutes, the 911 operator received six calls on a rusty Plymouth beater with a woman's arm hangin' from the taillight. Now, one call— that's probably a crank. But six? In Marsh Point, they were lucky to get six calls all night. 'Course not a single damn caller got the plate number.

"What'd I tell you," Billy crowed. "Hell if that ain't a woman."

Pete flicked the siren as they pulled up behind a limping woman. Leaving the engine idling, they approached cautiously. She turned to face them, swaying on her feet like a Friday night drunk.

"Holy Mother 'a God."

Blood oozed from an ugly laceration on the side of her head. Long, blond hair straggled from a fancy hairdo, covering half her battered face. Glowing in the moonless night, an icy blue sweater hung from one shoulder, covered in blood spatters and mud.

"Ma'am? I'm going to approach. Place your hands where I can see them." His gaze never leaving the woman, he muttered to Billy. "Get an ambulance. She ain't gonna be standing much longer."

"You're sayin' she can't remember anything?" Captain Jonas paused for the hospital intercom, his weary eyes looking every minute of his fifty-nine years. "Amnesia's in the movies, Jeb."

"Is it permanent?" Matt Barnes rose from his chair, relieved to suspend his argument with the small town cop. Jonas should have called yesterday. Since he'd landed in Marsh Point two months earlier, Steve had called him on just about everything. Instead, he'd received the news from the Boston drug team. A Jane Doe found in the middle of nowhere . . . *his* middle of nowhere. With distributor quality heroin under her nails.

"Too soon to tell." The doctor glanced from Jonas to him. "It's a common side-effect from a blow to the head."

"How long?" Just because Matt was on medical leave from the agency didn't mean he had *nothing* better to do. Well— almost nothing. PT on his useless shoulder and . . . Cable wasn't exactly great out at the lake.

The doctor shrugged. "Memory usually returns in fragments. The more she can string together, the more enabled she'll be to remember."

"What's typical?" Jonas turned his attention to the doc.

"Everyone's different. Could be days; maybe weeks. Some take longer."

"Could she be faking?" Matt voiced the question he and Jonas both wondered. It was pretty convenient the woman who'd rolled around in pure grade heroin couldn't remember a damn thing.

Jeb grinned. "Anything's possible, but pressuring doesn't work— so don't upset her." The paging system interrupted their discussion. "That's for me." Waving, he headed down the corridor.

Jonas scratched his head. "So, DEA's taking over my case?"

"You've said you're spread too thin. Why would you want to take lead on this?" *When you're seriously unqualified.*

The old man shrugged. "It's a good case. Fifteen years of Friday night DVs after Gus or Ricky has too much to drink-" He sighed. "Wives never leave 'em . . . and every time I gotta worry about gettin' shot." He scratched his salt and pepper crew cut. "Wife beaters and DIBs. That's my life now."

"DIBs?" Matt stifled a yawn. He wanted coffee that didn't come from a nursing station pot.

"Drunk in daddy's boat." His smile didn't reach his eyes. "So, you got a lead then? This tie back to Boston?"

"Looks like it might." He pushed off the corridor wall, grimacing as pain lanced his shoulder. Ten weeks after surgery and he was still worthless.

"Okay, Mattie. Let's do this." Graying whiskers creased into a smile. "We don't see many heroin dealers in Marsh Point. And I damn sure haven't come across amnesia before."

Matt pushed through the door. "Can't help on the amnesia, but drugs . . . I know." A battered, sleeping woman met his gaze. Blonde. Late twenties. Maybe thirty, he corrected, his gaze methodical. An ugly purple bruise marred her right cheekbone, the color seeping into her eye socket, giving the appearance of a shiner. A sweep of dark lashes stood in stark relief against parchment skin, leaving him with a disturbing sense of innocence she couldn't possibly live up to.

He drew closer. Bandages covered the head injury that had taken seventeen stitches to close. The contusion spreading into her hairline was a nasty rainbow of purple and yellow. Doc was right. She was lucky to have awakened at all.

"Ma'am? You awake?" Glancing at Jonas, he hauled a chair to her bedside.

When her eyes fluttered open, fear flared in their depths, warring with the arresting color for his attention. Terror, followed by confusion. Matt acknowledged both before conceding they were possibly the greenest eyes he'd ever seen.

"I'm Captain Jonas," Steve explained. "Marsh Point PD. This is my colleague, Matt Barnes. We'd like to ask a few questions, Miss-"

Her eyes widened. "Julie. That's all I remember."

"You've sustained a serious head injury. You remember how you got that?"

"Someone— hit me." Eyes unfocused, she appeared to be concentrating on a memory. She raised her arm to mimic the action. "Maybe a pipe?"

Matt's imagination filled in the sound of the thud— a weapon against skin and delicate bone. Her shudder caught him off guard, crawling down his skin. He catalogued it— comparing it to the database in his head. Faking fear was easy, he reminded himself. After a decade in drug enforcement, he'd pretty much seen it all.

"Did you know him?" Steve's elder statesman voice encouraged.

"I don't . . . remember." Grass green eyes went vacant. "My head feels— thick, like . . . it's not working right."

Her voice quavered on the last bit. *Nice touch*, Matt acknowledged. Avoiding him, her gaze remained on Jonas. Clearly, she preferred the fatherly figure she could trust. Or play.

"Where you from?"

Slender shoulders lifted, appearing helpless. "Not here." Restless fingers plucked at the sheets covering her. Once manicured, her nails were ragged. "Marsh Point is in the Berkshires?"

"Pretty much the last stop before the New York border," Steve offered.

Matt hid his smile. Already charmed, Jonas would be damn near useless. The old man may have started his career in the city, but after fifteen years in Marsh Point, he'd lost his edge. The tox report on Julie's clothing indicated she'd rolled around on a carpet laced with dangerously pure heroin. A batch of drug that sure as hell hadn't been cut to street grade yet. Her fancy sweater saturated in blood and drugs. Expensive black pants from Talbots— this season's style. Hot lookin' designer shoes that probably cost a week's pay. All dusted with smack.

The paydirt had been under her nails— drugs and a drop of someone's blood. Matt was eager to learn who owned the sample. "Do you remember anything about the night we found you?"

"Fragments— feeling late for . . . something." Her voice trailed off. "Maybe I was lost?"

Okay, so the scrunched nose thing was sorta charming, Matt admitted. Her gaze remained glued to the wall, leaving the impression she really couldn't remember what the hell had happened to her. Or she was damn good at trying to convince them.

"I remember the sound of the car . . . I thought he'd come back."

Jonas shot him a look. "Who?"

"The man in the ski mask." Her expression confused, she glanced up. "He put me in a closet. No— that doesn't seem right," she muttered. "It was noisy. I think I was lying down."

When Steve glanced at him— none too subtly, Matt wanted to groan. The old man was *seriously* out of practice. Her memory of the trunk should be organic— confirming what they'd gleaned from 911 calls. "What else?"

She reluctantly shifted her focus to him. "I think I had a meeting."

"With the man?"

"I can't believe I would associate with someone like him— yet . . . something felt familiar." Long lashes fluttered against translucent skin. "Is that crazy?"

Jonas muttered something reassuring. Matt remained silent, intrigued by her choice of words. 'Associate' implied someone beneath her stature. Was she someone important? That tended to complicate things. Her tailored clothes sketched a picture of a comfortable, monied lifestyle— certainly not what a street dealer wore. He filed the question away for later.

Removing himself from the temptation of his downtown office— from the well-meaning, visits of family and co-workers, from the *sorry-you-effed-up, Barnes* expression in their eyes— he'd hunkered down at the lake house for the grueling months of physical therapy his rebuilt shoulder required. Nearly three months after surgery he wasn't close to being duty-ready. At least not undercover. But sheer boredom had him consulting with the Marsh Point PD.

The call from State had been a godsend. They wanted him back— in some role. Lab analysis of Julie's clothes tied her to the Boston Harbor haul two months earlier. Their first real break since he'd been shot. But this wasn't shaping up as a typical case. Julie was a beautiful woman with a suspect story. The drumbeat of warning hammered his brain. This time, his shields would remain firmly in place, immune to manipulating, green eyes. Instinct told him this woman spelled trouble.

"They found her?"

"Yeah." Matias fumbled for loose change as he inched through the drive thru line.

"You have confirmation she's no longer . . . with the company?"

"Nothing in the paper yet." An icy warning whispered along Matias' spine. He resisted the urge to explain his latest screw-up. "The job was handled as ordered," he lied.

"You followed the plan?"

The silky voice raised hair on his neck. *Here it comes.*

"Because I don't remember discussing driving the bitch all over town."

Matias' pulse ratcheted a notch. How was it his fault the boss lady surprised him? Like— no one coulda warned him? When she'd discovered him standing over the old man's body, the *plan* had gone out the window.

"She showed up *unannounced,*" he reminded. Based on her— observations, I took action."

"This was an immaculately planned operation-"

How the hell could he predict her wakin' up in the trunk? The bitch kicks out a tail light, waving at every hayseed in the stupid town? He shoulda just capped her at the warehouse. Instead, his dick had gotten in the way. The *plan* involved doin' Blondie in the woods. His hands tightened on the wheel . . . feeling her throat. Her pleading with him. Tryin' to run. No one to hear her scream. . .

Heat rolled over him, his breath quickening. Dios, his luck sucked. "I thought-"

"We don't pay you to think."

Matias' blood pressure spiked with the desire to reach through the phone and choke the bastard 'til his eyes popped. He was sick of takin' orders-

"Provide verification on her status by tomorrow. Otherwise our employment arrangement will experience a rather abrupt end."

Fog surrounded Julie, the thick, powdery clouds nearly suffocating. When she stumbled over the body, her phone flew from her hand. Cold, black eyes behind the mask mocked as he raised a hand to silence her-

"Tori . . ." She jolted awake, her eyes wet.

"Was that a memory?"

Caught in the wispy tentacles of her dream, Julie shrank from the familiar voice.

"Ma'am, I won't hurt you."

It was Barnes. The one who didn't like her. Sensing him standing over her, she blinked to clear her eyes. "A dream." Brain still hazy, her shudder was involuntary. "He's still out there-"

"What's he look like?"

Julie hesitated. How to explain the ominous sense of dread without sounding crazy? Barnes' casual demeanor was betrayed by the wariness in his eyes. Despite his relaxed perch on the chair near her bed, she sensed a readiness to spring into action if required. "I see his eyes— they're dark. Scary."

"Is he white? Black? Hispanic?"

She summoned the memory she wished to forget. "He has olive skin."

"If he wore a mask-"

She raised fingers to her lips. "Around the mouth hole." Absorbing his scrutiny, she stared back. "You're with the police, too?"

"I'm consulting with Captain Jonas."

Consultant. She inhaled at the singe of memory. Straining for more, it dissolved in the air between them.

"What was that?"

Frustrated, she ignored his sudden interest. "That word— means something."

"Consulting?"

Something about Barnes didn't add up. His uniform- a polo shirt and faded jeans. "Where's your Tom Ford briefcase?"

Intense blue eyes studied her, this time from behind a pair of thick-rimmed glasses, reminding her more of a disgruntled professor than a small town cop. Ignoring her, he picked up his phone.

"You're pretty good at not answering questions."

He smiled. "I could say the same about you."

"For the record, I don't believe I'm usually this difficult." She hoisted herself into a sitting position so he wouldn't tower over her. "Were you wearing glasses yesterday?"

"I forgot to order new contacts. My luck ran out this morning." After scrolling through his phone, he slid it in his pocket. "Who's Tori?"

Call Tori. "My dream— I was trying to call Tori— but there was so much white dust- I couldn't breathe. I couldn't see the numbers. Then ski mask guy showed up."

"The officer who found you three nights ago indicated you said the name Tori several times."

Her pulse rocketed. "What about a last name? It must be someone I know."

Barnes flipped open a pad, scanning several items before speaking again. "He said it sounded like stash. You said 'cake' several times, too."

Frosting side down. Her smile was fleeting. "I was thinking about cake."

Barnes glanced up, closing the pad. "Stash refers to drugs. Maybe that's what you meant."

Drugs? She frowned. "No."

"How can you be sure?"

Because it seemed completely foreign? Was that a valid answer? "I just . . . know."

"Clouds of white dust? Doesn't that sound strange?"

"It was a dream," she emphasized. "I dreamt I tripped over a bod-" A shudder rippled through her. His eyes narrowing with interest, Julie realized too late it was probably the last thing she should have confessed. "Forget I said that."

His gaze intensified. "Not sure I can do that."

Great. By the time she finished blabbing, he'd have her under arrest for a murder she couldn't even remember. "It's been three days. Doesn't anyone miss me?"

"Not so far." His fingers drummed a restless beat on the bed frame.

She winced over his matter-of-fact tone. Voicing her fear only smothered the hope she'd carried. It didn't feel as though she were alone in the world. "I have no clothes, no money. I don't know where . . ." Forcing back the knot of fear clogging her throat, she turned to the window. "How do I get home when I don't know where home is?"

"You've got a little Fenway in your voice. Maybe Boston?"

Sensing his gaze challenging her, she didn't want to confirm the cynicism in his eyes. Barnes didn't trust her. Hell, he'd already convicted her— of something. "The doctor says I might be released tomorrow."

"They're not likely to dump you on the highway."

Frustrated tears burned behind her eyes. She hated the logic in his voice. Hated that he didn't trust her. Hated *him*. A ridiculously attractive man . . . Under normal circumstances his confident gaze likely caused hearts to flutter . . . with anticipation. Instead, hers was clutching with fear. Barnes had already decided she was the enemy.

Maybe he was right. "Captain Jonas said I could stay with him . . . but I don't know if that's appropriate." When Barnes startled, she wondered why. When *she* was the one with everything to lose.

Matt had studied her for hours. While she slept, blonde curls slipping free of a braid, the silken strands curling into her neck. While she tried to ignore him, full, red lips compressed in an intimidating line. A futile attempt at control. And now, as she began to unravel. Her expression shell-shocked, she held it together— barely. Dark smudges under weary, emerald eyes painted a fragility that didn't match the frustration in her voice. But he wasn't fooled. She was one of *those* women . . . beautiful. Pampered.

Her reference to a Tom Ford briefcase . . . Hell, he'd had to look it up. And no wonder. A briefcase costing two grand? Okay, so she was rich. A rich, sexy blonde— content to let her angel face do the heavy lifting.

"We'll find somewhere for you to stay until we get to the bottom of this." And it sure as hell wouldn't be with Steve. What was Jonas thinking? Sorority Barbie was a link— to something. Possibly a big something. She sure as hell wasn't leaving town. The drug residue on her clothes was too good a lead. While her personal labwork was clean . . . she remained their only link. And thus far— their only suspect. But to what?

"Has anything come to you? Memories? Images?" He'd called Dr. Bannett— voluntarily this time. She'd obliged him with a crash course in amnesia. Matt figured it couldn't hurt to give the agency shrink someone else to focus on for a change. He'd met with her on and off since the shooting— and he was damn tired of 'resolving' his feelings. The resolution was he lived and Pam died.

"Fragments-"

A flush of color stained her cheeks. Something embarrassing. "Memories can take the form of symbols," he suggested. Dr. Bannett had explained that in some amnesia patients memories were trapped in dream-like images.

"I see a lion's paw. How's that for obscure?"

Her disgruntled expression suggested he probably shouldn't smile. "You know it's a lion's paw?"

Annoyance flashed in increasingly pretty eyes. "It's just . . . a really big paw."

Relief flowed at Julie's improbable story. She was likely guilty— of something. That knowledge— *that belief*— would keep him in line. Because otherwise she'd be dangerously appealing. "Your inability to recognize animal prints will have to go in my report."

"I must've missed that day in kindergarten." Her bruised mouth lifted in a fleeting smile. "If we're done, can you-" She made a shooing sign toward the door.

"Why?"

"I'd like to hobble to the bathroom."

"Why don't I call the nurse?" Sensing her temper might lead to disaster, Matt instinctively rose. Her expression determined, she landed unsteadily on a bruised and swollen ankle before her face crumpled with pain.

"Ow. Ow. Ow." She teetered on her good leg, frozen between moving and retreating. Before she face-planted, he hauled her against him.

"You need crutches." When his shoulder spasmed a warning, he shifted her to his hip. Great. His lame ass rescue attempt had probably undone a month of physical therapy.

Matt studiously ignored the soft curves thrust against him. The cranky troll exterior housed a soft, curvy body that was wreaking havoc on his nervous system. Giving himself a mental headslap, he acknowledged maybe he'd been in the woods too long.

"Ready for a step?" His fingers tightened on a slim waist. Once he returned to Boston, he'd dust off his dating profile. Maybe reconsider Madeline's perpetual set-ups. His thrice-married mother and her busybody friends maintained a stable of eligible daughters. Brushing against the hint of a perfect breast, he felt perspiration slide down his spine.

Julie lurched away in surprise, her cheeks staining a flustered shade of pink. "Uh . . . sure."

His thoughts turning grim, he shuffled her the fifteen feet to the bathroom, conscious of her fingers digging into his hip . . . branding him. His spine tingling where her arm rested. Her damned curls swinging in his face. The huffing little breath that probably spoke volumes about her pain level . . . but to a groin at code red registered as sex sounds-

He skidded to a stop. What the hell was wrong with him?

"Are we resting?"

Her words muffled somewhere in the vicinity of his ribcage, but their heat scorched through the rest of him like an arcing current. Christ— could he act any *more* unprofessional?

"No," he said through clenched teeth. If she went down, he'd catch hell from the nurses. By the time they reached their destination, his shoulder was signaling the exhaustion of this month's white knight allowance. Relief and disappointment mingled when she pulled away from him. "Think you need a nurse?"

Despite her trembling limbs, she dismissed him with a limp wave before closing the door in his face. Uneasy, Matt retraced his steps.

"Don't go far." Her demand filtered through the door.

His smile was grim. "Not a chance, sweetheart."

Perched in the window, Matt raised his head when the shower turned on. Was she out of her mind? Five minutes earlier, she'd barely been able to stand upright. Clearly, this called for reinforcements. Tucking his notebook in his pocket, he moved for the hallway and the relative safety of the nurses' station.

Jerking the door open, he nearly plowed into the dark haired man blocking the entrance. "Excuse me."

The doctor muttered an apology before taking two steps back. He hesitated . . . glancing at his flipchart, then turned in the opposite direction. Matt's senses immediately flared. A vibe of uncertainty hung over the doctor. And something else. A vague flicker of familiarity. Dark eyes. Hispanic. He walked away— slowly at first, then more rapidly as he approached the corner, green coat flapping against his legs.

There was no doubt he'd been about to enter Julie's room. So, why the about-face? Instinct had his legs moving in pursuit before Matt's brain arrived at the same conclusion.

He doesn't belong here.

By the time he rounded the corner, Matt fought the urge to run. The stranger was already at the opposite end of the hallway. Glancing over his shoulder, they locked eyes. Heart ricocheting with certainty, he read the man's fear from fifty feet. Before he took off running.

Ski Mask Guy has olive skin. Why hadn't they accounted for the possibility of another attempt? Frustrated, Matt skidded to a stop. He knew why. He'd slammed the door on Julie's version of events. Ten weeks on leave had made him rusty. There was no hope of catching him now. And Julie was alone in a hospital bathroom. Unprotected.

OUT OF THE MIST, Available April, 2016

Dear Reader:

Thank you for reading CHASING MARISOL. I hope you enjoyed spending time with the Traynor family as much as I enjoyed creating them. If you liked this book, please consider leaving a review on Amazon or Goodreads. I hope you'll return for Hank's story. In the fourth installment of Blueprint To Love, solitary widower Henry Freeman crosses paths with Annie McKenna. SHELTERING ANNIE will be available summer, 2016. The first books of the series, Trusting Jake and Falling for Ken are available at all retail sites. Other books include my traditionally published novel, a romantic suspense, FOR HER PROTECTION released in 2010.

Blueprint To Love Series
Book 1: Trusting Jake
Book 2: Falling for Ken
Book 3: Chasing Marisol (January, 2016)
For Her Protection

To learn about upcoming books, please visit my Website or at Lauren Giordano Amazon page. Visit Lauren on Goodreads, follow Lauren on Twitter or Facebook.

Happy reading!
Lauren Giordano

ABOUT THE AUTHOR

Lauren Giordano is an award-winning author of eight novels ranging from contemporary romance to romantic suspense. She also blogs about the endless, troubling encounters she experiences on the journey to 'create' in her kitchen. Her Cooking Disasters blog can be found at laurengiordanoauthor.com. Originally from the Northeast, Lauren makes her home in the Mid-Atlantic with her husband, daughters and two vacationing cats.

Printed in Great Britain
by Amazon